Praise for *The Fight*

"Found myself hooked from the very first page . . . an astonishing debut novel. With well-developed characters, a strong moral, and an engaging finish . . . compares favorably with the finest male-orientated action novels in the mainstream today. Highly recommend."

> **—DAVIS BUNN**
> bestselling author

"I loved *The Fight*. It is so realistic and true to life. I can't recommend this book enough."

> **—NIGEL BENN**
> two-time world champion boxer

"A powerful page-turner—brilliant and deeply compelling."

> **—ANDY HAWTHORNE**
> founder of The Message Trust

"A high-paced, gritty, and beautiful redemption story."

> **—SARAH WYNTER**
> editor of *Youthwork* magazine

The battle over a man's past.
A fight for a boy's future.

THE
FIGHT

LUKE WORDLEY

TYNDALE HOUSE PUBLISHERS, INC.
CAROL STREAM, ILLINOIS

Visit Tyndale online at www.tyndale.com.

Visit Luke Wordley's website at www.lukewordley.com.

TYNDALE and Tyndale's quill logo are registered trademarks of Tyndale House Publishers, Inc.

The Fight

First published in Great Britain by Downton Press Ltd in 2011. First printing by Tyndale House Publishers, Inc., in 2014.

Boxer photographs taken by Alex Stanhope/alexstanhope.co.uk. Used with permission.

Designed by www.profiledesign.net and Dean H. Renninger

The author is represented by MacGregor Literary Inc., of Hillsboro, OR.

Lyrics in chapter 25 from "The Lord's My Shepherd" by Stuart Townend. Copyright © 1996 Thankyou Music (PRS) (adm. worldwide at CapitolCMGPublishing.com excluding Europe which is adm. by Kingswaysongs) All rights reserved. Used by permission.

The Fight is a work of fiction. Where real people, events, establishments, organizations, or locales appear, they are used fictitiously. All other elements of the novel are drawn from the author's imagination.

Library of Congress Cataloging-in-Publication Data

Wordley, Luke.
  The Fight / Luke Wordley.
    pages cm
    ISBN 978-1-4143-8949-3 (sc)
  1. Young men—England—London—Fiction. 2. Self-actualization (Psychology)—Fiction. 3. Christian fiction. 4. Boxing stories. I. Title.
    PR6123.O666F54 2014
    823'.92—dc23
                                                    2013040119

Printed in the United States of America

20 19 18 17 16 15 14
7   6   5   4   3   2   1

To Jenny—my wife and best friend

Acknowledgments

I first self-published *The Fight* in England in 2011, mainly thanks to the contributions of a couple of key people. First, to my aunt, Rita Carter, whose successful writing career inspired me to try my hand and whose expertise, "tough love," and encouragement through the grueling editing process was central to this book being completed. Second, to Rebecca Anderson, my UK editor and friend, who remains instrumental in improving and polishing my manuscripts to the end.

I would also like to thank a number of people who read early versions of *The Fight* and gave general and specific advice in various areas—namely Naomi Lloyd-Jones, Richard Pennystan, Denise and Duncan Murray, Tris Dixon of *Boxing News*, Andi Artze, Rosemary Longhurst, Ian Henderson, and Heather Andrew. Thanks also to Peter Hamilton at Profile Design for your brilliant original cover and for organizing the photos that have graced the covers of both versions.

For *The Fight* to now be republished in 2014 by Tyndale is just a dream come true. They have been an absolute pleasure to work with, and I can't believe how lucky I am. First, thanks to Karen Watson for being prepared to step out and take a risk on a quirky little boxing story by an unknown British author. Then to Jeremy Taylor, who has patiently held my hand through a second editing process and has helped improve the manuscript considerably. And to Jan Stob, Cheryl Kerwin, Dean Renninger, and Shaina Turner for all your skill and enthusiasm. I'm so enjoying working with you.

I am also thankful to my agent, Chip MacGregor, for introducing me to Tyndale. But none of these connections would have been made without Davis Bunn, a generous man to whom I owe a great deal. Thank you very much.

Finally, I would like to thank my family. To my wife, Jenny, who has provided steadfast encouragement and support over the many years this project has been in existence. To my children, Ben, Olivia, and Barnaby, for their fun and friendship—I hope you enjoy this one day! And to my parents, who have always believed in me. Thank you.

PART
ONE

1

Sam Pennington crouched in the filthy concrete stairwell, his eyes scanning the wasteland that the boys would have to cross. Slowly the three brothers emerged into view across the rubbish-strewn ground.

Gypsies. Sam was sure of it. They might live in the flat across the road and not in a caravan, but they were gypsies nonetheless. The white van and their dad's two greyhounds gave it away. They were the type who had stolen tractor diesel from Sam's family's farm and chased the rabbits and hares with their dogs, trampling all over the fields without a care about the crops they were ruining.

Yep, these boys were going to be trouble. Sam had seen them across the street, talking and staring when he and his mum were moving into their flat. The next day the oldest one had knocked on the door and asked if Sam wanted to play football. Sam had refused. He knew what they were try-ing to do—lure him out. A fight was just a matter of time.

Sam crouched even lower as the boys, unaware of him lying in wait, got closer. The brothers jostled, competing to kick an empty Coke can into an imaginary goal. Their easy sibling manner jarred Sam and made him even more determined as they walked forward, oblivious of the danger a few yards ahead.

He jumped up and sprinted from the stairwell, going straight for the biggest brother. The boy didn't even have time to raise his hands as Sam punched him hard in the mouth. He crashed to a heap on the ground, screaming. Perfect. Sam had felt teeth break and knew the boy wasn't getting up. That left one kid about his own size and the runt.

Sam turned toward the bigger boy, whose gaze shifted fearfully from his screaming brother to his assailant. The boy lifted his hands to protect his face, so Sam lowered his aim and smashed his fist into the boy's chest. He fell on his back-side, fighting for air.

Sam glared at the youngest brother, who was standing a few yards away, frozen in fear. A large wet patch appeared on the little boy's trousers. With one last look at his brothers, he turned and ran away as fast as he could.

"I'll get you later!" Sam shouted after him, letting him go. The kid wasn't important. Sam had done what was needed. Both older boys were sniveling on the ground, cowering in the dirt.

"You scum. Leave me alone," Sam snarled.

The younger boy glanced at Sam warily. "We only wanted to play football."

Sam looked down at the boy. "Leave me alone," he repeated before walking casually back toward his flat.

When he knew he was out of sight, he broke into a run and sprinted home. Order had been established.

/ / /

Janet Pennington sat by the window and watched the street below, her back turned to her new home. The second-floor flat, part of a run-down public-housing complex, consisted of just four rooms—a living room with a built-in kitchen, a moldy bathroom, and two bedrooms so small that the beds touched the walls at both ends. The flat had been filthy when they moved in, the threadbare carpet covered in dirty marks and nicotine-stained wallpaper peeling at the edges. She had spent three days scrubbing, but the floor still stuck under her feet.

They were lucky, the housing officer had said. With the government's big public-housing sell-off in full swing, unless you were a teenager with babies, you stood little chance of getting one. They had gotten one. Their unusual circumstances had obviously struck a chord with the world-weary housing officer. Janet had felt that perhaps their luck was changing when it was confirmed that they had a place. There were some charming government-owned houses in the villages near Copse Farm, where she had lived for seventeen years since marrying Sam's father. However, her hopes had plummeted when she first drove into the Mandela complex eight miles away in Romford, Essex. Litter was strewn everywhere, and intimidating gangs of kids stared as their Land

Rover pulled in. It couldn't have been more different from the life they had known. But now 28C Soweto Rise was her and Sam's new home.

As Janet gazed out the window she saw Sam charging down the street. Seconds later he burst into the flat, slamming the door and bracing himself against it.

"Hi, darling. How was your first day at school?" she asked brightly, craving communication after a day alone in the flat.

"Crap," he said, panting.

Janet noticed his hands were shaking. "Come on. It can't have been that bad," she said with little hope.

"It was crap, and I'm not going back."

"Please stop swearing, Sam. You never used to swear."

"My life never used to be screwed."

Janet's eyes welled up with tears. "Well, that's not my fault." Her voice quivered, unconvinced.

Sam grunted and made for his room.

"No, please stop and t-t-talk." Janet's last word was drowned by the sound of Sam's door slamming shut.

She sighed heavily as her gaze returned to the street below. It hurt so much to see her only child like this. Once he had been a happy boy, full of laughter and smiles. But he had changed completely. Since the accident, he had assumed an almost permanent aggressive frown. Indeed, the only time she had seen him smile was when he had admitted with a satisfied smirk that he was responsible for the black eye miserably worn by an older boy at the guesthouse where they had stayed for a while before moving to the flat. From that moment, Janet had known she was losing her grip. Since they had moved, little had changed. Sam was out of control. She couldn't cope with him. And he knew it.

Just then Janet saw two of the brothers from across the street hurrying up the road before disappearing into the stairwell of their flat. The older boy was cupping his mouth as if about to vomit, while his brother held on to his shoulder. Their mother soon appeared, looking furious as she stood with hands on hips, searching up and down the street. *Those kids look like they're in trouble,* Janet thought, noticing the mother's scowl as she kept glaring up at their flat. Janet could almost feel the mother's anger. She sighed again. If only she could muster up something similar, perhaps she might have a bit more control over Sam. Janet's husband, Robert, had done most of the disciplining in their house, although, in reality, apart from a bit of overexuberance that had to be checked once in a while, Sam had been an easy child.

The smallest brother appeared, his little legs a blur as he ran up the street. Even from this distance, Janet could see the boy was upset. His mother didn't tell him off but gave him a brief hug and quickly checked him over as she questioned him. In between sobs, the boy was clearly retelling a story, pointing back down the street and then up toward where Janet was sitting.

It was only when the mother sent the boy indoors and marched straight toward their flat that Janet realized what might have happened. A wave of nausea rose in her stomach as she counted the steps to her flat in her mind. Her gaze lifted to the door and the security chain hanging loosely by the doorframe. She jumped up, rushed to the door, and fumbled with the chain, trying desperately to secure it. The safety chain found its slot just as the door shook violently under the onslaught of hammering fists on the other side. Janet jumped back, terrified.

"Open the door! I know you're in there. I saw you at the window," the woman shouted.

Janet stood rooted to the spot.

The banging got louder. "Open the door now!"

Janet opened the door to the limit of the chain and stood back. "Can I help you?" she said timidly.

The other woman's face appeared through the gap, her eyes full of fury. "Can you help me? Can you *help* me? I've got three boys scared witless, and one is missing a front tooth. Thanks to your son in there!"

"I'm . . . I'm sure it wasn't Sam," Janet stammered instinctively. But she didn't believe her own words, and it showed in her voice.

"Well, let's ask him, shall we?" And with that, the weighty woman began throwing herself, shoulder first, at the softwood door. After three hefty barges, the door smashed wide open as the chain bracket splintered off the doorframe. Janet screamed as they came face-to-face.

"Where is he?" the woman shouted, scanning the dingy flat.

"Please leave," Janet whimpered, standing between the woman and her son's bedroom.

"Get out of my way!"

Janet staggered and fell awkwardly against the sideboard

as the woman pushed past her and opened Sam's bedroom door.

"No, please . . ." Janet sobbed. She had never seen such aggressive behavior from anyone before, and she was terrified. Sam was tough, but this woman would kill him.

The furious intruder left the bedroom and searched the rest of the flat.

"Where is he?" she yelled as Janet sat confused and frightened on the floor, shaking her head. The woman moved closer and demanded an answer.

Janet, looking up at her with terrified eyes, started to stammer. "I don't . . . I don't know."

The woman bent over Janet and pointed in her face.

"You better pray I don't get hold of him and that my kids never get touched again. If either of you mess with my family again, you're dead."

With that, the woman left as quickly as she had arrived.

Stunned, Janet pushed herself to her feet and limped to the door, slamming it shut. With shaking hands she attempted to push the shattered chain bracket into the hole it had been ripped from. It was futile. Janet dragged an old armchair they had brought from the farm across the thin nylon carpet. She jammed it against the door before staggering in confusion toward Sam's bedroom.

He wasn't anywhere to be seen. She knelt by his bed and looked underneath, but the space was full of boxes with nowhere to hide. There was only one possibility left. Janet stepped with trepidation toward the open window, hoping she wouldn't find her son's broken body on the concrete twenty feet below. Sam wasn't there. Janet's relief lasted only a moment before the shock of the last two minutes overwhelmed her. She slumped to the ground. A second later the small flat was filled with desperate sobbing.

Janet finally rose, limped to the kitchen, and took a dirty mug from the sink. She opened the cupboard under the sink and, reaching to the back, pulled out a half-empty bottle. Her hands shook violently as she clasped the cool glass, causing the wine to spill as she filled the chipped porcelain mug. She grasped the mug in front of her face. The remnants of tea gave the pale liquid a murky, grayish-brown color. Janet shut her eyes, took a large gulp, and swallowed. She took another swig and exhaled deeply to calm her racing heart. Filling the mug again, Janet crossed the room and sank into the old upright armchair that, a month earlier, had been in the corner of the sitting room at Copse Farm.

2

THREE YEARS LATER

"His dad died, squashed under his own trailer! They were tenants, so they got thrown out the family farm three years ago and shoved in the roughest complex in Romford."

"So what?" the headmaster replied forcefully. "I've got lots of kids with tragic backgrounds. It doesn't mean they go around beating the living daylights out of everyone. I'm sorry, Bob. I'm not budging on this decision."

Bob frowned back at his balding friend. Normally the social worker proved quite successful at talking the kind-hearted headmaster around. But this time he sensed a determination in his friend's voice that would be difficult to overcome. He tried anyway. It was his job, and he actually cared about this one.

"Come on, Norman. This kid's different. He's clever. We just need to reach him."

"I've tried, Bob. I've really tried. But he's not having any of it. He just doesn't want help." Norman sighed and began to smile. "I know he's bright. We've got this science teacher, Alex Swann. Between you and me, he's a moron. Anyway, Swann has an ongoing hate-hate relationship with our Sam. Last month he gave his class a test, and Sam actually took it for some reason. He came out on top by a mile, got 98 percent or something! I swear he did it just to make Swann mad."

The two men laughed together. Their friendship dated back forty years; they had grown up on the same street in Romford. Although it was good to see a familiar face at work, they both preferred their occasional evenings in the pub when they could forget about their positions and responsibilities.

Their laughter died away quickly. They were both dreading their impending meeting with the boy's mother. It had been fourteen months since Sam Pennington's file had landed on Bob's desk at social services. He had met Janet a number of times on his home visits to the Penningtons' flat. Over the past year, he had watched her change from a frightened, hurting lady doing her best to cope with a difficult situation into a miserable alcoholic. With a dead father and a drunk mother, the poor kid didn't stand a chance.

Bob glanced at his watch and pushed on. He now had only five minutes to change his friend's mind and perhaps a child's future. This would be the third school Sam had been expelled from in just under three years. The fifteen-year-old was on a course to self-destruction. After expulsion from three schools, the department of education would normally deem a child to be beyond the help of the conventional educational framework. He would then receive token individual tutoring until he was caught for some misdemeanor worthy of the prison system, whereupon he would become the responsibility of a different government department. Bob had seen it many times and was determined to prevent Sam from going the same way.

"But you know," Bob continued passionately, looking at his friend, "he's different from most of the kids we have to deal with. He's got problems, I know, but I'm sure there's hope for him. We have to try, don't we?"

"Look," Norman replied with exasperation, "I know he's different. He doesn't do or sell drugs. He doesn't touch up the girls. Or the boys, for that matter. But it's his temper, Bob—his temper and his attitude. He's not a bully. He never has a go at anyone smaller than him. It's always older kids or groups of kids. I've had loads of incidents, including four requiring medical treatment. We're not talking scrapes and bruises, you know; he really smashes them up." The headmaster picked up a notebook from his desk and started reading. "In two terms we've had a broken nose, several smashed teeth, two black eyes, and a broken rib." He threw the pad down and pushed away from the desk. "A broken rib! Bob, these are fifteen-year-old kids."

"But you can't tell me he was unprovoked in all those," Bob said, nodding at the list disdainfully.

"Absolutely not. Most of them are right troublemakers. But he brings it upon himself. He even seems to enjoy it. The whole school's scared of him. Even the teachers are scared of him."

"But give me a chance to get him over this temper of his.

Come on, Norman, just one more chance. He's clever—98 percent! He obviously listens in class. I remember you had a temper when you were his age, but you had a dad to discipline that out of you." Bob looked appealingly at his friend. He knew he was getting somewhere because Norman was looking rattled. Bob looked at his watch again—three minutes to go.

The headmaster slammed his hand on his desk. "For crying out loud, Bob! I've given you three chances with this kid already, and I was reluctant to take him in the first place! To get expelled from the Grange and County High in five months! I don't know how I let you talk me into it in the first place."

"Because you're a good man, Norman."

"Don't start," Norman growled, pointing at his friend. "I'm warning you. Don't start."

Bob backed off and decided to change tack. "I'm trying to think of a way to channel his aggression," he said carefully. "I spoke to his old headmaster from the boarding school he was at before his dad's accident. He was pretty sad to hear about Sam. Said he had been a lovely kid. . . ." Bob caught his friend's eye as he said it, but Norman picked up the list of injuries and shook it. Bob continued. "He also said he had been a heck of a rugby player."

"Boxing would be more appropriate from what I've seen," Norman offered sarcastically.

Bob paused as Norman's comment lodged in his mind, but immediately the thought was interrupted by an intercom on Norman's desk. The nasal voice of the headmaster's secretary informed them Mrs. Pennington had arrived.

Norman stood up and adjusted his jacket. "I'm sorry, Bob. I've written my recommendation to the education authority." He held up a letter to show his friend. "I have to expel him permanently. I'm starting to look weak over Pennington in the staff room and to other parents." He turned and walked to the door.

"Norman, this is it!" Bob blurted in desperation. "You're the last chance this kid's got."

The headmaster glanced irritably back at his friend as he grabbed the door handle. Then he took a deep breath and swung the door open. "Mrs. Pennington, please come in." He beamed at the woman and shook her hand, ushering her into the office.

Bob studied her carefully as she entered, her eyes flicking nervously around the room. He shook her limp hand. The slight stagger as she sat down confirmed that nothing had changed since he had last seen her.

"Mrs. Pennington," Norman said gravely as he returned to his seat. "I'm afraid Samuel has been fighting again."

Bob saw the woman feign an unconvincing look of surprise. She was not a good actress.

"He attacked a group of boys yesterday in the playground," Norman continued. "One of them sustained a serious facial injury."

The headmaster paused, waiting for a response. None was forthcoming. The woman sat unsteadily, her hands grasping the arms of the chair.

Norman looked across at Bob, and they exchanged a mutual glance of sadness. "Is there anything you want to say, Mrs. Pennington?"

Janet stirred and attempted to focus on the headmaster.

"I'm very sorry," she said, slurring slightly. The way she apologized made it sound like she personally had punched the injured boy.

There was silence for several seconds as the headmaster gave Mrs. Pennington the opportunity to speak up for her son. She said nothing.

Bob glanced at his colleague and, for the first time, sensed a flicker of uncertainty in his friend's face. He held his breath as the headmaster spoke again.

"I'm very sorry this has happened again. This is the fourth serious incident we've had. I am left with no choice but to—" Norman glanced up at Bob and hesitated—"suspend Sam for two weeks. If his behavior improves before the summer break, he can return again next term. But let me make this very clear. If we ever have another repeat of any fighting what-soever, Sam will be expelled immediately and permanently."

Bob breathed again with relief. But Janet showed no reaction at all. She just sat with her eyes fixed on the bare wall behind Norman.

The headmaster scratched his head. "Mrs. Pennington?"

"I'm—I'm . . ." She stuttered to a halt as she evidently forgot what she had been about to say.

Norman shifted in his seat and shot Bob a desperate look, which the social worker could clearly read: *Please get her out of here before she comes apart completely.* "Don't worry, Mrs. Pennington," Norman said reassuringly. "I'm sure Mr. Knowles has a plan to help Sam with his behavior."

Bob shook himself into action. "Er . . . yes, Mrs.

Pennington. I understand Sam was a keen rugby player at boarding school?" He looked for signs of acknowledgment. None came. He battled on. "Well, I was wondering whether you would approve of my introducing him to a local rugby club?"

Again there was no response. Bob spoke louder and more slowly, realizing he sounded like a British tourist speaking to a foreign waiter. "Mrs. Pennington? Rugby club?"

Finally she came around. "Uh, yes, whatever you think."

Bob sighed. At least he had consent, but parental support was clearly going to be lacking. The room was silent for a few seconds. "Do you need a lift home, Mrs. Pennington?" Bob finally asked.

"Yes, please."

Both men jumped up and helped her from her seat and toward the door.

"Thank you for coming," Norman said.

"I'm very sorry," she said again as she disappeared out of the office. Bob followed but a moment later poked his head back around his friend's door.

"Thanks for the break, Norman."

"Get out of here, you bully," the headmaster said as he tore up the now-irrelevant letter to the education authority.

Bob grinned and retreated before leaning around the door again. "Friday night? King's Arms?"

"Friday," his friend replied. The two men nodded solemnly to each other before Bob quietly withdrew and closed the door behind him.

3

"Ten minutes, lads."

Sam sat, watching the room before him. His new team-mates all wore their navy-blue rugby shirts with large white numbers embroidered on the back. Numbers one, two, and three—the front row—had formed their scrummaging clinch and squeezed together for a few seconds before releasing their grip. They were going to be under serious pressure, and they knew it. The hooker was the undoubted leader, and he was instructing his henchmen carefully. The two props stood and listened intently. Already weighing two hundred pounds and ugly, both boys had shaved their heads for this match. Now the hooker was slapping and shoving them, provoking more intensity. The three faced toward the wall, grabbed each other by the sides of their shorts, and squeezed together again, grunting like sea lions. They were ready.

The rest of the forwards paced around, grabbing and shoving one another to key themselves up. The backs, smaller and younger looking, were mainly sitting still or nervously lacing their boots.

Sam sat alone. He didn't need to psych himself up. He already had three years' worth of anger stored inside. He grinned as he looked at his new teammates. It was good to be back in the game.

When the social worker had suggested joining a rugby club, Sam hadn't been sure how to react. Up until then, he had automatically rejected everything the old corduroy bloke had said. Yet when he mentioned rugby, Sam had paused rather than answer with his normal silent shake of the head. He had missed rugby desperately. After his dad died, it was the only thing he had enjoyed in that final term at boarding school. But then he had started going to rubbish schools that didn't even play the game. Sam hadn't known that there were rugby clubs outside of school, but Bob had said Romford had a club with a junior section. Sam agreed to try it out.

The first session had just been fitness training—tackling bags and running through some moves. For many of the kids, preseason fitness training was not the thing they looked forward to most about the summer holidays. But for Sam, it was the first time he had enjoyed himself in over three years. The other boys hadn't seemed too bad, and a couple of them were even friendly until Sam was recognized by a kid from his previous school and word got around. Since then no one had spoken to him. That was fine by Sam. He was there for the rugby. If the others were scared of him, so be it. He didn't need friends.

/ / /

Pete Sanderson entered the changing room and looked around at his boys with satisfaction. The rugby coach saw his forwards slapping and shoving one another roughly, building each other up to a frenzy. Pete grinned. He could almost taste the teenage testosterone in the air. Today was going to be his day. The day he was finally going to get one over his old club. That would serve them right for letting him go as a player fifteen years earlier.

The coach looked to his right and saw his backs, now on their feet and shoving and slapping each other too, if a little less convincingly. They'd be fine once they got out there, he reassured himself. Finally his eyes alighted on the one boy still sitting. Sam.

Pete could still remember the phone call. He didn't have time for charity, but he had invited the drippy social worker to bring the boy by anyway. It had happened once or twice before, and Pete had always enjoyed watching the spotty little misfits embarrass themselves when it came to playing a man's game.

However, one sprint up the pitch identified this new kid as a potential find. He had incredible pace, outsprinting all the other players. He tackled the bags with fury and had good hands. He had clearly played rugby before.

The bearded weirdo social worker said the kid had aggression problems. Good. Pete had drafted the boy straight into the first team for today's opening match of the season.

Pete nodded as he saw Sam look up at him. Their eyes held for a second, and the coach was immediately pleased. The boy's face held no fear, despite his silent sitting. Pete nodded curtly and then strode into the middle of the room, sinking his thumb and forefinger into his mouth and whistling shrilly.

"Gather round, lads."

The eighteen boys formed a tight circle around their coach, linking arms behind each other's backs. Pete Sanderson slowly rotated, meeting the eyes of each player in turn. Finally he spoke.

"Right, lads. This is it. The big one, first up. There's a real crowd out there. Even a guy from the newspaper. This is our chance. If we beat this lot today, we won't look back all season. I believe in you. I think you've got everything you need to win today. Just because they train with Harlequins, that doesn't mean anything. You're not playing the men's professional team out there. I wanna see it hard and rough. Most of them are private-school wusses, born with a silver spoon in their mouth. So let's send them home crying to Mummy.

"I want to see hard tackling. If he's there, take him out. Bang. I don't want to see anything halfhearted. Not on my team. You hit him hard enough, and you'll have a nice soft landing. Fast to the breakdown. Recycle and spin. Nothing fancy first game. Let's just get it out wide through the hands, and get Mac and Sam into it."

Pete turned to his left, where most of the smaller boys were standing. "Backs, I wanna see that line steep, running from deep. And in defense, no drift; just pick your man and nail him." He turned to his right. "Forwards, I want it hard and fast. When you've got the ball, keep your support. No running off down blind alleys. And all of you—I want it tough. If your man is lying on the ball, make him feel it! No dirty stuff, but don't let them get away with anything either." Pete punched his fist into his open hand. "Let's show them who's boss. Right?"

"Right!" Everyone on the team began shouting as they moved toward the door. "Let's have 'em! Let's kill 'em!"

Pete Sanderson smiled as he watched the boys filing out. They were ready. His attention fell on the last boy in line. As Sam filed out behind his teammates, Pete caught his wrist.

"Your social worker said you were a tough one. Are you going to show me today?" They held each other's eyes before Sam nodded and ran after his teammates.

/ / /

Sam buzzed. He hadn't felt like this in years. As he sprinted to his starting position, he felt like a bullet in a gun.

4

"What happened, Bob?"

Bob shook his head. He reached into his briefcase and pulled out a copy of that week's *Romford Herald*.

"Let me give you the view of our esteemed rugby correspondent, Mr.—" Bob peered at the byline—"'Dave-Your-Man-at-the-Match.'"

"'Explosive Start to London Colts League.' That's the headline. 'After a bruising first half—' blah, blah, Harlequins were on top until, I quote, 'Sam Pennington, a newcomer to the Romford team, picked up a loose ball, sidestepped three players, and sprinted the length of the pitch to score.' Then . . . uh . . . here we are. 'Pennington scored again, smashing through a last-ditch tackle.'"

Bob looked up at the headmaster. "I tell you, I'm there cheering on the sideline. I felt like a dad on sports day." Norman laughed as Bob clenched his fists in triumph.

"Then," Bob continued, looking back down at the newspaper. "Here we are. Second half: 'A fight broke out. . . . Pennington was even seen to punch his own player. . . . deservedly sent off. . . . Romford went on to lose.' Blah, blah, blah—er, where is it? Here we go: 'Coach said afterward, "I will not accept violence of any kind on my team. The player is not welcome back at this club."' The end." Bob laid the newspaper down on the desk and rubbed the bridge of his nose.

"So have you seen him?" Norman asked.

"Not since before the match."

"It's a shame. He's been doing really well here. I've been meaning to ring you. Doing his lessons, polite, no fighting. His English teacher even told me that he blushed and smiled the other day when she complimented him on his work." Norman shook his head. "Any idea where he is?"

"None at all."

"His mother?"

"Nope. She said that last year he was gone for a week."

"A week! Where does he go for a week?"

Bob shrugged.

"Any ideas what to do next?" Norman asked.

"Not really," Bob replied dejectedly.

"How about another rugby club? He had been improving."

"I don't know if any would take him after this." Bob tapped the newspaper with his hand. "He lost it big-time. He was savage. I can see now how you got your list of pupil injuries. Mind you, the newspaper shouldn't be printing this stuff in such detail—and giving his name. It's kids' rugby, for crying out loud, not professional sport. I think Dave-Our-Man-at-the-Match wants a job at the *Daily Mirror* or something." He crumpled the newspaper into a ball and threw it into the wastebasket. "Anyway, I'm not sure after this that encouraging him into any sport is a good idea. He could start a fight playing tiddlywinks."

Norman shrugged. "Well, nothing more I can do, I'm afraid, Bob."

"I know. I know. I won't be able to do anything myself in two months. Once he's sixteen, it'll be out of my hands."

The two men avoided each other's eyes. They both knew what happened to boys who slipped through the system. It was best to look away.

5

Jimmy Davis sensed more than saw a movement out of the corner of his eye. Looking up, he caught a glimpse of a man disappearing around the corner of the grain silo. The farm laborer picked up a shovel and followed.

Jimmy had been a farm laborer for over twenty years—his entire adult life—and he'd been at Copse Farm for going on two years now. He'd chased off plenty of stray dogs, foxes, and the occasional hobo or gypsy over the years. Whoever this was, he wouldn't get far.

The shadow ahead of Jimmy ran past the edge of the silo and squeezed through the thin gap between the tractor barn and the chemicals shed. Jimmy quickly circled the tractor barn, feeling the same excitement as when he stalked ducks on the marshes. Pausing at the end of the wall, he took a quick look around the corner. A teenager emerged from the gap, covered in cobwebs and filth, and disappeared into an old shed. The laborer quietly crept down the back of the tractor barn until he stood in the doorway of the shed, peering into the darkness.

The growing brightness of the day didn't penetrate the shed's dim interior. Jimmy stood squinting in the doorway, too late realizing he was silhouetted against the early morning sun. His vision adjusted just in time to see the wiry youth halfway across the shed, approaching in full flight. Suddenly losing his nerve as the sizable lad tore toward him, he flung the shovel aside and gripped the metal handle of the sliding door. The rusty runners screeched as he slid the heavy elm door shut. The kid inside never slowed.

The whole end of the wooden shed vibrated violently as the intruder barged into it with all his weight and velocity. Jimmy stepped back in astonishment. A second later the door began to slide open. Jimmy grasped the handle again. The two wrestled the door, but Jimmy had a better grip. Forcing it closed, he fastened it shut with a rusty old shackle and pin that hung below the handle.

The kid immediately began shoulder-barging the door but soon gave up. Jimmy breathed a silent thanks to whoever had constructed the door using such solid wood.

He stood back from the door and picked up his cap, which had fallen to the ground, and replaced it on his head. He was breathing heavily, shocked at the ferocity of the stranger's assault. With the captive still grunting in anger, the laborer walked shakily to his vehicle to radio his boss.

Sam sat down, taking great lungfuls of dusty air. The commotion had caused all the filth from the straw on the floor to swirl around the shed's interior in clouds. It irritated his lungs and made his eyes water. He coughed several times and hacked up a ball of phlegm, which he spat into the straw.

He was furious with himself for getting caught. He had been visiting his old farm on and off for two years. Catching a bus from Romford to the nearby village, he would wait until dark before walking across the fields and bedding down among the old bales. He was careful to avoid the house, where some people had moved in with a flashy BMW and a Range Rover. But they were rarely home, and even when they were, they never strayed from the house and garden, so they were easy to avoid. The landlord's farm workers were around quite a bit, but the huge, noisy tractors they drove normally forewarned Sam of their approach. So Sam had felt pretty safe. Until now. The boy buried his face in his hands.

"Where is he?"

The fat farm manager fell out of the door of his four-wheel-drive vehicle.

Jimmy pointed to the locked shed.

"Who is it—a gyppo? Did you clobber him?" The manager was pink and panting with excitement.

Jimmy shook his head. "No. He was pretty lively."

The fat man paused, looking at the shackled door. "Police," he said eventually. "Not that I wouldn't like a go at him myself. I flippin' would, but they'd probably put *me* away for it."

He lumbered back to his pickup truck and grabbed his phone, stabbing at it with his pudgy fingers. "Is that Harris? It's Brian Smith. The manager at Talbot Farms. I'm calling from Copse Farm." He paused for effect but apparently didn't get the recognition he'd hoped for, because he scowled and continued. "I've caught one. . . . A gypsy, who do you think? Yeah. Round the back. In a shed. Well, someone has to catch them, don't they, 'cause none of you lot seem to be able to. Yeah. Five minutes, fine. Bye."

The manager ended the call and turned to Jimmy. "They're coming. Five minutes."

/ / /

"He's in there!" the farm manager said excitedly as Will Harris climbed out of his police car.

"Is he armed?" Harris asked.

The farm manager looked back blankly. Evidently he hadn't thought about that. Harris looked at the other man standing nearby, apparently a laborer, who replied with a shake of his head. "He wasn't. I don't think so. Unless he's picked up something in there."

Harris noticed the laborer's nervous shuffle. *This is going to be interesting,* he thought wryly. He turned back to the door and called out. "Hello—who's in there?" There was no response. "This is Police Constable Will Harris. I am going to open this door now. I don't want any nasty surprises. Do you understand?"

Again there was no response. Harris took a deep breath and lifted the pin out of the shackle, his heart beating rapidly. Behind him, he heard the laborer backing even farther away. He glanced quickly over his shoulder and saw the fat manager bending down to pick up a shovel that was lying in the nettles.

Harris slid the door open to a man's width and peered inside. Just as it opened, a figure burst through it, smashing headlong into the hefty policeman. The momentum carried both of them several feet into the yard. Harris did a complete backward roll in the dirt, landing on his knees. His assailant scrambled to his feet to make good his getaway. But he was too slow. The fat man took careful aim with his shovel and smacked him across the back of his head. The boy landed face-first in the dirt, unconscious.

"I got him! I got him!" the farm manager squealed as he danced around the stricken boy.

"You could've killed him," Harris wheezed, winded and fighting for air. He crawled across to the prone figure and turned him over. The filthy boy was beginning to regain consciousness. Harris patted the boy on the cheek, and the kid's eyes opened blearily. The policeman caught his breath as he recognized a boy he once knew. He cursed.

"You know him?" the fat man asked, still squealing.

"Yeah, I know him," Harris answered quietly.

"Regular troublemaker, is he?"

Sam Pennington blinked and groggily looked up at the two men stooping over him.

"Regular scum, are you?" the farm manager goaded Sam.

"He used to live here," Harris said angrily. The manager fell silent.

"Come on, Sam, son. Sit up." Harris helped Sam into a sitting position. The boy rubbed his eyes.

"Okay. Let's stand you up, and I'll take you home." Harris lifted Sam to his feet.

"Aren't you gonna charge him?" the manager said, squealing again. "I want him charged!"

Harris helped Sam into the police car and then turned around. "What am I going to charge him with? You're the one who attacked him." He challenged the manager with his eyes.

The fat man considered it briefly. "He was trespassing," he said weakly.

"Fine," Harris replied. "I can charge him with trespassing. There's just one thing you might want to think about. If you accuse him of trespass and I arrest him, we will be duty bound to appoint him a lawyer. The lawyer would, I'm sure, quickly hear you hit him over the head with a shovel and no doubt demand you be charged with assault. In court, I, under oath, would sadly have to say I'm not sure that you were directly threatened or that your action was justified." The policeman smiled. "It would be interesting to see which way the judge would go on that one."

Harris climbed behind the wheel, gunned the engine, and

wound down the window. "Ring me if you want to press charges."

/ / /

Jimmy Davis grinned to himself as his deflated manager watched the departing police car, hiding it quickly when his boss turned around.

"Get back to work," the farm manager snarled. "I still want that job finished by lunchtime."

6

"Are you all right?" Will Harris asked, looking sideways at Sam, who was holding the back of his head.

The boy dropped his hand and shrugged.

"He gave you a decent clonk. I think you put a dent in his shovel!"

Harris watched closely to see if Sam would laugh or smile. He did neither.

"Where are we going?" Sam demanded.

"I'm just going to get someone to look at your head at the hospital."

"I'm fine," Sam retorted immediately. "I don't need a doctor." He lifted his hand to the door handle.

The experienced policeman chose his words carefully. "Let's go, mate. I could get in a lot of trouble if I don't at least get you checked out. You were unconscious back there."

"I don't need a doctor. Let me out."

"Come on, Sam. Your dad and I were good friends. Give me a break."

Sam flinched and fell silent, looking shocked at the reference to his father and the realization that the policeman knew who he was.

Harris bided his time as he drove to the hospital. He had enough experience with adolescents to know that their confidence was not gained by bombarding them with questions. They pulled into the hospital complex and parked right outside the accident and emergency department.

As they entered the busy reception area, the policeman turned to Sam. "Can I trust you, as the son of a friend, to sit down for a minute and not run off?" Sam looked at his feet and paused before nodding. Harris turned and walked to the admissions station.

The duty nurse recognized the policeman and greeted him warmly. "Hi, Constable Harris. How are you?"

"Fine, thanks. Are you busy?"

She looked up at him and then glanced ruefully over his shoulder at the roomful of patients.

"Hmm, sorry. Stupid question."

The nurse sighed and smiled up at him. "Just another day in our sunny health service. How can I help you?"

"Well—" he nodded to where Sam was sitting looking at his feet—"he's had a bit of a bang on the head. He was unconscious for a couple of seconds and a bit dizzy. He seems all right now, but I just wanted to get him checked out. Trouble is . . ." He nodded at the roomful of people.

"That's fine," she interrupted. "Bring him through."

"Thank you. I owe you one." Harris beckoned Sam over.

"Hi," the nurse said sweetly to Sam, who blushed. "Come with me, and we'll take a look at your head."

/ / /

The policeman hurried outside to his car and picked up the police radio.

"Hi, Julie. It's Will Harris."

"Go ahead, Will."

"Julie, can you do me a favor and run a check on the name Sam Pennington? I don't know his current address, but there can't be many with that name."

The dispatcher came back a minute later. "There are four Sam Penningtons in the system. Any other info?"

"Well, he must be about fifteen, sixteen years old."

Julie was another few seconds before replying. "It must be this one. Sam Pennington. Fifteen years old. 28C Soweto Rise, Mandela complex, Romford. Not a lot on record. Do you want the detail?"

"Yes, go ahead."

/ / /

Sam and the nurse emerged from a treatment room. Harris strolled over.

"The doctor says he's fine," the nurse said, patting Sam on the shoulder. "Just a big bump and a headache. Sam, tell your parents they must bring you back if you start vomiting or become more sleepy than normal. Okay?"

Sam nodded. "Thanks," he mumbled.

"You're welcome. Nice to meet you."

The policeman winked at the nurse and mouthed a silent thank-you before laying his hand on Sam's shoulder. "Come on. Let's go and get some food."

/ / /

"So, what's the story, Sam?" Harris finally asked when the boy had finished eating. The policeman had been studying the kid carefully, deciding on his approach as Sam devoured a large plate of chips and fish fingers. "You're hiding in places that no longer belong to you, presumably bunking off school."

Sam sullenly picked up his fork again and began prodding at the remaining bread crumbs on his plate.

"How are you getting on at school, Sam?"

Sam shrugged. "All right," he mumbled without looking up.

"And what school's that? Number one, two, or three since you've lived in Romford?"

Sam prodded harder.

"What about your mum? What does she think about you disappearing off?"

"She wouldn't notice," Sam shot back angrily. "She's a drunk."

The policeman grimaced. *Poor kid,* he thought. *Life's not fair.* He was beginning to regret his tough approach. But he had started now.

"C'mon, Sam. What are you doing with your life? Fighting, skipping school. I don't think your dad would be very proud of you."

After a long silence, Sam raised his eyes to the older man. "Leave me alone."

7

Robbie Dixon climbed onto the railing and negotiated the few yards to the bus stop like a tightrope walker, swaying his arms to balance. Shoving off the railing with his feet, the rangy youth landed on the bus-shelter roof with a thump, unintentionally scaring the life out of the old lady sitting inside. He rolled over and sat cross-legged in the drizzle. *Why sit in a bus stop when you can sit on it?* he thought with satisfaction. It didn't occur to him he'd be drier inside.

That was Robbie. He fitted no convention. He didn't drink or take drugs. He listened to ABBA when all his mates listened to hip-hop. He preferred lawn-bowling clubs to nightclubs and wrote poetry—though not very well. Up until the week before, he had been the proud driver of an old brown Volvo, his pride and joy. The lads at school mercilessly ribbed their friend for his dreadful taste. He didn't care. It might be the slowest thing on the road, but he loved it. Only now it sat broken on his grandma's driveway after he had parked it in a bog while trying to find a secluded spot to serenade his new girlfriend. She had not been impressed at having to cross a field and climb a hedge in her skirt and heels.

"Why couldn't we just find a spot in some parking lot like everyone else?" she had complained bitterly. It had cost him two hundred pounds and a broken front axle to get his car recovered from the mud. Robbie had no money to fix it, which was why he was catching the bus.

It wasn't just his car that had foundered in the bog. Mandy hadn't returned his calls either, despite the rhyming apology he had shoved through her letter box. He had been very proud of it. It wasn't easy to find words that rhymed with *Volvo*.

Much as he loved his car, Robbie's real passion was boxing. And, unusually for Robbie Dixon, he was actually good at it. He had been training since he was twelve years old and was now one of the best young boxers at the Ilford Boxing Club. He wasn't a brawler or a particularly strong puncher, but his speed and ring craft, learned in hundreds of hours of careful sparring and instruction with his trainer, meant he could more than hold his own.

From his vantage point atop the bus shelter, Robbie glanced up the street for the number 73 bus that would take him to the boxing club. Instead, his eyes fell upon three skinheads walking down the other side of the street, spanning the entire pavement. An Asian woman, moving in the opposite direction, ducked her head and scurried across the road as all three spat in her direction.

Robbie instinctively scanned the rest of the street. It was clearing rapidly as other pedestrians ducked into shops or hurried across the road to avoid the threat. All except one. Robbie frowned as he noticed a teenage boy walking directly toward the intimidating trio, apparently unaware of the danger ahead. As the gap closed, Robbie willed the kid to look up while he still had time to get out of the way. The skinheads had spotted him and immediately picked up their pace.

"Come on, kid, get out the way," Robbie said under his breath as he noticed his bus turning onto the street. But the boy carried on walking with his head down and eyes on the pavement directly ahead.

"Come on. *Come on.* Cross the street!" Robbie muttered, climbing onto his haunches. The skinheads and the clueless boy were now twenty feet apart, level with Robbie's bus stop. Robbie quickly glanced to his right to see the bus stopped at the light fifty yards away. He looked back at the impending confrontation.

The moment the boy reached them, one of the skinheads shoved him roughly backward, swearing loudly. Robbie watched in disbelief as the youngster steadied himself and then threw a huge overhand right. The punch caught the startled skinhead in the face, and he slithered to the ground. Before either of the other men could react, the young kamikaze threw a ferocious left uppercut at one of the remaining attackers. But the man saw it coming, and the punch only grazed his shaved head as the fist went flailing past. Now the boy was in trouble.

The remaining skinhead lashed out at the kid, catching

him on the side of the throat, while the other one grabbed the boy's shirt and head-butted him across the bridge of his nose. A knee crashed up into the boy's chest. He collapsed to the ground as the two men began kicking and stamping, burying their steel-toed boots into the kid's exposed body and head.

Robbie could no longer stand by and watch. The boy might deserve a beating for picking such a stupid fight, but a few more seconds of this and he would be dead. Robbie vaulted off the bus shelter roof, landing in front of the approaching bus, and bounded toward the fight.

Bang, bang, bang. In a flurry of punches he had knocked both remaining skinheads to the ground. He reached down and yanked the bleeding boy to his feet with a strength belied by his skinny frame.

"Come on!" he yelled, dragging him in the direction of the number 73. As he looked up at the bus, Robbie noticed the driver staring past him in alarm. One of the skinheads, with blood all over his face, had clambered to his feet and was staggering toward them. The boy beside Robbie turned to confront him.

"Move, you idiot!" Robbie screamed and shoved the boy into the bus, landing on top of him as he jumped through the closing door.

The bus took off like a rocket, sending the standing passengers hurtling up the aisle. Someone screamed. Two skinheads were now on their feet and giving chase, violently kicking the side of the bus as it sped wildly down the street in an explosion of revving engine and gray exhaust fumes.

Robbie leaned against the door, trying to catch his breath.

The bloodied boy beside him was struggling to a seated position. The two young men caught each other's eye and silently sized one another up while the bus driver swore fluently down at them.

Sam wiped the blood from his nose. "Thanks," he said quietly.

"Did you know them?"

Sam shook his head.

"Then . . . why?"

Sam shrugged his shoulders, and Robbie broke into laughter. "You're nuts, mate."

Sam began to laugh too, but his damaged ribs forced him to stop. He coughed again, the pain clear on his face.

"Does he need a hospital?" the bus driver said to Robbie, finally gathering his composure.

Robbie looked at the boy, who shook his head vigorously. "No. I'll get him checked out."

"Well, if you're gonna stay on the bus, at least take a seat."

Robbie helped the boy to his feet, and they staggered back toward an empty seat. The shaken passengers looked aghast at the two boys as they passed. Robbie nodded apologetically.

"And don't bleed on anything," the bus driver yelled up the bus behind him.

Robbie turned to the boy. "I'm Robbie," he announced, thrusting out his hand. Sam looked down at the outstretched hand and then at his own, which was smeared in blood. He showed it to his rescuer, who didn't withdraw. He wiped his hand on his trousers and reached out slowly.

"Sam."

/ / /

When the bus turned onto Ilford High Street, Robbie stood up and motioned Sam to follow him to the front. He held out his bus pass and dropped two coins in the tray. "Sorry about that back there, mate. Is that enough for him? I doubt he's got a pass."

"Er—yeah . . . that's fine," the driver said, shocked. The unpaid fare had clearly been the last thing on his mind.

Sam followed his rescuer painfully down the street. He ached all over and struggled to keep up with the tall boy ahead of him. Robbie dived down an alleyway between a betting shop and a grocery store and walked up to a big red door with the letters *IBC* painted roughly on the outside.

He led Sam through the heavy door and up a flight of stairs, then opened a swing door and ushered his new friend through.

Sam stopped openmouthed and stared.

8

The blaze of light and bustle of activity were almost overwhelming. The room was long and wide with wooden floor-
boards. The glass in the high Victorian windows had been
painted with white emulsion up to head height. Above the
paint, the sun streamed in, bathing the room with shafts of
light.

To the right of the doorway, three young men hugged
leather punching bags that hung on chains from the ceiling, turning them toward their attackers. Next to them,
another group pounded away on small, round punching
bags that dangled from a rack and vibrated back and forth
rhythmically. To Sam's left, grown men skipped rope at a
pace unseen on the school playground. Others were dancing
around, punching the air, snorting through their noses as
each punch landed on an imaginary opponent. Against the

far wall, muscled athletes lifted steel bars toward the ceiling, while still others hauled medicine balls above their heads.

But what attracted Sam's attention above all else was the raised boxing ring in the center of the room. Two men wearing head protectors danced around each other, sparring, while others hung over the ropes, watching the fast flurries of punches. Every thirty seconds or so, a tall black man leaning on the ropes stopped the fight and called both boxers over. He would demonstrate a technical point and then set them off again. Sam felt drawn toward the ring like a bee to a pot of honey.

"Come on," Robbie said, smiling. He led Sam to their left, where a small, wiry man was massaging a young boxer's shoulders. He looked up as the two boys approached.

"Hey, Robbie, have you written any more poetry?" he said in a broad Italian accent.

"I'm not showing you any more, you ignoramus."

The older man laughed loudly, playing to the crowd. "Oh, but Robbie, I like your poetry! It makes me go all goose pimply!"

"Mario, you wouldn't know talent if it smacked you in the face."

"Eh, how can you say that?" Mario said with a wounded look. "You see this?" He pointed at his own flattened nose. "This face has been smacked by a lot of talent, no?" He cackled loudly at his own joke. "But I tell you, Robbie. Your poetry? It hurt me the most of all!"

Mario erupted in laughter again and smiled at Robbie before frowning as he spotted Sam. His expert gaze took in the bloody face and pained movement immediately. He looked back at Robbie.

"You been sparring with locals?"

"He's had a bit of a shoeing, Mario. Can you have a look at him?"

Mario slapped the boxer he was massaging on the shoulder and grabbed a towel for his hands. He beckoned to Sam. "Come here. Take your top off."

Sam gingerly pulled off his T-shirt, conscious of Robbie's assessing gaze. He flinched as Mario ran his thumb gently along the ugly red patches on his ribs.

Mario turned his attention to Sam's face. Sam grunted in pain as the man felt the bones of his nose with his fingertips.

"Broken," Mario said in a matter-of-fact way, and gently sandwiched the nose between his thumb and forefinger. "Breathe in."

As Sam took a breath, Mario, without warning, squeezed Sam's nose and forced it sideways. There was an audible crack as the bone reset, and Sam yelped with pain. He instinctively slapped Mario's hands away and rose to retaliate but stopped as he realized the pain had eased.

Mario watched him warily, and Sam was conscious of how close he had come to striking him. "Sorry I not give you warning," the older man said gently, "but I promise it would've hurt more if I had. I have done this many times."

The Italian stood in front of Sam and studied his handiwork. "Pretty good, actually." He smiled and wiped blood from Sam's face with a towel.

"You're fine. Go and have a shower."

Sam stared helplessly at him until Mario pulled a towel from a hook on the wall, threw it to Sam, and pointed to a door in the corner.

Sam gingerly eased himself off the bench and headed away.

/ / /

"Who was that, Mario?" Jerry Ambrose asked as the new kid disappeared into the showers.

"Dunno, Jerry. Ask him." Mario nodded to Robbie, who was hurriedly stripping off his street clothes.

Robbie looked over. "I was sitting waiting for the bus on Romford High Street and saw him get into a fight with three big skinheads right in front of me. He took one out but then got a good kicking."

"And then they let him go?" Jerry asked.

Robbie glanced up at the tall black trainer and then down at his feet. Jerry clapped his hands in frustration. "Come on, Robbie. You know it stays in the ring!"

"He was gonna get killed, boss! I had to get him out of there. I promise I didn't do any damage. Just enough to get him away."

Jerry rubbed his head. "Sorry, Robbie. I'm sure you did the right thing. What's his name?"

"Sam."

"Do you know anything about him?"

"No. Nothing," Robbie replied, shaking his head. "Except he's got a death wish. Solid overhand right, though. The first guy never got up."

Jerry looked in the direction of the showers. *What have you brought me this time, Lord?* he asked silently.

/ / /

Sam stood in the shower, letting the hot water wash through his hair and down his back. While the water soothed his aching body, his mind was racing with excitement. He had found somewhere he wanted to be.

9

Jerry Ambrose leaned on the ropes, watching two boxers spar. His hair was just beginning to gray at the temples, giving him a distinguished look. But his thirty-nine-year-old physique showed no sign of middle-aged spread, and his black skin still held the sheen and tautness of a much younger man's. As he watched the boxing in front of him, his head and hands twitched as he sensed each punch before it was thrown.

"Spin away, Robbie! That's it. Nice! Good counter. Head up. Come on, head up!"

Jerry frowned as he saw Robbie ducking forward again.

"Okay, stop it there. Come here." He put his arm on the young boxer's shoulder. "Robbie. You're six foot two. Use it. You're leaning forward too much and ducking into punches. You're gonna come up against shorter guys at your weight, so let's wear them out punching uphill. Okay? Your feet are great, though. And I loved that feigned left lead you made. Just don't use it too much. Surprise, Robbie. Don't lose the surprise. Got it?"

Robbie nodded like a puppy dog.

"Okay. Ding-a-ling. You're on."

Robbie bounded away, panting. Jerry fought to conceal his smile. He loved this kid. Jerry had worked with him for five years, helping turn him from a bullied child into a young man equipped for life and happy to be himself. Boxing had worked for him. Robbie was honest and hardworking and sure to make a success of his life.

In the process, Jerry had also turned him into a very useful boxer, good enough to represent the club at quality amateur events. However, Jerry sensed that Robbie, like most young amateurs, dreamed of a glorious career as a professional. Much as Jerry wanted all his boxers to succeed, deep down he knew Robbie wouldn't cut it at the very top.

Jerry didn't fret. His passion was to see young lives turned around, as his own had been many years earlier. In his mind, success in the ring was of only secondary importance.

As Jerry watched the boxers sparring, he noticed the new boy, Sam, had emerged from the showers and was walking toward the ring. The boy stepped up to the ring surface and leaned on the top rope opposite, unconsciously caressing the rope in his hands. Jerry didn't acknowledge the lad, yet kept half an eye on him throughout the rest of the session. The boy's attention didn't waver for a second.

Finally Robbie maneuvered his opponent slightly to his left and threw two swift jabs that landed sweetly. The opponent covered up to protect his stinging nose, and Robbie immediately danced in a foot closer. His adversary lowered his guard, and Robbie's thumping overhand right found its target. The boxer stumbled backward into the ropes, causing Sam to jump out of the way.

"Okay, that's it," Jerry shouted as Robbie followed up. Both boxers instantly dropped their gloves. "Lee, are you all right?" The boy brushed his nose with his glove and nodded at the trainer. "Good lad. Thank you very much—that was perfect. You're coming along really well. Keep that work rate going and that jab snapping, and you'll be giving Robbie real problems. Well done! You can get changed."

Jerry turned his attention back to Robbie. "Hallelujah! That was beautiful. We're really getting there now. Just remember, head up and don't overextend. But really good, well done. Now go grab a drink, and then we'll do some work with the pads."

As Robbie filled up his water bottle at the tap, Jerry noticed the other boy circling the ring toward him.

"I wanna fight," the boy said firmly as he reached Jerry.

"Why?" Jerry answered immediately.

The boy fell silent, clearly lost for a reply.

"I tell you what," Jerry intervened after a few seconds. "You go home and nurse those cuts and bruises. Come back next week, and if you've thought of a good-enough reason, I'll think about it."

Jerry saw the boy scowl at him but chose to ignore it, turning instead to Robbie, who was climbing back into the ring.

"Okay. Let's go, Robbie," the trainer said, ducking between the ropes as he pulled on two hand pads. "See you next week, Sam."

Sam turned away and walked sullenly toward the exit. Jerry watched him go.

"Just give me a second, Robbie." Jerry lifted the large pads and buried his face in the soft leather, shutting his eyes. "Please bring him back, Lord," he whispered. A feeling of peace replaced his concern. "Thank you, Jesus. Thank you."

The trainer clapped the pads together and began bouncing on his toes.

"Come on then, Robbie! I'm Goliath! I'm a Philistine, man! I'm nine foot tall, and I'm coming after you. I wanna knock you clean out the ring!" Jerry swung the pads with exaggerated sweeps toward Robbie. "Pick up your slingshot, son. Fire those pebbles. I want you scoring points but not risking yourself at all. I'm really gonna come for you and try to pin you down. Hit and move, hit and move. Okay?"

Robbie nodded, tapping his mouth guard into place with his glove.

Jerry clapped the pads together again. "Let's go."

Jerry advanced like a grizzly bear. The boy spun away, dancing on his toes and firing jabs as he went.

10

Janet Pennington pushed through the bathroom door, scrunching up her eyes against the sunlight that made her head throb harder. Sam was standing in the kitchen with his cereal bowl to his lips. She ignored it. Five years earlier she might have gently scolded him, but she had long since given up remonstrating with her son about table manners.

"Morning," she said quietly, pushing back a strand of lank hair that hung across her face.

Sam returned the greeting automatically, without meeting her eye. "I've gotta go," he said, setting his bowl down in the sink and picking up his bag. "See you later."

"Bye, sweetheart. Have a good day," Janet replied. But Sam had already gone, the front door clunking behind him.

She sighed. Nowadays they hardly ever exchanged cross

words, but the lack of depth or warmth in their communication tore Janet apart.

She looked across the room at her reflection in her grandmother's antique mirror, which hung incongruously against the swirling wallpaper, and shuddered. Even from ten feet away, she could see it. The previous five minutes of scrubbing in the bathroom had had no effect. Her skin was turning yellow. There could be only one explanation.

"Today," she vowed aloud. Today was the day she was going to turn it around. She glanced up at the clock and was pleased to see it was just after eight, at least two hours before she normally surfaced. It was Thursday—the day she collected her benefits and child allowance from the post office. Today she would take the money straight to the supermarket and buy some proper food.

"Roast dinner," she said. "I'll make Sam a roast dinner." Immediately the thought of the cost and what she might have to go without hounded her mind. She looked up again at her yellow reflection in the mirror. Even her eyes were yellow. "No drinking," she said firmly. "Not this week."

Janet pulled on her coat, gathered her handbag, and headed for the door.

/ / /

An hour and a half later, Janet was feeling really proud of herself. She carried several more grocery bags than usual, and only a small chinking of glass reminded her that she hadn't ignored the liquor aisle completely. She had stood in the shop for ages, struggling in panic to remember all the ingredients she needed for a pork roast with all the trimmings. Back at the farm, this had been her specialty, and most of it had finally come back to her. She was, so far, only aware of forgetting corn flour to thicken up the gravy. She had remembered the key ingredient—applesauce. At Copse Farm, they had made their own with fruit from the old Bramley apple tree that stood in the corner of their front garden. Throughout the late summer, she and Sam would pick up the windfalls. Later, they would have an enormous cook-up, producing enough applesauce for the whole year. It had been Sam's favorite.

Janet paused for a moment and checked again that the sauce had made it into her bag. There it was, nestling against a familiar green bottle. That had been what was chinking in her bag, she thought with a smile—applesauce! Not gin. Well, not just gin. Her eyes lingered on the green bottle.

Not yet, she resolved. *I've got a roast dinner to cook.* She looked up to see the ugly concrete structures of the Mandela housing complex coming into view in the distance and hurried forward.

By the time she reached the complex, she was almost running, determined not to stop and have a drink. If she did, she knew it would be the end of her romantic notion. And today, just for one day, she was going to be the Janet Pennington of old again. Robert's Janet. The Janet Pennington who could cook a meal standing on her head. She smiled inwardly at the thought. She could pull her life together. A roast dinner for Sam was just the start. She hurried toward the underpass leading to the complex, lost in these unfamiliar yet happy thoughts.

As she approached the concrete tunnel she saw three men

leaning against the wall ahead. Two of them had their backs to Janet, while the third, dressed in a baggy gray tracksuit and a white baseball cap, was facing her. Janet shivered as she walked forward, heading for the remaining gap between the youths and the opposite wall of the narrow underpass. Just as Janet reached them, the man in the baseball cap looked up and saw her.

"Hey, mama," the man said casually, stepping out to block her way. His two friends turned around. Janet nodded silently, glancing back to see an empty path behind her. She was alone.

"You been shoppin'?" the man continued in the same soft yet threatening voice. Janet looked down at her shopping bags and nodded again. This time her eyes remained on the ground.

"Poor you," the young man said mockingly. "You must be so tired." The two other men began to snigger.

"Nice one, Dwayne."

"Here," Dwayne said, reaching forward and grabbing Janet's bags. "Me and my boys will carry these for you."

Janet held on grimly. "It's fine. I'm fine," she replied in a high-pitched voice that quivered with fear. "I'm almost home. I can manage. Thank you."

Dwayne refused to let go. "I insist. We must all help our neighbors, mustn't we?" He roughly pulled the bags from Janet's grip and handed them to his friends before theatrically stepping aside and gesturing Janet forward. Janet clutched her handbag to her body and headed for the square of light ahead of her, mourning the joint of pork and her bottle of gin.

They emerged into daylight. To Janet's surprise, the boys didn't run off. For a moment she allowed herself to believe that they were really trying to help. But as she turned around and saw the face of the man who had accosted her, she knew that this was no act of charity. And immediately a worse truth dawned on her. She was now leading them to where she lived. She stopped, took a deep breath, and turned to face the men.

"Thank you so much. I can manage from here," Janet said, smiling as sweetly as she could and gesturing toward the bags of shopping.

Dwayne touched his baseball cap and smiled menacingly. "That's fine, lady. We'll carry them right to your front door. All part of the service!" He winked at his two friends, who laughed again.

Janet turned slowly and moved with dread toward the concrete stairwell that led to her flat. As she climbed the stairs, she had an idea. She fumbled urgently for her key inside her handbag. Reaching the middle landing, she saw her opportunity and scuttled up the remaining steps. She ran to her front door and jammed the key in the lock, swinging the door open as she heard running footsteps behind her. She ducked inside and swung the door hard, but it came to a jarring halt. She looked down to see the toe of a big white trainer wedged in the gap between door and frame.

A moment later the door was forced open. Janet stepped back in resignation and wearily raised her eyes to face her fate.

Dwayne stood in the doorway with a mocking grin. He slowly shook his head, tutting gently. "You almost forgot your groceries."

He thrust out his hand and shoved her roughly backward into the flat. He reached around and grabbed the shopping bags from his friends and threw them across the room. They landed with a crash on the linoleum floor.

"Delivered!" Dwayne said, smirking as Janet backed away toward the far corner of the room, still clutching her hand-bag. A sob escaped as she saw milk seeping across the floor.

"So." Dwayne sneered, crossing his arms in front of his chest. "Are you gonna give us our reward?"

Janet instinctively reached up and clutched the top of her blouse. Dwayne grimaced in a deliberately insulting way. "Dream on. I wouldn't want an old hag like you." The other men laughed again, but more nervously this time. One of them glanced over his shoulder at the open door and swung it shut behind them.

"Money!" Dwayne barked.

Janet was frozen for a second before suddenly springing into action. She pulled the purse from her bag, but her hands were shaking so hard she couldn't open the zipper. Dwayne strode toward her and snatched the black leather purse. He ripped it open and turned it over, flicking through the flaps but finding nothing. He unzipped the coin section and shook out seven coins. "Is this all you've got?" he shouted in disgust.

"I'm sorry," Janet said, looking forlornly at the electricity meter money in his hand. "I only get forty pounds a week. That's all I've got after shopping."

With contempt on his face, Dwayne dropped the coins in his pocket. Then, with stunning speed, he grabbed Janet by the lapels of her blouse and drew her face to his.

"Right then," Dwayne yelled in her face. "Every Thursday from now on, I'm having half of that! Got it?"

Janet shivered and looked down.

"Otherwise . . ." He paused and scanned the flat. "You got kids?"

Janet shivered again and shook her head as convincingly as she could.

"Okay," he said, leering at her. "Well, if you don't come up with the money . . ." He paused again and turned her toward the two lads who were standing nervously by the door. "These big black boys—well, they're not as picky as me. Don't get as much, you know." He reached down and grabbed Janet's buttock with his hand. "They might just fancy a bit of white middle-aged action. You get what I'm saying?" He turned Janet back to him, his face now inches from hers. "Have we got a deal?"

Janet nodded miserably.

Dwayne held on to her for a couple seconds more and then released her. Her knees buckled, and she collapsed onto the sofa. The two men laughed nervously as Dwayne stood over her. He leaned forward and patted her on the head like a dog. "See you next week. I'll bring my boys just in case."

With the threat still lingering, he strode across the room, pulled the door open, and left, his two friends close behind. Janet sank onto the sofa, burying her face in its brown velour cover.

Eventually her sobs died down, and she slid painfully from the sofa to the floor. On her hands and knees, she crawled to the pile of shopping bags. She pushed aside the bag containing the pork roast and reached for another. She had heard the smash of glass as the bags had hit the floor, and she feared the worst. Another sob escaped as she saw that everything was covered in applesauce.

But not everything had shattered. She reached through the broken glass and retrieved what she was looking for. Her hands slipped on sticky applesauce as she tried desperately to open the bottle. Wiping the cap on her blouse, she finally succeeded. Janet slugged the gin until she gagged and the clear liquid escaped down her chin. Then she crawled back to the sofa.

Twenty minutes later, the bottle lay half-empty on the floor next to her hand.

11

The school bell finally rang. The week's wait was over at last. Sam jumped up from his desk and grabbed his bag before the teacher had even finished speaking. Sprinting out of the school, he set off toward Ilford, five miles away, running along the edge of the road. As he did so, the number 73 bus, which he didn't have enough money for, trundled past.

/ / /

Jerry was at the gym, waiting and hoping. His week had dragged too. Ever since Sam had walked out of the gym seven days earlier, the young man had been on the trainer's mind. Jerry had gone home that evening and, after bathing the children, had told his wife of the unsettling burden he felt for a boy he barely knew. They had reached across the kitchen table and prayed together.

"Yes!" Jerry said under his breath as he saw Sam enter the gym. Their eyes locked, and Jerry fought the smile that began to spread itself across his face. *Thank you, Lord,* he prayed instead. The trainer dragged his eyes back to the boxers in the ring and pretended that his attention hadn't been disturbed.

Sam walked directly toward Jerry and, with one bound, landed on the narrow walkway surrounding the ring. He circled toward the trainer, who looked up as he approached.

"So, Sam, why do you want to fight?"

"Well . . ." Sam hesitated. "I want to learn how to defend myself."

Jerry raised his eyebrows at the rehearsed answer and rubbed his chin thoughtfully. "Well, stand up straight and let's have a look at you."

Sam straightened and flexed his muscles a little.

The trainer looked him over. "Have you got a brain, son?"

Sam nodded.

"Good." Jerry's eyes moved downward until they rested on the boy's battered old sneakers. "Have you got quick feet? Can you run?"

"Yes, I can," Sam said, sounding more confident now.

"Then God has blessed you richly indeed! A brain and the ability to run fast." Jerry looked deep into the boy's eyes. "You want to learn to defend yourself?" He slapped Sam's upper arm. "God has given you everything you need already."

Jerry jumped down from the ring, leaving Sam standing bewildered.

"Brain and feet, brain and feet." Jerry chuckled. "It's

all you need." He stopped and turned. "A free tip, Sam. Attacking skinheads is not using your brain."

Sam erupted without warning, yelling a curse and jumping off the ring platform toward Jerry. The loud cry alerted all in the vicinity. Almost before Sam had landed, two men were standing between him and Jerry. Sam stopped and glowered, aware of the sudden silence in the gym and of dozens of pairs of eyes boring into him.

Jerry was startled but waved the other boxers back to their stations. He walked up to the boy and spoke gently. "Why do you really want to fight, Sam?"

The boy floundered silently and then finally looked up at Jerry. "Because it feels good."

Jerry nodded gently. "Okay. That's honest at least."

The two of them appraised each other until Jerry nodded at Sam's bag. "Have you got any shorts in there?"

Sam nodded.

"Well, go and put them on. I'll take a look at you."

/ / /

"So, are you a professional?" Sam asked as he mimicked Robbie's stretch.

Robbie shook his head. "Not yet. But I will be one day. Most people here are amateurs. Just do it for fun. I think there's about twenty professionals here. Most of them are just . . . well, they call them journeymen. They've fought a lot of fights. Lose as many as they win, but they get a bit of cash out of it. Most of them have other jobs as well. There's a few good 'uns. They earn quite a bit more. Pretty good records, too."

"Who's the best?"

"Frank McCullough," Robbie answered. "He's brilliant. Fifteen wins out of fifteen! Jerry and Bert are trying to get him a British title fight."

"Who's Bert?" Sam asked as they rolled their shoulders.

"Bert Stubbs. He owns the place and organizes all the fights. He's called a promoter. That's his office over there." Robbie pointed to an office in the corner with a window through which Sam could see a bald man working at a desk.

"And who's the Italian bloke?" he said, nodding at the man who had fixed his nose the week before.

"That's Mario—he's the cut man."

"The what?"

"Cut man," Robbie said. "When boxers get cut in a fight, he has to stop the bleeding. He's also a masseur. He knows everything about sorting out injuries."

Sam nodded silently as they stretched their necks, rolling them backward and forward gently, then side to side.

"What about Jerry, then?" Sam asked, nodding at the black man on the far side of the room.

"Jerry? He's the trainer. Trains all the fighters—pro and amateur."

"Seems like a jerk."

"No." Robbie bristled. "He's brilliant. He's been like a dad to me."

Sam looked at Robbie curiously but said nothing.

"He's also the best boxer here by a mile," Robbie added proudly. "He's almost forty, but he could still kick anyone's butt here if he wanted to."

"Was he a professional?"

"Dunno. He'll never talk about it."

Sam looked hard at the trainer again, then turned to point at a weight rack nearby.

"What's that?"

"That's a chest press. Have you ever had a go?"

Sam shook his head. Robbie glanced toward Jerry, who was deep in conversation with his back turned. "Come on. I'll show you."

/ / /

Jerry realized he had lost sight of the boys warming up as he chatted to a couple of the boxers he hadn't seen for a while. He scanned the gym and spotted a small crowd gathered in the weights area. Jerry excused himself and sauntered over. As he got closer, Jerry could see Robbie bouncing around excitedly as other men watched someone lifting a heavy barbell on the bench press. It was Sam. Jerry instinctively counted the circular weights hanging on each end of the steel bar and took a sharp breath.

The boy's strength was extraordinary—he was lifting in excess of what most men at the club could manage after years of training. As he easily bench-pressed 240 pounds, a greater crowd began to gather.

Jerry had seen enough. "Come on, pack it in," he said, wading in. "I told you to warm him up, Robbie, not knacker him out."

"Sorry, boss. But did you see how strong he is?" Robbie said, grinning.

"Yes, I did. Very impressive," Jerry replied flatly. "Get your gloves on, and we'll do some pads."

Robbie bounded off, and Sam stood up from the bench sheepishly.

"Come with me," Jerry said, beckoning. He led Sam to a small room in the corner of the gym, crammed from top to bottom with boxing equipment.

"Hold your hands out," Jerry commanded.

Sam obeyed, and the older man expertly wrapped a long bandage around each of Sam's hands and wrists before looping the coarse white fabric around the thumb repeatedly and locking it in place with some white tape. Sam flexed his newly wrapped hands, seemingly unaccustomed to the extra support the tight bandages gave his wrists.

"Clench," Jerry ordered. The trainer reached out and smothered Sam's bandaged fists with his own cupped hands. He then turned and selected a pair of gloves and handed them to Sam.

Sam pulled on the red gloves and clenched his fists. Jerry watched the boy's face as he unintentionally grinned.

"Good. Let's go."

/ / /

Sam watched carefully as Robbie bounced rhythmically, punching Jerry's hand pads at the trainer's command.

"Left," Jerry demanded. The thud of glove on pad followed almost immediately. "Left." Thud again. Robbie was jabbing beautifully. "Good. Left-right-left." *Thud, thud, thud.* "Excellent."

After several minutes, Jerry lowered his hands and turned to Sam. "Your turn."

Sam stepped forward and adopted Robbie's pose, his gloves in front of his chest.

"Okay, Sam. Turn a bit more sideways and hold those hands up higher. Yeah. Up to your face." Satisfied Sam was roughly in position, Jerry lifted his right pad.

"Okay. Left," Jerry barked. *Thud.* Jerry swallowed. "Right." His voice croaked slightly. *Thud.* "Left-right." *Thud, thud.*

Jerry's heart raced. The boy's punching power was incredible. His posture was naive, and he was only punching with his arms and shoulders, not with his legs. Yet Jerry couldn't stop his hands from recoiling backward with each vicious punch. He kept Sam going, partly out of wonder, waiting for the boy to tire. But he didn't. Indeed, he even seemed to be building up to a greater intensity as he got the hang of punching the pads.

Jerry studied Sam's face as the boy stood throwing punches. His eyes were wild, and he wore a fearsome, slightly unhinged expression on his face as every punch landed. Minute after minute they pounded on, Sam responding quicker and harder to the prompting as Jerry unsuccessfully tried to get Sam to throw the wrong fist.

Jerry finally called a halt. As they both lowered their fists, the trainer realized with exhilaration that his hands were both throbbing with pain and shaking with excitement.

"Are you left-handed, Sam?"

"Yeah."

Jerry nodded knowingly. "I thought so. Your right's particularly weak."

Jerry immediately flinched at his own words as he saw a flash of pain register on the boy's face. He wondered why he had made such a harsh and untrue statement. For the first time in a long time, Jerry felt flustered. "Right," he said hurriedly. "Let's move on to some other exercises."

After a further twenty minutes, Jerry was even more astonished. Sam had taken to each exercise in seconds. In addition to his punching power, the boy's timing and coordination were excellent. He even managed to master the speed ball within a couple of minutes—a skill that a couple of the journeyman pros still struggled with after years of trying. And when Robbie and Sam had taken turns on the large punching bags, it was as much as Robbie could do to hold on to it as Sam pounded away. Eventually Jerry brought the session to an end.

"Okay. Well done, Sam. Good first session. There's plenty to work on, but you're definitely a natural. Now go and have a shower while Robbie does some sparring in the ring."

Sam's face fell as he glanced at the ring. A look of fury suddenly clouded his face. "But I wanna fight!" he said angrily.

"Sorry, Sam," Jerry said, shaking his head. "You're a long way from climbing in the ring. Most don't start sparring for at least six months. We've got a lot to work on before that. I'll see you next week."

"No way, I'm ready now. I'll take anyone on."

Jerry looked down at the angry boy slamming his gloves together and considered his options. Ignore him? Or give him a lesson? Deep down he knew what he should do, and all his wisdom and experience screamed at him to walk away. But something inside drove him down another path. "You'll take anyone on, will you?" he asked.

"Anyone," Sam replied defiantly. The man and the boy held each other's stare.

"Okay. Give me a moment." The trainer climbed down from the ring and wandered over to a group of men chatting in the corner. Annoyingly, only one of them had his gloves on, and Jerry grimaced when he saw who it was. He knew again that he should walk away, but he succumbed once more.

"Frank," he said, turning to the gloved boxer, "can you do me a favor and teach this kid here a lesson?"

"It'd be a pleasure," the featherweight replied with a grin, looking over at the boy. "How much of a lesson do you want me to give him?"

"First time in the ring. So just dance around him while he flails and sting him once or twice. Don't hurt him. I just want him to know there's more to boxing than brawling."

The fighter nodded, and Jerry returned to the ring via the kit room, collecting a head guard, which he threw to Robbie. "Put that on him, Robbie."

As Sam faced Robbie to allow the head guard to be put on, Frank McCullough sidled up and silently climbed into the ring. Other people in the gym began to wander over, intrigued by the curious matchup.

When Sam's head guard was in place, he turned around to face his opponent. At 112 pounds and only five feet tall, the young Irishman was a clear head and neck shorter than Sam and probably fifty pounds lighter. Sam immediately turned sideways to Jerry.

"I'm not fighting him."

"Why not?" Jerry replied.

"I only fight proper-sized people," Sam said, gesturing at his opponent disdainfully.

The featherweight closed the distance between them in an instant and threw a lightning-fast overhand right. His gloved fist struck Sam square in the face much, much harder than Jerry had asked him to.

"Cheeky git." McCullough sneered as the boy reeled backward.

"Argh!" Sam yelled, bending at the waist and cradling his face in his gloves.

"Frank! What are you doing?" Jerry shouted angrily, rushing around the ring to the rope Sam was now leaning against. "That wasn't what I asked for." The trainer grimaced as he saw the boy's nose. It had just begun to heal from its encounter with a skinhead's forehead a week earlier, but now it had opened up again like a squashed tomato. "Mario!"

The trainer immediately felt two gloves push him firmly away. Jerry's attention lifted from the boy's nose to his eyes. They were full of pure rage.

The boy turned and lunged toward his assailant like a wild animal, throwing two huge punches. Frank McCullough easily ducked the flailing fists. Sam lunged again as Jerry grabbed the middle rope to duck underneath, intent on ending the fight. But he suddenly stopped as he saw something remarkable. The boy caught hold of his temper and adopted a crude but recognizable boxer's stance and advanced carefully toward his opponent. The Irishman was still far too quick, though, and jumped forward, firing unreturned jabs at Sam's injured nose. The boy grimaced and growled in pain yet relentlessly forged ahead, trying to shepherd the smaller man into a corner. Jerry watched with fascination.

Extricating himself both left and right from Sam's advances, Frank McCullough landed another fifteen or twenty unanswered punches to Sam's head and torso. Yet Sam absorbed the barrage of blows with seemingly little effect and continued to advance with a steely determination.

Frustrated, the Irishman stepped inside and delivered a devastating nine-shot combination. It finished with a vicious uppercut to Sam's chin. Sam reeled backward, turning away from his opponent and staggering toward the ropes.

"That's enough, Frank!" Jerry shouted. A flood of regrets crashed through his mind as he climbed into the ring. Yet while his outward anger burned toward his prize boxer, Jerry knew deep down that he alone had caused this ugly situation.

Sam bounced off the ring rope and staggered back to where Frank McCullough was smiling, waiting for the boy's knees to buckle.

Without warning, the punch-drunk stagger turned into a perfect side step and lunge. Sam rugby-tackled the Irishman around the middle and slammed him hard into the corner post. An explosion of frenzied punches rained down on McCullough's stomach and midriff, and the featherweight simply could not escape. Blow after blow hammered into the smaller man's body.

The barrage ended as quickly as it had started when a hand reached across Sam's throat and yanked him backward. In one movement Sam was swept away from the other boxer and planted face-first on the floor of the ring.

"Calm down," Jerry said firmly, kneeling on the boy's back and twisting his arm behind him. Sam squirmed angrily but couldn't move and eventually became still.

Jerry watched and prayed as Mario coached the completely winded McCullough to catch his breath again. Finally the featherweight drew a tortured breath, and his lips turned back from blue to pink as oxygen reached his lungs.

"Are you all right?" Jerry asked his best fighter, who was still sitting against the corner post, looking as if he might vomit.

The Irishman nodded slowly. "Flippin' heck, Jerry. Which zoo did you find him in?"

12

Sam finally came to a halt on the road outside his flat. He leaned on the old family Land Rover, panting for breath. He had run the six miles from the boxing club in thirty-six minutes, and his clothes were wet through with sweat.

But now anger was giving way to pain. As he stretched his cramping calf, his eyes settled on the vehicle's dented hood. Sam's mind wandered back to the last summer he had shared with his father on the farm. Age eleven, Sam had driven this same vehicle around the fields after harvest while his father sat on top shooting rabbits in the glare of the headlights. Sam had loved it and still remembered the excitement when his father had thumped on the roof to indicate a rabbit ahead, the creature's eyes shining red in the bright light. Sam would accelerate hard to get his father in shooting range before the rabbit disappeared into the hedge.

A lump quickly formed in Sam's throat, and he tried hard to swallow it away. He had loved his dad more than anything in the world. How he wished he could talk to him about what had happened at the boxing club.

Sam took a deep breath as he acknowledged another truth. He had loved his mum, too. He still did, even though they hadn't really talked in years. He knew his mother desperately wanted to communicate with him, but Sam just couldn't. He knew he had hurt her. Every time he ignored her, he could see the pain on her face. But for some reason he just couldn't bring himself to reach out.

Now, though, after what had just happened, Sam felt desperate to talk to someone. And it slowly dawned on him that there was only one person in his life who understood what he had been through. He looked over his shoulder at the front of their flat. He knew she would be in. She rarely went out these days, except to pick up her benefits and go shopping before hurrying home and locking the door again. Everything seemed to terrify her, which seemed odd to Sam. Since the accident nothing scared him anymore.

He stood away from the Land Rover and made up his mind. He was going to do it. He was going to talk to her. He turned and entered the stairwell, already rehearsing what he would say.

But his words were wasted. As he entered the flat, there was a pungent whiff of alcohol. Sam saw his mother slumped on the settee, the half-empty bottle lying by her side. The boy moved toward his mother nervously, wondering whether she had killed herself this time. With weary relief, he heard her snoring lightly.

"Mum," he said. There was no response.

"Mum!" he repeated, louder this time. Again his mother didn't move. Sam leaned down and gave her a firm shake. Her breathing shifted slightly, but it was clear that no amount of shaking would wake her from her stupor.

"AAAGGH!" Sam yelled at the top of his voice, shockingly loud in the crummy little flat. He jumped up and down on the floor, screaming with anger, his fists clenched in front of him.

"*Shut up!*" A voice resonated through the floor, followed by three thumps as the old man in the flat below banged a broom on his ceiling. Sam ignored him. The shriveled old man was no challenge.

The boy took one last look at his mother, then turned past a pile of shopping bags on the floor and sprinted to his bedroom. He grabbed the mattress off his bed and flung it upright against his dresser.

"I HATE YOU! I HATE YOU! I'M GONNA KILL YOU!" Sam shouted as he threw punches and kicks at the victim before him. Like a defeated boxer, the flimsy mattress kept bending in the middle as if trying to drop to the sanctuary of the floor. But Sam kept throwing uppercuts, forcing it back to its feet.

Sam knew it wasn't his mother. It wasn't even the skinny runt at the boxing club who had punched him so many times that afternoon. He didn't know who it was. But it didn't matter. Sam punched and kicked until every bit of energy was gone.

Exhausted, he returned the mattress to its base and slumped on top of it in a sweaty heap. Silent tears ran down Sam's face before tiredness finally gripped him, and he dropped into a deep sleep.

13

Jerry woke with a start and gripped the side of the bed. He took a deep breath and calmed his racing heart before lifting his head to see the red neon digital clock across the room. 5:27 a.m. He flung the duvet off his sweating body and lay still.

It had been the same dream again—the second time in a week. Jerry hardly ever dreamed, and certainly not about boxing, despite a lifetime in the sport. Yet this one was so real. He could still picture it clearly. He frowned as he tried to work it out.

It was clearly a big fight night—big crowd, big noise, big atmosphere. Jerry could see every detail, from the faces of familiar commentators to the lights shining down from above the ring. Looking out into the crowd from his position below his corner, Jerry could see rows of people standing and shouting, throwing punches of encouragement.

Bert was there in the front row sitting next to someone Jerry almost recognized yet couldn't quite place. Both were holding long, fat cigars from which contented wisps of smoke rose gently. Next to them sat a tall, striking brunette, her scarlet ball gown incongruous against the tattoo-clad crowd that bellowed behind her.

In the dream Jerry's gaze now turned back up to the fight. From the noise and frenzy in the arena and the flashbulbs of a dozen cameras, the fight was clearly reaching a climax. A white-shirted referee circled the two fighters in the ring above. Although Jerry couldn't identify their faces, he knew the boxers were familiar to him. One of them was badly beaten and almost finished, in stark contrast to his fresher opponent. Yet for some reason the winning fighter was holding back, seemingly unwilling to deliver the final punch that would surely end the fight.

The winning boxer suddenly turned and looked directly at Jerry. His curious expression seemed to say, *Are you going to finish this, or am I?*

Jerry looked down at his hand to see it tightly gripping a white towel. And in that split second, Jerry knew he had a decision to make.

That was when he woke up.

Weird, Jerry thought to himself as he lay in the darkness, trying to figure out what was happening. As a trainer, he could save his defeated fighter by throwing a towel into the ring and thus conceding the fight. He had done it many times in real life and had never had a problem before. So why couldn't he do it this time?

Stupid dream.

Jerry rubbed his eyes and sat up. Turning his head toward his sleeping wife, he gently placed a hand on her side and prayed. He then went through to his children's bedrooms and prayed for them, too. It was a daily ritual he never missed, a precious secret moment between him and God.

/ / /

Half an hour later, Jerry sat in the ring at the boxing club, flicking through the pages of his crumpled old Bible. He was restless and couldn't settle on a Scripture. After a few minutes of searching, he heard some heavy steps on the concrete stairs. He looked up to see Geoff, a heavyweight who had been a gym member for years, pushing through the swing door of the gym, clutching his Bible in one hand and a paper cup of coffee in the other.

"What time of the morning is this?" Geoff grumbled loudly as he walked toward the ring. "This is the last time, I tell you. Who's stupid enough to organize a prayer meeting at six thirty on a Monday morning?"

Jerry put down his Bible and smiled at the familiar complaint. Most weeks Geoff swore he wouldn't come again, yet the fighter hadn't missed Jerry's Monday-morning prayer meeting for over a year. Geoff climbed into the ring, taking care not to spill his coffee, and sat down next to Jerry. The two men greeted one another with a warm handshake.

"What time did you get to bed?" Jerry asked.

"Half two."

"Trouble?"

"Nah." Geoff sighed. "My car conked out on the way home again."

Jerry smiled and shook his head. Geoff was a bouncer at a nightclub in Romford but lived in Dagenham, near the river. He was the proud owner of an old green Ford with a red door. The only reliable thing about it was the frequency with which it broke down.

"What was it this time?"

"Crud in the carburetor. Needs a service. I was stuck on an overpass in the rain."

Jerry scrunched up his face in sympathy. "That car needs to be put out of its misery."

"What?" Geoff clutched his chest in mock pain. "It's practically a new car."

"They stopped making that model twenty years ago," Jerry said, laughing.

Geoff smiled. He lay down, rested his head on the canvas, and closed his eyes. "Well, it'll be a classic soon, then." The heavyweight sat up with a start. "It'll be worth a fortune," he quipped, playfully flicking out his hand and striking Jerry's shoulder before draining the rest of his coffee and lying down again.

Jerry looked down at his friend, horizontal on the canvas. He smiled. He had seen him like that a few times over the years. Not that Geoff wasn't a good fighter. He had heart, commitment, a good right hand, and a solid chin. Being six foot three and nearly 250 pounds, the heavyweight also had presence and was universally accepted as the senior pro at the gym. Geoff just lacked that little extra ability needed to reach the top league of boxing in the country. He had always been found out when put up against the better heavyweights in the UK. Jerry had helped him become the best his talent would allow, and Geoff seemed content enough, picking up a couple hundred quid every month or so. And he still won more than he lost.

/ / /

Geoff, unaware his friend and trainer was studying him, lay still with his eyes shut. Despite his grumbling, he loved this time of peace in the gym before they prayed, invariably waiting for Dave, the third member of their prayer group, to turn up.

Geoff smiled to himself as he thought about how his life had been transformed over the last three years. Apart from getting up earlier on Monday mornings, his outward life hadn't changed that much. Geoff still lived happily with his mum, who doted on him. And he still worked as a nightclub bouncer. But it was more about how he had changed inside. He still found it difficult to explain to people, but he now had a peace and contentment he had never experienced before.

Geoff hadn't been sure what to make of Jerry when he'd first joined the club as a new professional. He hadn't really met a Christian man before. Geoff's mum went to church every Sunday and occasionally dragged him along, but the congregation was made up almost completely of women, apart from the vicar, who also wore a big frilly white dress. He, more than anything else, had reinforced Geoff's conviction that religion just wasn't for men like him. Even when Jerry first began training him and Geoff heard him singing Christian songs and saying Bible quotes, Geoff brushed it off as the way some black people were.

But it was just before Geoff's first professional fight, when Jerry said he wanted to pray for him, that Geoff realized there was more to the trainer's faith than funny language. Although Geoff thought praying seemed a pretty strange thing to do, especially before a fight, he let Jerry do it anyway. It surely couldn't do any harm. Later the other boxers at the gym told him Jerry prayed for everyone before a fight.

Anyway, Geoff had won. And when he won the next four fights too, he found himself starting to half believe in this praying lark! Then he lost. Having started to think he might have a lucrative career in boxing, he'd been pretty gutted and said to Jerry in a more aggressive tone than he meant that his praying clearly hadn't worked.

"Yes, it did," Jerry had replied. "You just weren't listening to what I prayed for." The trainer went on to explain that he never prayed for his boxers to win. "You should listen next time," he added with a smile.

When Geoff's next fight came around six weeks later, he paid more attention. After lacing up Geoff's gloves, Jerry put his arms lightly on the heavyweight's shoulders. "Can I pray for you?" he asked. Geoff nodded, shut his eyes, and listened.

"Father," Jerry began, "I pray for Geoff tonight. I pray that you will bless him, that you will protect him from harm, that you will give him courage and strength, and that he will come to know you and love you as his Lord and Savior. Amen."

Geoff had won the fight, but that night, lying in bed, he couldn't get Jerry's prayer out of his head. The next week in the gym, he had asked the trainer what being "his Lord and Savior" meant. Jerry had taken him to a nearby café and, over a cup of tea and a bacon sandwich, had told him.

Geoff hadn't fully understood it all—the dying-on-the-cross thing still confused him three years later. But when Jerry talked about God loving Geoff so much and desperately wanting to have a relationship with him, the heavyweight had been blown away. He knew immediately it was what he wanted. There and then in the café, with Jerry leading him through a simple, whispered prayer, Geoff had given his life to God.

While there had been some really tough times since, including his mum's cancer, Geoff had never looked back. God had made it all good. *Even these six-thirty prayer meetings,* he thought, grinning to himself as he lay on the canvas floor of the ring.

/ / /

The swing door opened with a bang, shaking the two men from their thoughts.

"Sorry I'm late, boys," Dave apologized, hurrying across the room.

"No problem." Jerry shook the gray-haired newcomer by the hand. "So what's going on in your worlds?"

Geoff went first, reporting on the main things happening in his life. Dave followed.

"And what about you, Jerry?" Geoff asked when Dave had finished.

Jerry frowned. "Everything's fine away from the gym. Gloria and the kids are on good form."

"And what about here?" Geoff probed.

Jerry looked up to see both men studying him carefully. He took a deep breath. "Well, I don't know how much you've heard. But it's been a pretty lousy week, really. And it's all my fault."

"Go on. What happened?"

"Robbie brought this new lad to the gym a few weeks ago. . . ."

Over the next ten minutes, Jerry poured out the whole story, culminating in the impromptu fight between Sam and Frank McCullough.

"So anyway," Jerry continued, "the whole gym was involved by now. And as soon as Frank got his breath back, his ego rises up and he starts kicking off at the boy, whom I've still got pinned to the floor. So I got pretty angry and told him to get lost and go cool off somewhere. And then I told the boy he should make himself scarce too, before he got into any more trouble." Jerry shook his head before continuing. "The truth is, though, that I'm shouting at them, right? But in reality, it was *me*. *I* caused it all from start to finish. It's the first time in eight years I've lost control of the gym like that." Jerry scratched the back of his head in agitation.

"Anyway, an hour later Frank rings me to tell me that if that's how I look after a boxer of his talent, I'm not fit to be his trainer, and he's moving on. By the time Bert caught up with him that evening, he'd signed with another manager."

Jerry grunted. "You can imagine what Bert thought of that. I'm not his favorite employee at the moment."

"Well, don't worry about that," Geoff intervened. "You're his only employee—full-time at the gym, at least. Anyway, Bert knows the score and how important you are here."

"Yeah," Dave agreed. "And I've heard Frank McCullough's been itching for a contract with one of the big-boy promoters for ages. I reckon this is just a convenient excuse for what he would have done anyway."

"You're probably right," Jerry replied. "You can't sign up with a new gym and manager in a few hours without a lot of chats having taken place beforehand."

He shook his head again. "It's not really Frank McCullough I'm upset about, though. He's a good fighter, but, you know, between us—and this goes no further . . ." Jerry looked up to see Dave and Geoff nodding. "I never trusted or liked him much. No. What I'm really upset about is the way I've mishandled this new lad. I totally lost my brain."

"Why was that, do you think?" Dave asked.

Jerry took a long, deep breath.

"Because . . . he's the best prospect I've ever seen. And I'm scared."

"Why are you scared?" Geoff asked, confused.

Jerry frowned again. Until he said it moments earlier, he hadn't realized he was scared. The three men sat in silence while Jerry examined this new revelation. "Because when he first walked in, I saw a sad, wounded kid, and I wanted to help him. Now I just see potential glory, title fights, and championship belts. I thought I was beyond all that."

"Well, you can do both, can't you?"

"I guess," Jerry said, sounding unconvinced even to himself. "It probably doesn't matter anyway. I asked Robbie to get the lad to fill out a form, but Robbie forgot, so we don't know where he lives. We've got no way of contacting him. And we didn't exactly part on good terms. I suspect we'll never see him again."

A gloomy quiet descended on the men as they listened to the distant noises of Ilford waking up, with vehicles driving past and industrial roller doors being opened on nearby shop fronts. Dave eventually broke the silence.

"We should pray," he said quietly.

"Yeah," Jerry replied. "That would be good."

14

Jerry leaned on the top rope, watching Robbie and another of the young boxers sparring.

Thankfully, life at the gym had returned to normal pretty quickly since the fight between Sam and Frank. Bert had seemingly forgiven Jerry for losing McCullough, and they were working well together again. Indeed, after a recent fight night, Bert, with a few pints in his belly, had confessed to Jerry that Frank McCullough had issued him an ultimatum a month earlier—pay him a massive retainer or lose him to another promoter.

Jerry had accepted Bert's apology with good grace. It turned out there wasn't a lot of love lost for Frank McCullough anyway, so nobody else had left the gym in protest, and morale was high.

Sam hadn't returned, though. No doubt everyone else at

the gym had forgotten about him, but Jerry just couldn't. He frequently found himself thinking about the boy. Just that morning he and Gloria had been praying about Sam, after Jerry had woken in a sweat following the same dream. In some way, Jerry knew the two were linked.

Robbie threw three successive left jabs, followed by a terrific straight right that rocked his opponent back on his heels. Quick as a flash, Robbie was on top of him, harrying and punching, forcing his opponent backward. But Robbie's opponent fended off the punches and managed to spin away. Jerry saw Robbie grimace in frustration.

Same old problem, Jerry reflected. Robbie's performance was great at amateur level, where you win and lose fights based on the number of clean, scoring punches you land. However, professional bouts were normally won by knocking your opponent down—something Robbie just didn't seem to have the punching power to achieve. Sam, on the other hand . . .

"Come back. Please come back," Jerry pleaded quietly.

/ / /

"I'm sorry, my love. You can only take four books at a time. I know it's daft, but it's the rules."

Gloria Ambrose looked down at the boy from her raised position behind the desk of Romford Municipal Library. A nasty scowl grew on the kid's face, but Gloria's gentle smile stopped it before it was fully formed. The boy's eyes returned to the books he held, and he began to filter nine books down to four.

Gloria studied him carefully. "You're into boxing, huh?" The book on the top of the pile showed a bloodied but defiant Muhammad Ali standing over a vanquished George Foreman.

The boy nodded, blushing a little.

"Well, that one's a must," Gloria continued, tapping Muhammad Ali on the chest. "Muhammad Ali is the greatest boxer who's ever lived."

The young man looked at her quizzically as she smiled at him again.

"Do you box yourself?" Gloria asked as she checked the library ticket inside the front cover. The book hadn't been borrowed in more than a year.

The kid nodded again as he thumbed through the remaining eight books.

"Where do you box?"

"Wherever." He grunted, slamming two more books down on the counter a little harder than he must have intended. "Sorry," he muttered.

Gloria studied the boy as he looked down at his final choice. There was something overwhelmingly sad about the teenager, and her heart went out to him. At least she could talk to him about boxing. The sport had been a part of her life since her earliest memories, her father throwing punches as a boxing commentary blared from the radio. Later she had married one of the most talented British boxers of his generation.

"I'm sorry," Gloria said after a few seconds. "I should mind my own business. I just love boxing."

A curious grin filled the kid's face.

Now it was Gloria's turn to set a book down with a mock-indignant slam. "What?" she demanded firmly, but with a smile on her face.

The boy shrugged his shoulders. "I didn't know girls liked b—" He blushed again before correcting himself. "Ladies liked boxing."

Gloria smiled, intrigued. She rarely heard youths in this neighborhood refer to women as "ladies." The boy had clearly been taught manners at some point in his childhood.

"Women can like boxing too, young man," she said, pretending to be insulted. "I think women can appreciate the art of boxing better than men. You see," Gloria added playfully, "we've still got brain cells because we're not dumb enough to take part in it!"

The boy smiled as he laid his final choice down on the counter.

"You got your card?" Gloria asked, picking up the final book to check the code.

"What card?"

"Your library card. You need it to take out books."

He scowled. "I haven't got a stupid library card."

"Hey!" Gloria said indignantly. The boy looked down only half apologetically.

"Right," Gloria said. "Now let's do something about you not having a library card." She reached behind her and picked up an application form. "What's your name?"

"Why?"

"Well," Gloria answered patiently, "when we fill out this form, we can issue you a card, and you can take those books away today. Without a card, you can sit down over there and read them, but you can't take them out of this building. It's your choice."

The boy stood still, considering his options. "Sam," he said eventually.

Writing the name down, Gloria got to the *m* before the realization hit her. *Sam.* The name she and her husband had prayed about a dozen times. Wow! Gloria took a deep breath. Whatever others might say, she would never believe this was a coincidence.

"What?" the boy asked aggressively.

Gloria shook herself. "Sorry. Miles away. Sam. Is that short for . . . ?"

"Samuel. Pennington." He mumbled the full name as if embarrassed by it.

"*S-a-m-u-e-l P-e-n-n-i-n-g-t-o-n,*" she recited slowly as she printed the name on the form. She decided to venture further. "So are you boxing at the moment?"

"No," he said gruffly.

"Would you like to?"

Sam paused. "Yeah," he muttered, bowing his head.

Butterflies danced in Gloria's stomach. "You should join a boxing club then," she offered as casually as she could.

"I tried. They didn't want me."

The words cut deep; Gloria knew how pained her husband would be when he heard.

"Well, I can't believe that's true," she blurted.

"What would you know?"

Gloria sighed inwardly. *So much more than you do,* she

thought to herself ruefully but couldn't say aloud. Instead she raised her eyebrow.

"Sorry," he said, backing down. "I'm not going back there, though. I'm going to teach myself."

"Oh," she answered, buying herself time to think as she busied herself completing the form and card. She quickly prayed as the boy signed the signature strip on the reverse of the new card.

"Well, I tell you what," she said when he had finished. "My husband's got a load of old boxing magazines and videos at home. As long as you promise to look after them, I'll see if he'll lend them to you. I think you'll learn more from them than you will from these books."

"You can get boxing magazines?" Sam asked excitedly.

"Oh yeah. But they're specialist, so you won't get them at the newsstand. My husband's got 'em all, though, going back decades. I'll lend them to you in batches. I'm always here until five on Mondays, Wednesdays, and Thursdays."

"Thanks," the young man said. A quizzical expression crossed his face. "Why are you being nice to me?"

Gloria was completely stumped. No one had ever asked her that before, and she momentarily considered saying, "Because Jesus loves you," or something similar. But she couldn't find words that wouldn't sound forced. "Well, er . . . it's good to be nice, I guess. It's . . . my job, too," she said nervously, immediately hating how lame that sounded.

Sam looked at her with an expression difficult to read. "So can I come back Wednesday and get those magazines?" he said eventually.

"Sure. I'll get my husband to put some aside tonight."

"And the videos?"

Gloria smiled and nodded again.

"Thanks." The boy smiled awkwardly, clutched the books to his chest, and hurried toward the exit.

"Well, would you believe it?" Gloria said to herself as the boy disappeared through the revolving door. "Thank you, Lord."

15

Robbie was in his sixth round of sparring. He looked sideways at Jerry. The trainer read the boy's frustration.

"Okay. Stop it there." The two youths immediately dropped their gloves.

"Thanks, Johnnie," Jerry said to Robbie's opponent. "Good defense. Strong chin. I like it. You okay?"

Johnnie nodded.

"Right," Jerry continued. "My only criticism is your ring positioning. Don't let your opponent keep pushing you into a corner. If he's pressing you backward, spin out sideways and reset."

Johnnie nodded again.

"Good lad. We'll work on that next week. Go take a shower." The trainer turned to Robbie. "Well done, Robbie—that was really great."

"It was rubbish," Robbie moaned. "I can't knock him down."

"But you're scoring points all the time," Jerry countered. "You'd have got eight or nine points from that last round alone."

"Yeah, but that's amateur bouts. I'm not going to make it as a pro if I can't knock 'em out."

"But you don't have to, Robbie! You're a class act. And you've got a great amateur future ahead."

"I don't want to be an amateur. I wanna be a pro," Robbie said painfully.

Jerry looked down at the dejected boy, and his heart went out to him. An idea suddenly came to mind. Jerry knew that he should really clear it with Bert first, but he reached out and put an arm around the young fighter's shoulders.

"Robbie, I've been holding off telling you, but Bert and I want to put you forward for the British Amateur Championships in Birmingham later this year. Is that okay with you?" The trainer watched with relief as a huge grin broke out across Robbie's face.

"Okay? That's fantastic! Thank you!" Robbie jumped up and down and let out a loud whoop of joy.

"Shhh," Jerry hissed. "I don't want everyone to know yet." *Especially Bert,* he thought to himself wryly. His boss was generally unenthusiastic about amateur tournaments, particularly when they involved overnight accommodation and travel expenses. Anything outside Greater London was to Bert "at the other end of the dang country" and "would cost a flippin' fortune."

"Sorry, boss. But that's fantastic!" Robbie whispered, still struggling to contain his excitement.

"Well, that's great," Jerry said. "Bert will be delighted. If you see him, though, let me tell him what your answer is first. Is that okay?"

"No problem, boss. Thank you so much."

Jerry squeezed the boy's shoulder. "You deserve it. But we've got a lot of work to do over the next four months. Are you sure you're up for this?"

"Boss, I'm gonna be here every day. I'm gonna run here and run home again. I'm gonna eat just good stuff," he said, before adding wistfully, "And I'm gonna win the title."

"Okay, Robbie," Jerry said, chuckling. "This will be a higher level than anything you've faced before. If you get through the first bout, that will be a good result. Let's just work hard and see what happens. Got it?"

"Got it." Robbie nodded with almost comic determination.

Jerry laughed inwardly. He knew Robbie would already be thinking about victories and titles—probably even Olympic medals! Jerry felt a pang, knowing that Robbie's ability, even in amateur boxing, would never match his dreams.

"Go and have a shower, Robbie."

Jerry watched as Robbie ducked under the rope and skipped toward the showers, almost colliding with Bert as he came out of the bathroom and disappeared back into his office.

Jerry frowned. *No time like the present,* he thought, climbing down from the ring.

/ / /

As Jerry framed the request, Bert began to complain about costs but stopped midsentence.

He smiled slightly and nodded back at Jerry. "That's fine," Bert declared.

Jerry looked at him. He had expected much more resistance than that.

"Ah, he's a good lad, Robbie. Do you think he's got a chance?"

Jerry paused, pondering whether to stretch the truth, but decided against it. "No," he replied simply. "But it will be good experience."

"Fair enough. So that will only be one night's lodging, then?" Bert said, grinning.

Jerry nodded. "I expect so."

"Okay," Bert said, scribbling a note to himself on his pad. "Right, now you're here, shall we run through the matchups for the Walthamstow card next month?"

"Sure," Jerry replied, delighted but still a bit suspicious that Bert had sanctioned Robbie's trip so easily.

"So," Bert said, looking down at a sheet of paper on his desk, "no amateur or kid bouts—too rough over there. We're starting with four-rounders for Darren, Bobby, Robbo, and Tommy Flood. All against their club boxers." Bert looked up at Jerry, who nodded his approval. They were all club journeymen who had no records to protect and, win or lose, would be glad to have forty pounds for their efforts.

Bert continued. "Then we're looking at a six-rounder for Tony J. at welterweight, against a guy called . . ." Bert squinted at the paper as if trying to decipher his own writing. "Joe Brock. Er, sounds quite handy. 21–4 record." Bert looked up. "You heard of him?"

"I've seen him, I think," Jerry replied as he shut his eyes to recall the memory. "Yeah, down at the Circus Tavern at Purfleet a year or two ago. Joe Brock. That's all right. He's well conditioned, but Tony should be able to turn him over."

"Okay," Bert said, ticking his sheet. The two men ran through a few more matchups before they got to the last fight.

"And . . ." Bert paused. "For the finale, we're going to put Geoff up in an eight-round bout at heavyweight." Bert looked down, opened his desk drawer, and dug around for something he couldn't find before eventually closing the drawer again.

"Aha," Jerry said suspiciously. "Against who?"

"Ray Butcher."

"No way!" Jerry barked. He knew now why Bert had suddenly agreed to Robbie's trip to the British amateurs.

"Now before you start," Bert said quickly, "this was the deal breaker for the night. Without this bout, none of the rest of the card is viable. Ray Butcher's a big draw over there, and they rely on him to bring in the punters."

"That's because he's an animal. He should be in a cage—not a boxing ring." Jerry felt aggravated just hearing Ray Butcher's name again. The East End boxer was the most vile and dirty fighter Jerry had ever encountered. Any fight night with his name on the bill invariably turned into an ugly affair. "And anyway, what about Geoff?" Jerry said angrily. "He could get seriously hurt."

Bert countered immediately. "Geoff can look after himself fine, and you know it." The promoter hesitated before continuing. "Anyway, I've checked it with Geoff and he's dead keen. Three hundred pounds, they've offered him."

"You've talked to Geoff already?" Jerry exploded. "That's not how we do it, and you know it. *We* agree on the match-ups before any of the boxers even hear about them."

Bert sighed. "Well, I knew you'd kick off about it, and I wanted to check he was up for it before we . . . got into this."

Both men glared at one another.

"Well, I don't like it," Jerry stated firmly. "Regardless of whether Geoff can handle himself, I don't want to put any of my fighters in a ring with Butcher. And that's that."

"Look!" Bert said, losing his temper. "We've no choice. We're overdrawn at the bank, and we need these bouts. At the end of the day, this is a business, not social flippin' services. If you want jaunts up to the British amateurs with no-hopers like Robbie, we have to take fight nights like this, whether we like it or not." Bert softened his gaze, pleading with his eyes for Jerry to back down.

"No," Jerry said. "I'm not going to put anyone in against Ray Butcher again. Ever."

Bert stood up and slammed his folder down on the table, pointing at Jerry. "Look, mate. Since we lost Frank McCullough, we've got no big fighters who are gonna bring in proper money anytime soon. If we get a reputation for not even being able to put on full cards against other clubs, we're finished."

Jerry stood up to unleash a tirade but stopped himself. He

knew Bert had a valid point. He sat down again, as did Bert a couple of seconds later.

"Come on," Bert said. "We can't turn fights down that support our boxers and our gym just because we don't like the opposition. You need to equip Geoff to take Butcher out."

While they both waited, hoping the other would buckle first, Jerry's mind wandered back to the two times his boxers had fought Ray Butcher. In both defeats, his men had been shaken by low punches and head-butts, not to mention foul-mouthed insults after Butcher had won. One of his men had even quit boxing as a result.

As he recalled both miserable experiences, a thought crept into Jerry's mind. Maybe, just maybe, if he prepared Geoff right, together they could teach Butcher a lesson. The thought grew in appeal.

"Okay," Jerry said finally. "Book it. I guess Geoff and I have got some work to do."

"Thank you," Bert said.

Jerry nodded. "Thank you for Robbie." He looked at his watch. "I'm gonna go home—I was in early this morning. Can you make sure someone locks up?"

"No problem."

/ / /

Twenty minutes later Jerry turned the key in the lock. He opened his front door to see his children running toward him.

"Daddy!"

"Hi, my beautiful girls!" Jerry said, bending to catch them

and swing them both to his chest in a bear hug. Jerry's wife appeared behind them.

"Hiya, gorgeous," Jerry said, leaning forward to kiss his wife. "You had a good day?"

"Oh, okay," Gloria said. "Just a normal day. Except . . ."

"What?" Jerry said, intrigued.

"Oh, nothing," Gloria teased. "I'll tell you later. Maybe at dinner."

"Now, you can't do that," he said, putting the children down. "Tell me."

"Nah."

"Tell me, or I'll tickle it out of you." Jerry grabbed his wife in a part tickle, part hug. The children quickly joined in.

"No," Gloria squealed, as the tickling became more vigorous. "Okay, okay, I'll tell you if you stop."

Jerry let her go, and Gloria looked up at him. "Had a visitor to the library today. Borrowing boxing books."

Jerry raised his eyebrows.

"He went by the name of . . . Samuel Pennington," Gloria said, grinning.

Jerry's face was momentarily blank until the shortened version of the name struck him. "No!" he said. "You're kidding, right?"

"I'm not!" Gloria beamed. "Had a long chat with him."

"Wow! I can't believe it. We were only talking and praying about him, what . . . this morning?"

"Uh-huh!" She smiled.

"Thank you, Lord," Jerry said, shaking his head. "Tell me all about it, then."

16

"Left!" Jerry barked.

His hand recoiled as a large gloved fist slammed into the pad he held with a resounding thud. "Right-left-right!" Jerry commanded, twisting the face of his hand pad toward the floor to indicate he wanted an uppercut. Geoff delivered smartly.

The pounding continued as Jerry put the heavyweight through his paces. Geoff and Jerry had been training every other day for five weeks. Now, with the Ray Butcher fight just five days away, they were training every day. While there had been less fun than usual, a new intensity to their sessions meant Geoff was the sharpest Jerry had ever seen him.

"Okay, good work," Jerry said, bringing the drill to a halt. "Have a drink."

As Geoff swigged from a bottle, Jerry scanned the gym

and was pleased to see it almost empty. Two guys were lifting weights in the corner, and Mario was sitting on his massage bench talking to an old friend. None of them were taking any interest in the ring. Jerry made the decision quickly.

"Okay, Geoff. We're going to do something else. Just give me a minute." Jerry climbed through the ropes and trotted toward the storeroom.

Geoff looked curiously at his friend as he climbed back into the ring. He had never seen Jerry wearing a head guard, let alone boxing gloves. As far as Geoff knew, Jerry hadn't fought in a ring, sparring or otherwise, since he had retired more than eight years previously.

"Right," Jerry said, relieved the four other people in the gym were still engrossed in their own business. "We're going to do a bit of sparring."

"I can't fight you, Jerry," Geoff teased immediately. "You're giving me about seventy pounds. And ten years!"

"Ha-ha! Shut up and concentrate," Jerry said seriously. "Your sparring has been good, and Bob and Glen are a similar size to Ray Butcher. You've been picking them off real nice, and Ray Butcher ain't much more talented than either of them. But . . ." Jerry checked to see he had Geoff's full attention before continuing. "Ray Butcher has a lot of . . . let's call them tricks, which I am not going to teach Bob or Glen, in case they're ever tempted to use 'em. So I apologize in advance, but I'm going to fight like Ray Butcher will fight. I might not be as heavy as him, but I'm just as tall, so don't alter your style. And don't worry about hurting me. I can look after myself. You just pretend I'm Ray Butcher. Okay?"

"Okay," Geoff chuckled.

Jerry frowned. His friend's playful manner showed him that this session was absolutely necessary. The trainer lifted his gloves up for Geoff to touch them, indicating the start of the bout. As the heavyweight reached out to touch gloves, Jerry threw a ferocious punch that landed squarely on Geoff's unprotected nose.

"Aagh!" Geoff shouted. "What was that for, Jerry?" He backed away, his eyes watering from the pain. Before he knew what was happening, Jerry was on him, throwing a flurry of punches, forearms, and elbows into his face.

"My name's Ray Butcher, you idiot," Jerry snarled menacingly. "And I'm gonna kill you."

Jerry threw a punch into his opponent's groin, causing Geoff to double up. As his head dipped forward, Jerry slammed his shoulder into Geoff's face, barging the larger man back into the ropes. The trainer then threw a vicious overhand right at the heavyweight's head as he bounced off the ropes toward him. Geoff, catching on quickly that this was no friendly sparring session, took the punch on his raised gloves and roughly shoved Jerry away. As Jerry advanced toward him again, spitting insults, Geoff wasn't grinning anymore.

/ / /

Three minutes later Jerry abruptly called the session to a halt and ripped his head guard off. As they stopped, both breathing heavily, Geoff eyed his friend warily.

"You all right, Jerry?"

For several seconds Jerry didn't respond, lost in a world of his own. "I'm fine," he replied eventually. "You?"

"Just about."

Jerry, his heart still racing, turned away and slowly removed his gloves, then stood trancelike, studying his knuckles as Geoff hurriedly pulled off his own gloves and strapping. Jerry didn't have the stomach for any more training tonight. After the initial shock of the early punch and the low shot to his groin, Geoff had begun to get the idea and was able to ward off most of Jerry's assault. Yet in the last minute, Jerry's onslaught had unconsciously become a smothering frenzy, and Geoff had simply covered up and hung on for the end.

Jerry finally shook his focus from his hands and glanced anxiously around the room. To his relief, he saw that the two young boxers were still lifting weights in the corner, oblivious to the drama that had been unfolding. He swung around to look for Mario. The friend was gone, but Mario was still sitting on his massage bench, now facing the ring. Their eyes met, and Jerry knew that Mario had seen everything.

The two men nodded to one another. Jerry hoped Mario would know exactly what he had been trying to do and how important these discreet late-night sessions were if Geoff was going to combat Ray Butcher. But as they held each other's gaze, Jerry sensed the Italian had also seen something else, and he looked away, ashamed.

"Sorry about that early punch," he said to Geoff. "But you needed to know just what you're going to be facing. I'm sorry I overdid it a bit at the end. Ray Butcher will be just as vicious, but he won't be able to keep that up for a whole three minutes. You'll get your chances toward the end of each round when he's knackered himself out."

Geoff nodded.

"Tomorrow," Jerry continued, "I'll start to teach you ways to counter all of Ray Butcher's tricks."

"Okay."

Jerry lifted his hand to his friend, and Geoff reached out and took it. Jerry wasn't yet sure whether their friendship had been deepened or damaged in the preceding few minutes.

"I'm glad I never faced you fifteen years ago," Geoff said.

"I'm glad you didn't know me then either."

/ / /

Jerry pulled off the road five minutes from home and killed the engine. He gripped the steering wheel with both hands. In the gloom of neon streetlights, he studied the knuckles of his hands, still tingling from their earlier workout. Before tonight, he hadn't thrown a real punch in eight years. Yet in those three minutes of fighting, he had felt the same old emotions overwhelm him again. The desire to hurt. The desire to cause pain.

"Crap!" Jerry shouted, slapping the steering wheel with his open palm. He had thought God had changed him, that those desires were all in the past. But they were still there. He had just hidden them away.

"All crap," Jerry said, quieter this time. His shoulders slumped. His faith hadn't changed him at all.

/ / /

Gloria had put the kids to bed by the time Jerry got home, and she met him at the door with a hug. "How was your day?"

"Okay," he said gruffly. "How was yours?"

"Good. Everything all right?"

"Fine," Jerry said sharply. "I need a bath."

Gloria went to the kitchen and flicked the kettle on. She frowned. It was unusual for Jerry to return home in such a mood. As the kettle boiled, Gloria began to pray.

Jerry was already in the bath, swishing bubbly water around himself and adjusting the temperature with short blasts from the cold tap, when Gloria arrived. She paused by the door and smiled.

"Mmm. You're gorgeous," she said, giving his still-toned body an approving look.

"Hmm," he answered without looking up.

As Jerry reached up to accept the cup of tea, Gloria spotted an angry purple bruise on the outside of his arm. "Jerry! What have you done?"

"Huh?" Jerry replied, twisting his arm. "Nothing," he said, a little too quickly. "Just a bruise. Must have banged it at the gym or something."

Gloria frowned but decided against pushing the point. "Can I come and talk to you while you have a bath?" she said instead.

"Fine," he replied curtly.

Gloria pretended not to notice his unfriendly manner. She sat down in the doorway and busied herself shaping her nails. "Sam came in again today," she ventured after a couple of minutes of sullen silence. Out of the corner of her eye, she saw Jerry look up.

"Aha," he replied casually. Gloria smiled. However grumpy he was, he couldn't disguise his interest.

"Yeah," she continued. "He said he loved the last magazines. He took the new ones too and asked if he could hold on to all of them. Promised he'd look after them. He's clearly a bright lad. He could probably make something of himself with the right support."

Jerry nodded his agreement.

"He also asked if I had any videos of Sugar Ray Leonard. He said he's read Leonard had good footwork."

"Wow. He's studying carefully, isn't he?" Jerry seemed to have forgotten his grumpiness for the moment. "At the gym, I've got a couple of videos of Leonard's fights. I'll bring them home tomorrow. Did he say anything else?"

Gloria paused nervously, but she couldn't lie. "Yeah. He said something about going to a boxing thing on Saturday."

"Did he?" Jerry said excitedly as he sat up before suddenly groaning a curse. "Saturday? I'm taking the kids swimming."

Gloria bit her lip. "I don't think it's your gym he's going to, sweetheart. He said it was in town somewhere."

Jerry cursed again, slamming his fist down into the tub, sending soapy water across the bathroom.

Gloria was speechless for a moment, shocked at his outburst. "Jerry! What has got into you tonight?"

"Well, we're going to lose him to another club, aren't

we? All because you won't give me the address off his library form."

"We've covered this," Gloria countered indignantly. "That's confidential. I'm not going to break the law. Anyway, we've prayed about it. If God can enable me to meet Sam right out of the blue, he must be on the case. We just have to be faithful to that and trust him."

Jerry brooded as silence filled the room. He then took a noisy breath and ducked under the soapy water, rinsing his hair.

"What happened today, sweetheart?" Gloria asked when her husband finally surfaced. He glared at her for several seconds, but his expression softened.

Slowly Jerry told her about the sparring session with Geoff. By the time he finished, his voice was cracking.

Gloria stared at her husband, a raft of emotions running through her mind. She was furious that he had fought again when the risks to his health were so high. Yet she knew that Jerry was talented enough, despite his age, to protect his injury. Gloria looked down at her husband as he swallowed awkwardly and glanced away. She moved over to the bath, took her husband's face in her hands, and kissed him softly.

"Oh, sweetheart. Violence doesn't define you anymore. We do." Gloria gestured toward the children's bedrooms on the other side of the bathroom wall. "They do. . . . And God does."

"I don't know about God," Jerry snorted. "He seems a million miles away from me at the moment."

Gloria kissed him on the forehead and ran her hand down

onto his chest. "That's all right. I'm only a few inches away. And I love you so much. It will be all right."

Jerry looked into her eyes and finally nodded, taking her hand. They held each other for a few seconds before Gloria lifted his chin once more. She leaned forward and planted a lingering kiss on his lips.

A few minutes later, the troubles of the day were no longer at the forefront of Jerry's mind.

17

Sam squinted in the sunlight streaming through his thin bedroom curtains. Today was the day. Saturday had finally come. Even at this time of the morning he felt excited. For two months he had been reading about boxing and watching videos. Tonight he was going to experience fighting again firsthand. He couldn't wait.

Sam turned over and reached for the boxing magazine that lay beside his bed. He had read it from cover to cover a dozen times yet couldn't resist flicking the pages open to have another look. Since the woman at the library had started lending them to him, Sam had lived and breathed boxing from morning until night. He had watched the videos endlessly, rewinding them to study the knockout combinations so many times that he had noticed the picture was beginning to distort as the videotape got worn. Every day, while his mother slept off her latest bender in the bedroom next door, Sam would shadowbox around the living room in front of the television. He could now mimic every knockout combination thrown by Muhammad Ali, Sugar Ray Leonard, and Marvin Hagler. Sam had learned how to dance on his toes, how to stand southpaw and regular, and how to throw every type of punch and combination.

In one of the magazines he had found a training regimen for young boxers, which he now followed religiously. Twice a day he went for a run around the wasteland, recording his times on the black Casio watch his dad had given him. His times were falling remarkably. He could now sustain a virtual sprint for almost three minutes and do 150 push-ups in under two. The only part of the regimen he couldn't maintain was the diet, as there was hardly ever any decent food in the flat. However, he made up for not being able to stick to the suggested diet by doing twice the exercise regimen. And he did get food at school, which proved his main incentive for going.

Sam rolled out of bed and dropped to the floor. He pushed his legs out straight and did a hundred push-ups without stopping, his arms quivering on the final few. Annoyed at his arms, after a moment to catch his breath, he did another ten to defy his weakness. He then rolled over into a sitting position and began his sit-ups, holding his legs suspended in midair to add to the difficulty. He gave up at 176 repetitions, collapsing on his back as he clutched his cramping belly. That wasn't bad, though—twice what he could complete just two months earlier.

For the next few hours, Sam watched his favorite Muhammad Ali tape over and over. First run-through, he focused on the great man's footwork, mimicking his steps and ring positioning. Then he rewound the tape and added the punching elements. Finally he watched it again, combining footwork and punching to mimic the entire compilation of fights. The only deviation was adding a few savage extra punches at the knockouts in frustration that the opponents didn't stand up longer.

Sam finally stepped away from his vanquished opponent and released his clenched fists. He glanced up at the clock. Three hours without stopping. Good. He walked back to his bedroom to take a nap before the long walk ahead.

///

Jerry hurried into the gym.

"What's going on?" he asked, spotting Mario by his physio bench. "I took the kids swimming, and when I got back Gloria said I had to come straight here."

Mario shook his head. "You'll never believe it. Geoff's knackered his knee."

"What happened?"

"He was watching two boys sparring, and when they finished, he must have tripped as he stepped down from the ring, 'cause he went splat on the floor." The cut man slapped his hands together dramatically as Jerry glanced at the fading blue fabric curtain that surrounded the raised base of the ring.

"When we finally got him to take his hands away, his

knee had blown up like a football." The Italian made a farting noise with his lips. "We stood him up after five minutes, but he couldn't put any weight on it." Mario shook his head again. "Dave took him to the hospital to check it out. I think it's torn ligaments. He definitely won't fight tonight."

"Poor old Geoff," Jerry said glumly. "He'll be gutted."

A pang of regret crossed his mind as he realized he'd lost the opportunity to put Ray Butcher in his place. All the turmoil he had gone through had been for nothing. Yet he also felt a weight of responsibility lift from his shoulders.

"I didn't want him to fight Butcher anyway." Jerry smiled. "No payday for old Ray, eh!" The trainer stopped smiling when he saw his friend's face. "What?"

Mario looked grim. "You not gonna like it, Jerry."

"Tell me."

"No way. You need to talk to Bert." The Italian gave a curt wave toward Bert's office window, through which the promoter could be seen speaking on the telephone.

"What is he scheming?" Jerry said, partly to himself. The cut man pursed his lips, shrugged his shoulders, and busied himself preparing his kit bag for the fight night ahead. Jerry walked with foreboding toward the office. As he opened the door, Bert was standing, shouting into the receiver.

"He'll be fine. He'll seem credible. He looks fantastic, and it will be another win on Butcher's record. Everyone will be tanked up by then on your cheap, crappy beer and won't even notice. They'll get the knockout they want and go home happy." The promoter acknowledged Jerry with a nod.

"No!" Bert barked into the phone. "We'll take a two-hundred-quid hit as I said earlier, but that's all. The rest of our lineup's top notch, and you're lucky we can organize anyone at this short notice. It could just as easily have been Ray Butcher who hurt his knee, and I can guarantee we wouldn't be screwing you around like this."

Bert paused and held the phone away from his ear as another tirade blasted out. Bert cut in angrily. "No! I cannot guarantee what round he's gonna last until. I'm not a bleedin' fortune teller. He'll do the best he can. I'm not holding back on anyone here. It's this guy or no one."

Jerry began to speak, but Bert held up a finger, warning him to wait. The trainer forced himself to keep calm, even though he knew what Bert was attempting. It was understandable. The stakes were high for the promoter, with a major fight night just hours away. Nevertheless, Jerry felt nauseous. Whatever Bert was negotiating, Jerry knew he would have to deal with the consequences.

Jerry watched as the muscles around Bert's eyes twitched before visibly relaxing. The promoter let out a silent breath.

"Okay," Bert said. "Good. See you tonight. Bye." He slumped in his chair, took another deep breath, and then looked directly at Jerry.

"Right, I know you won't like this, but I've got no choice. There's a five-thousand-pound penalty clause against us in the contract if we don't provide a credible opponent for the top three fights—including Ray Butcher. You don't need me to tell you that a five-thousand-quid payout without any revenue tonight, and we're finished. I had to put up someone." Bert looked away.

"Who have you offered up?" Jerry said, much more calmly than he felt.

"Billy's away visiting his sister in Glasgow. Can't get back in time. Mike's working a shift down at Ford, and his boss won't let him off under any circumstance. He's already told him if he calls in sick, he'll be sacked. I talked to them about Tommy, Pete, and Jimmy at light-heavy, but they would only take a genuine heavyweight."

"So who?" Jerry asked, genuinely confused. "We've got no other heavyweights . . . apart from Earl!"

Bert looked at Jerry and said nothing.

"You're kidding!" Jerry exclaimed. "You've put up Earl to fight Ray Butcher?"

"There's no one else."

"Earl!" Jerry said, raising his voice to a shout. "Bert, my great-auntie could knock Earl over. He hasn't got a chance!"

"He doesn't have to," Bert retorted quickly. "He just needs to look the part. He can flex a few muscles, bounce up and down at the beginning, take an early punch, and go down. The punters won't be any the wiser."

Jerry was standing by now. "Bert. You're mad. Earl is a million miles off being able to protect himself, let alone give Ray Butcher a fight."

"Look, Jerry," Bert said, raising his voice. "I don't like it any more than you do. But we've genuinely got no other choice, except to call off the night, and with a five-thousand-pound clause, that's curtains for this boxing club."

There was silence for almost a minute as both men stewed angrily.

"This is crazy," Jerry said, finally breaking the standoff. "If I see Earl's got any doubts, or I think he's not gonna take my instructions to go down at the first opportunity, I'll throw the towel in the moment that bell rings."

"Fine," Bert said curtly. "I don't want to see Earl get hurt either."

Silence filled the office once more.

"This is crap," Jerry said bitterly.

"I agree." Bert nodded.

"I take it you've spoken to Earl?"

Bert nodded again. "You might not believe me, but I told him he would probably get beat up bad, and I gave him a genuine opportunity not to take it."

"But I bet he didn't hesitate, did he?" Jerry sneered. "'Need the money,'" he said, mimicking the boxer's deep, slow voice.

Bert smiled. "Didn't even ask what the fee was. He always wants anything I can get him. He'd take fifty pence to get his head smashed in if that was all that was on offer."

"I hope you've offered him a good purse," Jerry said aggressively. "He'll bloomin' well deserve it."

"I offered him the whole three hundred pounds Geoff was gonna get," Bert said.

Jerry looked at his boss and nodded. "Good man." The opportunity had been there for Bert to rip Earl off, and he hadn't. Although they had been disagreeing a lot recently, Jerry knew Bert had the best interests of the boxers and the club at heart. "Okay. When's Earl coming in?"

Bert looked over Jerry's shoulder. "He's here now."

Jerry looked through the internal glass window of Bert's

office to see the enormous figure of Earl standing awkwardly. Jerry sighed. It was faintly reminiscent of a year earlier when Earl had first appeared.

/ / /

Jerry could still remember the sudden hush in the gym as everyone stopped to observe the huge black man-mountain. For a moment Jerry's boxing heart had fluttered.

But Earl was no George Foreman. In fact, he was the least talented fighter Jerry had ever encountered, incapable of coordinated movement or aggression. Jerry had taken him aside and suggested boxing wasn't for him. But Earl had the bit between his teeth by then and insisted on continuing, threatening to go to another club if necessary. Jerry had reluctantly relented. Earl got in tremendous shape, but his basic lack of coordination or aggression rendered him, in boxing terms, little more than a sitting duck. He lost every amateur fight he entered. With each amateur loss, Jerry had tried to discourage Earl from seeking a professional fight. Earl would have none of it, insisting he needed the money.

To Jerry's utter amazement, Earl won his first professional fight. At the sight of Earl's rippling mass of muscle, the opponent dived for the floor at the first opportunity and stayed there, despite the count being delayed by Earl's kneeling down beside him to check if he was okay. Since then Jerry had noted Earl was always happier to lose than win, which was a good thing as Earl had easily lost his subsequent six fights, though Jerry handpicked the poorest opponents.

Jerry stood, opened the door, and beckoned his boxer over. Earl shyly approached the office and sat down.

"Earl," Jerry said firmly, fixing the boxer with a serious gaze. "Bert was wrong to offer you this fight. You were wrong to accept it. Your opponent is a guy called Ray Butcher. He's a million times better fighter than you. And he's also an animal. I've been training Geoff for five weeks solid, and I think he still probably would have lost badly. Ray Butcher won't just beat you tonight. He will go out of his way to hurt you. You will get hurt bad. Three hundred pounds is not worth it. Three thousand pounds would not be worth the risk you are going to be taking. I beg you to not take this fight."

Bert shifted uncomfortably in his seat but said nothing.

Earl looked shaken by Jerry's words yet still shook his head. "Sorry, Jerry, but I need the money."

"Why do you need the money?" Jerry asked irritably.

"I just do. I need it."

"I'm telling you," Jerry repeated again, "you are going to get beaten up bad, and you are going to hurt. A lot."

"I know that, Jerry. You've both told me. But I'm decided. I need the money."

There was silence in the room as Earl looked back at Jerry dolefully.

The trainer pursed his lips in frustration and continued. "I am only going to let you fight if you promise you go down immediately when he starts to hurt you. And stay down."

Earl looked across at Bert, who shrugged. He glanced back at Jerry and inclined his head. Jerry studied him for several seconds, the debate raging in his mind, and shook his head in disgust. "Fine. Be at the bus at five o'clock."

"Do we need to do any work now?" Earl asked.

"No," Jerry replied grimly. "Unless you want to do some practice falling to the ground the moment you're hit. I think you can manage that."

18

Jerry stood in the ring, giving encouragement and tactical advice while Mario treated swelling and cuts. So far the club's fighters had given a good account of themselves, with more bouts won than lost. Nevertheless, Jerry felt sick in the stomach.

The cause of his nerves was seated fifteen rows back. Even from this distance, Earl cut a forlorn figure with fear clearly etched on his face, in sharp contrast to his teammates, who were vociferously engaged in the current fight.

There were still three bouts before Earl and Ray Butcher's finale, but already the packed auditorium was a cauldron of noise. Huge volumes of beer were being drunk, evidenced by the chants and cheering, which were getting coarser and louder by the minute.

Just as the bell rang for the start of the next round, a chant picked up in the crowd on the far side of the auditorium.

"Killer! Killer! Killer!" The chant spread quickly as the subject of their cheering came into Jerry's line of sight.

Ray Butcher.

His pale skin was covered in pockmarks, and his face wore an arrogant sneer. Green-blue tattoos were plastered up his neck to his ear and hairline. He slowly circled the arena, contemptuously distracting the crowd's attention from the ongoing fight.

Jerry fought the urge to watch him and concentrated on the fight above him. But individual cries of "Butcher" sounding out above the rhythmic "Killer" chant were difficult to ignore. Instinctively Jerry glanced back toward Earl.

Earl looked terrified, unable to tear his eyes from the intimidating figure who was slowly and deliberately moving around the arena toward him. Jerry knew a confrontation was imminent, but the bell rang again, and his professional duties were required in the ring once more. He sprang up and tried to concentrate on his fighter for the one-minute interval between rounds.

Only as the bell rang again did he allow himself to look up. Ray Butcher was standing ten feet away from Earl, who was sunk deep into his seat despite his huge frame. Butcher pointed at Earl before slowly and theatrically drawing the same finger across his throat.

"I'm . . . gonna . . . KILL YOU!" he shouted, raising his voice higher and louder with each word. The crowd echoed

Butcher's prediction, silencing Earl's fellow boxers, who were trying to stick up for their clubmate.

Jerry could stand it no longer. Abandoning the ring, he pushed past the throng around Ray Butcher and forced his way to Earl. Grabbing the huge man by his arm, he dragged him out of his seat toward the changing rooms. The crowd jeered at the humiliating retreat, although those in their path quickly stepped away as they saw Earl's size and the anger in Jerry's face up close.

Jerry pushed past the steward guarding the door and led Earl to their changing room. "Stay here," he commanded before turning and running back to the ring.

///

It was another half hour before Jerry was finally able to drag himself away from the ring, at the start of the interval before the final fight. He hurried to the changing room, unsure of what he was going to find. But Earl was nowhere to be seen. Instead a very irate Bert was pacing the changing room.

"Earl's disappeared," Bert shouted at Jerry, his face red and sweaty. "We can't find him anywhere. The boys are out looking for him."

Jerry sat down gently on one of the benches to take in the news. After a few seconds he was struggling to contain a grin. "Good on you, big man," he said under his breath.

But Bert wasn't amused at all. "We're done, Jerry. That's five thousand pounds, plus our fee! Not to mention causing a riot out there. We're finished."

Jerry said nothing. The financial ramifications

notwithstanding, Jerry felt nothing but relief that Earl wasn't going to have to fight Ray Butcher. The man was looking more vicious and thuggish than Jerry had ever seen him, and Earl had looked like a lost little boy despite his towering size.

Bert swore loudly and then turned and kicked a stray boxing glove across the room. It thudded against a closet door in the corner with a bang, followed by a quiet yelp. Bert and Jerry looked at each other for a moment before Bert strode over and swung the small closet door open. Among the mops and buckets sat the forlorn figure of Earl, blinking up as light filled his hiding place.

"Thank goodness for that," Bert exclaimed loudly. "I thought you had done a runner. Are you all right?"

Earl nodded.

"Well, come on, mate. You're on next. You need to get changed pronto."

"Okay. Sorry, boss." Earl extracted himself from the debris in the closet, slowly stood, and started unfastening his belt.

"You'll be fine, Earl," the promoter said, trying to instill confidence in his man. "Jerry'll stop the fight when he can, and you'll go home with a sore head but three hundred pounds better off. Can't be bad!" Bert slapped him on the back and looked at Earl's impressive torso. "Don't be scared to show those muscles off. And stay on your feet as long as you—"

"Get lost, Bert," Jerry said sharply. "He's going down straightaway like we agreed. Unless I can persuade him to drop out beforehand. Now leave us alone so I can prepare my fighter."

Bert looked indignant and a little shocked at Jerry's tone but chose to walk away.

"And gather up our boys," Jerry called after him. "It's getting really ugly out there. They should have shut the bar hours ago."

To Jerry's relief, Bert disappeared immediately. The trainer turned to look at Earl, sitting on the floor lacing his boots.

"Are you all right?" Jerry asked.

"I'm okay."

"Please don't do this."

"I have to do this," Earl said, his voice almost breaking.

Jerry tensed in anger as he saw the fear and determination in Earl's eyes. He took a deep breath and forced himself to be professional. "Let's get you ready."

The trainer bound Earl's hands, grimacing at the irony. Since Earl likely wouldn't land a single punch, his hands were probably the last part of his anatomy needing protection.

"Okay. Let's warm you up." Jerry quickly led Earl through a series of stretches and punching exercises. "Are you ready?"

"Pray for me then, Jerry."

Jerry winced, realizing he had hardly thought of God for days. Normally, for Jerry, a fight night was a continuous stream of silent prayers. Tonight he couldn't even remember if he had prayed with any of his fighters. Ever since his sparring session with Geoff, his faith had seemed almost nonexistent. He looked up at Earl, who was staring back with pleading eyes. "Sure," Jerry replied.

Jerry laid his hands on Earl's shoulders and began. But as he heard himself praying, he realized his words were just that. Words. Jerry felt wretched and ashamed and glad his wife wasn't there to hear them.

"Amen," he finally concluded, opening his eyes and lifting his hands from Earl's shoulders. Immediately Earl grabbed his hands.

"Pray some more, Jerry. Please, I'm scared."

Jerry snapped. "What are you doing this for, Earl? You're crazy! You can twist your ankle getting off the bench here, and we can end it now!"

"I need the money."

Jerry slammed his fist down on the preparation table. "What do you need the money for? Tell me."

"Please, Jerry. I just need it. Don't shout; just pray."

Jerry watched as the giant man scrunched his eyes tight in pleading anticipation of the next prayer. His heart tore. Three months earlier he would have been thrilled if a boxer had asked him to pray some more. Yet now Jerry just wanted to gather Earl up in his arms like a child, then go and fight in his place. Even at thirty-nine years old, Jerry would easily be able to dispatch a limited bullyboy like Ray Butcher. Indeed, there wasn't a boxer alive Jerry would more enjoy hammering. But instead he was going to have to stand and watch as this man he loved got smashed up.

Earl still sat with his eyes clenched shut.

Lord, what is this? Jerry mouthed at the ceiling. But there was no answer. Eventually he gathered his composure and laid his hands again on the big man's shoulders, shamed at his earlier effort and humbled by the value Earl placed on his prayers.

With the sound of the drunken boxing hall humming just thirty yards away, Jerry prayed again for his friend with all the sincerity he could muster.

19

Fourteen minutes later, Jerry and Mario bent by Earl's pros-
trate body. Ray Butcher stood over them, hurling insults
above the noise of the cheering crowd.

Mario growled at Jerry to ignore the fighter's taunts and
help lift Earl into a sitting position. The cut man reached up
and removed Earl's mouth guard. A thin trail of bloody saliva
momentarily strung from Mario's hand to Earl's bottom lip
before twanging and dropping to the canvas. Earl opened
his eyes again, his pupils wandering alarmingly in different
directions.

"Shut your eyes, Earl. Count slowly to ten."

Earl obeyed Mario groggily. When he completed the
count, he opened his eyes again. This time Earl's pupils finally
pointed in the same direction. Jerry watched with concern
yet could not completely shut out Ray Butcher's jeers.

"You can't be a very good trainer, Ambrose, if that loser's the best you can come up with."

Jerry concentrated on Earl, fighting hard to ignore Butcher's provocation. Finally Earl became more responsive and looked across at Jerry. "Sorry I didn't do better, boss."

"You did fine, Earl," Jerry replied with a lump in his throat. "You were very brave. I'm so sorry I let you in there." He reached out and gripped Earl's shoulder. "But next time, when I tell you to go down, you go down. You got that?"

"Yeah."

Mario plunged a wet sponge into the boxer's face. Jerry, still kneeling, scanned the ring, his anger bubbling up again. Ray Butcher was standing on the far corner post, holding his arms up to the baying crowd and orchestrating their chants of "Killer! Killer!"

"Where's that ref?" Jerry shouted angrily, realizing with frustration that the official had obviously fled the scene. Jerry was furious. Earl had been hurt from the first exchange when Ray Butcher had landed two punches and a forearm into Earl's exposed face. Earl had wobbled around the ring as Jerry yelled at him to hit the deck. But Earl hadn't. It wasn't unusual for boxers to be so disoriented and focused on warding off punches that they forgot they could end it simply by buckling their knees. That was when the ref should always step in.

He hadn't. Jerry had immediately thrown in the towel directly at the referee's feet. Instead of stopping the fight, the referee had kicked the towel off the ring surface and let the noncontest continue. It was the most crooked and dangerous piece of refereeing Jerry had ever seen.

Jerry scanned the raucous crowd and spotted the white-shirted referee disappearing through the changing room doors.

Suddenly the trainer was aware of someone standing next to him. Ray Butcher's voice bellowed in Jerry's ear.

"You should retire, Ambrose, if that dummy's the best you've got."

It was the final straw. Jerry leaped to his feet and threw a lightning right hook at his tormentor. The punch landed squarely on Butcher's cheek, sending him reeling backward across the ring. Two of Butcher's entourage jumped on Jerry as the heavyweight bounced off the ropes and came back swinging. Enraged, Jerry shrugged off the arms that held him and threw two more well-aimed punches that caught Butcher in the face. Within seconds there was chaos, with punches being thrown from all directions and a dozen bodies shoving each other around the ring. As more people tried to restrain the two fighters, Butcher spat a lump of bloody phlegm that landed on Jerry's shoulder, infuriating the trainer even more. Just as Jerry attempted to shrug off the restraining arms again, he was suddenly lifted off his feet.

Earl hauled Jerry through the ropes. Pinning him to his hip with his still-gloved hand, Earl barged toward the dressing rooms. Jerry realized he was completely overpowered and stopped struggling. While his bravado recoiled against it, deep down he knew it was for his own good.

Fighting had broken out all over the hall. Jerry watched in shock as a glass beer bottle flew across his line of sight, quickly followed by a folding chair being thrown the other way. Mayhem filled the room.

Earl continued to barge through the fighting crowd as Jerry looked around in a daze. Suddenly, out of the melee, a single face caught his attention. A familiar young man stood not twenty feet away looking straight at Jerry with an expression of shock and fascination. Their eyes locked despite Jerry's bouncing around horizontally, clamped against Earl's hip. Finally two brawling men obscured their line of sight.

Earl burst through the swing doors to the changing rooms. Jerry's last view of the hall before the doors swung shut was a heaving sea of fists, bodies, and flying debris. Five minutes later, without half their gear and with Earl still in his shorts and gloves, they were all in the club minibus heading away from the bedlam.

/ / /

Sam made his way along the town footpath toward Romford. A hundred yards away, a few cars still droned along the A12 dual carriageway. He had been walking for an hour but couldn't even remember the journey, he'd been so lost in the events of that evening.

From the moment he arrived as the first spectator in the hall, Sam had been transfixed. The buildup, the atmosphere, and, most of all, the fights had fascinated him all evening. Unlike those who sat around him, waiting for the intervals so they could fill up with more beer, Sam had stayed at his seat from start to finish.

He had been unimpressed by almost every skill aspect of the early fighters. Nevertheless, he had loved the confrontation and the ebbs and flows of all the contests. Some had been over quickly, ended by a good punch or combination. Others had finished in a final frenzy of wild, tired punches before the last bell. But unexpectedly Sam had also been intensely interested in the rest periods between rounds. And that was for one reason only. Jerry Ambrose.

It had been a shock to see the trainer walk into the ring with the first fighter. Sam had felt anger bubble up inside him. And when Jerry had returned to the ring again for the second fight, Sam began to feel cheated—his enjoyment spoiled by the bitter memories of his last visit to the Ilford Boxing Club. The poster he had seen advertising the evening made no mention of the club, instead featuring a fearsome-looking man nicknamed Killer.

While the rest of the crowd had ogled the bikini-clad woman holding a sign with the round number printed on it, Sam studied Jerry carefully. Throughout the evening Sam watched with growing fascination as the trainer, through a combination of words, body movements, and quick shadowboxing, instructed his fighters between rounds. Time and again, Sam watched the fighters putting Jerry's instructions into action, often resulting in a shift in fortunes. In one fight near the end of the evening, Sam had seen Jerry flick his own shoulder strangely to his fighter and then suggest a counterpunch. In the next round, Sam spotted the opposition fighter displaying the exact shoulder movement when he flicked out a jab. It happened three or four more times as the round went on. Finally Jerry's fighter stepped inside and threw a left hook as soon as he saw the movement. His gloved fist slammed into the momentarily unprotected chin of his opponent, who instantly crumpled to the floor.

The Walthamstow supporters surrounding him decried the lucky punch. But Sam sat down stunned. From that moment on he vowed that, despite their past, there was only one man he wanted to train him—if Jerry would have him back. During the last fight he moved around to the changing room door in the hope of catching Jerry and begging him to take him back.

But he hadn't had a chance. The last fight had ended in chaos, and Sam had stood rooted in place as the brawl broke out. By the time Sam had pushed his way past several groups of fighting men, Jerry had been carried out of the arena by the big black guy. Sam was just about to follow when a man to his left attacked.

Sam had just seen him in time to duck his head and raise an arm, taking the bulk of the chair's impact on his shoulder. Annoyed rather than hurt by the unprovoked attack, he had turned and caught the drunken man with a right hook to the temple, sending him sprawling across the deserted seats behind. Sam immediately knew he had hit him cleanly and hard, and he wasn't surprised to see the man's body slither down between the chairs and settle motionless on the floor. With that, Sam left and set out for home.

At just past two, Sam climbed into bed. He shut his eyes with only one thought. The next day would involve another long walk. To Ilford.

PART
TWO

20

Jerry sat on his sofa in a T-shirt and gym shorts, watching some Australian soap opera. It was an emotional scene with one of the characters threatening to leave while her friends begged her not to go. Jerry assumed she left in the end. He had just seen the actress on a morning chat show, trying to launch a pop career.

Jerry had watched a lot of daytime TV in recent days. His skin had the telltale pallor of someone who hadn't been outside in a while. Thick black stubble, speckled with gray, sprouted from his face, making him look much older than he was. He yawned at the television, bored, and his mind stewed on the events of a few weeks earlier.

The riot had made the national news on account of a man left in a coma in the local infirmary. Dozens of others had sustained minor injuries. For the first few days, the press had called him and even knocked on his door a number of times, but that had eventually died down. He had also had a steady stream of visitors from the gym, all trying to tell him it wasn't his fault. Mario had tried. Geoff and Dave had tried. Even Bert had been around to his house.

But Jerry didn't want to hear it. In the end he just stopped answering his door, drawing the curtains the moment Gloria left for work.

"Your whole faith's about forgiveness," Gloria had pleaded desperately. "You've preached forgiveness. Yet you won't accept it yourself! Please, Jerry."

It was no good. In his own eyes, he had undermined all his previous efforts. He had preached self-control and discipline to young boxers a hundred times. Yet he couldn't practice it himself. God hadn't really changed him.

Over the next week, anger with God had turned into indifference, indifference to self-pity, and self-pity, finally, to unbelief. He hadn't prayed since laying his hands on Earl, minutes before the last fight at Walthamstow. "That didn't have much effect, so what's the point?" Jerry had said bitterly to Gloria when she tried to encourage him.

Things had hit rock bottom the night before. Geoff had come round again, clutching a handful of mail and telling Jerry the gym was like a morgue and everyone wanted him back.

Jerry gave Geoff no encouragement. Geoff offered to pray. Jerry refused. They sat in uncomfortable silence until Geoff picked up the hint and stood to leave. Jerry showed him to the door. As the heavyweight limped away, he appeared completely crushed. Geoff had looked up to Jerry ever since the trainer led him to faith three years earlier. Jerry wanted to comfort his friend. But his new way of thinking prevented him.

In between letters of support in the mail Geoff had brought, a brown envelope caught Jerry's eye. *British Boxing Board of Control* was stamped in bold capitals across the envelope. In cold language, the letter informed Jerry he was being cautioned for bringing boxing into disrepute. Any repeat offense and his trainer's license would be revoked.

Jerry wasn't surprised. He had suspected he'd be lined up to take the fall. Following the riot at Walthamstow, the reputation of boxing had once again been dragged through the mud by a hungry press. There had even been calls for a debate in Parliament to consider banning the sport.

Gloria had fled to bed in tears when Jerry casually informed her. He was annoyed at her for encouraging Geoff to visit. And her constant praying was really beginning to irritate him. For some reason he was starting to take perverse pleasure in disappointing her spiritually.

Jerry knew he was behaving badly. Gloria didn't deserve it. While he now felt her faith was misguided, she was still the kindest person he had ever met. And the children had certainly done nothing to warrant Jerry's sullen lack of interest in them. He was in danger of ruining everything, but he just couldn't break out of it. All it would take was fifteen steps from the sofa to the bedroom, and, with a sincere apology, Gloria would be back in his arms. But he just couldn't do it. That would mean acknowledging and talking about God again—the last thing he wanted to do. He had switched on the television instead and spent the night on the couch.

When he awoke, his family had already left for school and work. There was a curt note asking Jerry to buy some bread and milk. But apart from eating breakfast and going to the toilet, Jerry hadn't moved.

/ / /

The shrill ring of the doorbell tore Jerry's attention from the TV. He grimaced. He wasn't in the mood for visitors.

He crept quietly to the door, stooping to look through the peephole. The unmistakable shape of Earl's torso filled the lens. Jerry paused. Anyone else and he would have pretended he was out. But he had wondered about Earl ever since the fight. Jerry took a breath and opened the door.

The two men nodded at one another.

"Jerry."

"Earl."

Earl stood up straight and delivered his well-rehearsed line. "Jerry, if you don't come back, I'm going to quit fighting."

"Good. Quit. It's what I've wanted all along."

Earl, taken aback, stood for several seconds digesting the answer he hadn't anticipated. His mind churned over a new approach. "Jerry. If you come back, I promise I'll quit fighting." Earl delivered the declaration with the same unerring sincerity as he had the one before.

Jerry couldn't prevent a smile, and for a moment he forgot about himself. "Earl, be honest with me. Why do you fight?"

Earl shifted his weight from foot to foot. "I need the money," he mumbled.

"I know. You need the money," Jerry said quietly. "Why do you need the money?"

Earl frowned and fell silent, as if fighting an internal battle. "For my daughter," he finally said, watching Jerry's reaction fearfully.

Jerry was genuinely shocked. He had wondered whether Earl's insatiable "need" for money was because of drugs or gambling, the two most common pits for men to sink their money into, but neither seemed to fit Earl's character. On the other hand, a child seemed unlikely too.

"You've got a little girl?" Jerry said, gathering his composure and smiling broadly. "Earl, that's great. That's brilliant! That's beautiful, man. Why didn't you tell me?"

Earl shrugged, relief clear on his face.

"You're a dad, Earl. That's great! What's her name?" Jerry continued.

Earl grinned shyly. "Ella."

"Ella. That's a beautiful name. How old is she?"

"Four."

"Earl, you've got a four-year-old daughter, and you've kept her a secret all this time? Man, I tell everyone about my kids. I'd be shouting from the rooftops."

Earl laughed again, clearly enjoying talking about his daughter.

"You got a photo?" Jerry asked.

The smile immediately disappeared from Earl's face, replaced by a worried frown. He looked down at his feet and shook his head.

Jerry stopped, surprised at the change in Earl's demeanor.

He sensed he was nearing the heart of Earl's desperate need for money.

Jerry recognized the irony. Months before, he had spent many hours praying for Earl, asking God to show him what was behind Earl's desire to fight. He had received no insight from God at all. Now, when Jerry felt at his lowest spiritual ebb in years, Earl was opening up. Jerry knew he had to listen to God. For the first time in three weeks, Jerry sent up a quick prayer. Instantly he knew what he should ask.

"Can I meet her?"

Earl flinched at the question and tried to ignore it.

"Earl," Jerry said firmly. "Let's go and see her."

Earl stood still, contemplating what to do. Then, turning on his heel, he strode to his car.

Jerry panicked, not sure whether Earl was running away or wanted Jerry to go with him. Either way, he knew he must go. Shutting his front door behind him, Jerry followed his friend to the car, still wearing his slippers.

21

Earl and Jerry drove in silence to a housing complex on the other side of town. The car came to a halt outside one of six gray concrete tower blocks. Jerry said nothing. He knew this was not Earl's home; the huge black man lived several miles away.

Earl retrieved a bag of groceries from the trunk, and they entered the building, ignoring the vandalized elevator door, which had been skewered by a galvanized fencing post. Earl began climbing the concrete stairs, two at a time. Jerry followed more cautiously, wrinkling his nose at the stench of urine and stepping over a pile of ashes where someone had lit a fire.

When they arrived at the eighth-floor landing, they exited the stairwell into a long corridor with doors every few yards. Earl stopped outside one. The word *whore* had been spray-painted across it. Putting a key in the lock, Earl pushed it open with his shoulder and stepped inside. Jerry followed, immediately hearing a high-pitched cry of "Daddy!" He watched from behind as Earl bent down to catch a running child.

"Hello, beautiful," Earl said softly. He turned to Jerry, revealing a pretty little blonde girl in his arms. "Ella, say hello to my friend Jerry."

Jerry found himself looking into two beautiful pale-blue eyes.

"Hello, Jerry," the little girl said with a shy smile.

Jerry smiled but couldn't answer. He had tried to visualize on the journey over how Earl's daughter might look. A pretty blonde girl with pale-blue eyes was not the image he had envisaged.

Ella buried her head in Earl's collar as his large fingers ruffled her hair. The two men looked at one another, each trying to read the other's thoughts.

A sound came from the neighboring room. Earl set Ella down and rushed for a door on the other side of the dingy living room. He was too late. A woman fell through the opening before catching the door handle and steadying herself. She blearily tried to focus on the two men across the room.

Jerry smiled, but in his heart he knew. This woman was the cloud that hung over Earl. Jerry guessed she was in her late twenties, although she looked much older. She was painfully thin, and her skin had a grayish tinge. Her face was covered in old makeup, and her hair was a mess from sleeping. An old pink T-shirt that had once borne a logo hung from her bony shoulders above a pair of gray underwear. She was half-wearing a dressing gown. The woman made a fumbling attempt to cover herself as she looked suspiciously in Jerry's direction.

"Hi, I'm Jerry," he said, walking quickly toward her with his right arm outstretched. She made a vain attempt to hook her own right arm through the sleeve of the dressing gown, but Jerry didn't give her time. He stopped a yard short of her and held out his hand, inviting her to reach out and shake it.

"Hi," she said nervously. "Kirsten." Her hand was cold and clammy. As Jerry shook her hand, he looked down at the inside of her bare arm.

/ / /

Jerry sat on a park bench outside the high-rise, watching Earl and Ella playing on the swing. The little girl squealed with delight as she was gently pushed skyward.

"Higher, Daddy, higher!" she pleaded as Earl shuffled back and forth behind her, hands out in case she fell.

Jerry sat entranced as they finally left the swing and began bouncing on an absurdly uneven seesaw. But as enchanted as he was, Jerry felt overwhelmed by the depressing reality of the situation.

Ella finally got bored with the seesaw and ran off in the direction of a slide. Earl wandered over toward Jerry, not taking his eyes off the little girl.

"She's beautiful, Earl."

"Yeah, she is," Earl said, smiling, waving at Ella as she sat on top of the slide.

"Watch me, Daddy!" the little girl shouted.

"I'm watching, sweetheart," Earl shouted back. Ella slid down with a squeal of delight before dismounting and rushing around to the metal steps. Jerry took a deep breath.

"Earl. You know she's not . . ." He paused, not able to say it. The words hung in the air.

"She's not what?" Earl said defensively, the smile falling from his face.

"Watch me, Daddy!" The words were faint as they blew across the park.

Earl waved again. "Daddy's watching, sweetheart." Ella went down the slide again. The two men sat in tense silence as they watched Ella climb the steps once more and this time stop her descent by digging her rubber-soled shoes into the stainless steel. Jerry put his hand on Earl's shoulder.

"I'm sorry, brother. None of my business."

Earl flinched but didn't push Jerry's arm away. "I wanna tell you. It's just—" Earl swallowed—"hard." Tears formed in the corners of his eyes.

Jerry swallowed as a golf ball formed in his own throat. He had seen Earl take numerous painful beatings in the ring but had never seen tears before.

"I know what you were going to say," Earl continued, still looking at Ella. "That she's not mine. I know that. I always have. People laugh at me because they think I'm so stupid that I don't realize. But I knew before they did because I never even, you know, went with her mum."

Jerry shook his head. "Then why, when she got pregnant, didn't you just say the baby wasn't yours?"

Earl paused and glanced up at the sky before continuing.

"I care about her." Earl looked at Jerry as if contemplating how much to say. He studied his hands before sucking in a deep breath. "We grew up in the same children's home. She was abandoned too. We weren't really friends. She used to tease me like the rest of them. Calling me slow and that. But then when the others weren't around, she'd come and sit with me. She never said anything. We just used to . . . sit." Earl swallowed awkwardly, fighting back emotion. "Once she came and saw me in prison. She was the only person who ever did." Earl looked away toward Ella, blinking back tears.

"Why were you in prison?" Jerry ventured after a few seconds.

"I didn't do anything," Earl said urgently, clearly concerned what Jerry would think. "My cousin got me a job as a doorman in Hackney. Five pounds an hour for standing outside a flat. My cousin told me it was a card game. Then one day the police turned up. I didn't know there were drugs and guns inside.

"So when I got out of prison, I used to see Kirsten around. Then after a few years she got pregnant, and everyone was calling her a slut and saying she probably didn't know who the father was. That was when she named me. I wanted to give her a break. When Ella was born, I was the only person who went and saw them in the hospital. I looked . . ." Earl paused again, battling with his emotions.

"When I looked down at her in her crib, so beautiful and small, I thought . . ." Fresh tears rolled down Earl's face as he struggled to get the words out. "I thought that she deserved a dad that loved her."

"Watch me, Daddy!" Ella shouted from the top of the slide.

Earl lifted both arms and waved. "I'm watching, sweetheart." She was too far away and too enthralled in her play to notice the quiver in her father's voice.

Jerry put his arm around his friend. "You're a great dad, Earl."

"No, I'm not," Earl replied. "If I was, she wouldn't be living in this *dump*!"

They sat in silence, watching Ella play. Her happy demeanor and excited squeals jarred against the bleak squalor of the high-rise behind her.

"Ella's mother is a drug addict," Jerry ventured finally. "I saw the needle marks on her arm."

"I know. That's why I need the money from boxing. All her welfare money goes for drugs, so I have to buy them food and give her money to keep the debt collectors from taking their furniture. But it's never enough. That's why I fought Ray Butcher. I wanted a bit extra to buy Ella a treat. Maybe a bike or something."

Jerry turned away, angry at the injustice of it all. He had seen the fear in Earl's eyes before the fight with Ray Butcher. Earl had been genuinely terrified. Yet he was willing to do it—to provide for a child who wasn't even his.

Jerry watched as Earl clapped and cheered encouragement toward Ella, who was now bouncing up and down on a crocodile mounted on a giant spring.

"Should she be living with her mum?" Jerry asked carefully.

"Ella's not going to a children's home," Earl said, shaking his head from side to side with wild, panicked eyes. "I won't let it happen."

"Earl, the woman needs help. They both need help."

"I know."

"Well," Jerry said, "you've got to let someone professional know."

Earl said nothing but descended deep into thought. Finally he jutted out his jaw. "Can you do me a favor?"

"Anything."

Earl glanced up toward the high-rise flat. An angry expression contorted his face, and Jerry followed his gaze. A man they had passed in the stairwell ducked out of the tower block entrance and hurried away.

"We can go back now," Earl muttered. He turned to Ella and spread his arms wide. "Ella, my love. Time to go."

The little girl ran to Earl, and he swept her up and swung her around. Ella giggled with delight. Earl then turned and strode toward the flats, still carrying her. Jerry stood up and followed.

"I've got a surprise for you, sweetheart," Jerry heard Earl say as they entered the stairwell and began climbing. He said something else, and then Jerry heard the little girl gasp with excitement as he hurried to keep up.

"Holiday, Daddy? Really?"

The rest of the conversation was lost to Jerry as he fell behind. When he finally reached the eighth floor, the door to the flat was closed, and he had no choice but to wait. A few minutes later Earl emerged, carrying Ella in one arm and a duffel bag in the other.

"Now be good, Ella. Jerry and his family are going to take good care of you."

Jerry looked up at Earl in shock. "Hold on—" Jerry said, as the child was passed into his arms.

But Earl cut him off. "Thanks for doing this, Jerry."

Ella wrapped her arms around Jerry's neck and jiggled up and down. "Holiday! Holiday! Holiday!" she chanted excitedly.

Jerry knew he had no choice. "How long?" he asked.

Earl shrugged. "I don't know."

"What are you doing?"

"Something I should have done a long time ago."

Earl bent forward and gently kissed Ella's forehead. "I'll see you soon."

When he leaned back, Jerry could see tears again in the big man's eyes. Earl pressed the duffel bag into Jerry's free hand. Then he turned and disappeared back into the flat, shutting the door firmly behind him.

///

Jerry almost laughed at the absurdity of his situation, standing in wet slippers in an unknown tower block, holding a child he didn't know but for whom he was now responsible. It had been a crazy two hours. Yet as heartbreaking as they had been, he realized that his gloomy mood of several weeks had suddenly lifted. He looked down at Ella, who was studying his face carefully.

"Where are we going on holiday?" she asked.

"To my house," Jerry said, then cursed himself for not making it sound more exciting.

Ella's eyes widened in wonder. "You live in a house? With stairs inside and everything?"

Jerry nodded at the earnest little girl's face.

"I'm going on holiday to a house!" she chanted.

Jerry smiled and carried her down the stairs. By the time he reached the bottom, he realized he had no car, no money for a taxi home, not even his house key. There was only one option left. As he set out walking toward the library in Romford, a couple of miles away, he prayed no one would question why a disheveled, unshaven black man wearing slippers was walking hand in hand with a white child through one of the roughest parts of London.

22

Gloria tried hard to concentrate as she typed on the new computer. She had never learned to type properly, so progress was painfully slow as she searched the keyboard for each letter. The updated computer system was going to save them all time, her supervisor had said. Yet completing three forms had taken Gloria half the afternoon.

Gloria knew she wasn't on her best form. Her attention kept wandering back to the troubles she faced. Life at home was miserable, and there seemed little hope of a breakthrough. Her husband—her kind, gentle, loving soul mate—had disappeared and been replaced by a grumpy ogre who moped around the house, snapping at her and the kids. Every morning for three weeks she had hoped and prayed that day would be the turning point. Yet every day it had seemed to get worse.

It was finally getting to be too much. That morning she had sat in her car after dropping the kids at school and sobbed her heart out. While she had always approached God in prayer with respect and reverence as her grandmother had taught her decades earlier, today she had screamed and shouted. Through angry tears she had ordered a break-through from God because, frankly, she couldn't take any more. Although five hours later she was ashamed that she had shouted at God, she nevertheless still felt anger and bitterness toward him. She shut out the thought and concentrated on the keyboard in front of her.

A few moments later, aware of movement beyond her desk, she looked up, longing for a distraction.

She got one. Twenty feet away, her husband, the source of so much heartache, was walking toward her in his slippers, hand in hand with a small white girl. While Gloria's mind was normally quick to build scenarios, she struggled to think of any circumstance that could possibly explain this strange vision before her.

"Hi," she said as he reached her.

"Hi," Jerry replied sheepishly, bending down and lifting the girl up. He sat her on the desk. "Ella, meet Gloria. Gloria, meet Ella."

"Hiya, gorgeous," Gloria said, smiling and holding out her hand. The little girl smiled and gently gripped Gloria's hand with her own.

"Ella is Earl's daughter, and she's going to come and stay with us for a little while," Jerry said in an enthusiastic voice that urged Gloria to respond positively.

"Er. Well. Yes," Gloria stumbled, looking at Jerry closely.

Ella smiled and fixed Gloria with an inquiring look. "Do you really have stairs inside your house?"

"We do," Gloria said. "With a lovely red carpet."

"Wow!" the little girl said as Gloria shot her husband a quizzical look.

"Now, Ella," Gloria said, "I bet you love drawing, don't you?"

The little girl nodded, and Gloria lifted her across the desk and sat her down with a pen and paper. The girl started drawing an enormous square detached house.

She's going to be a bit disappointed by our urban semi, Gloria thought to herself wryly before turning back toward her husband to ask him what on earth was going on. But before she had a chance, someone else approaching the desk caught her attention. She froze. Jerry, seeing the look on her face, turned around.

Five yards away, Sam stood holding a carrier bag of magazines and looking back and forth from Jerry to Gloria with a baffled expression on his face.

"You know," Jerry said, "this day is getting stranger by the minute."

/ / /

Ten minutes later, Jerry was driving Gloria's car. Sam sat beside him, while Ella bounced excitedly on the backseat, waving at passersby. It occurred to Jerry she had perhaps never been in a car before.

Jerry glanced sideways at Sam, wondering if the young

man was angry with him. Sam looked ahead with a faraway gaze that revealed nothing. They drove in virtual silence except for excited observations from the backseat.

Ella was already flagging by the time they reached Jerry's home. After running up and down the stairs a number of times and into every room in the house, she submitted to a brief story reading from Jerry before settling down for a nap in his youngest daughter's bed.

Jerry came down the stairs into the kitchen. Sam was sitting quietly at the kitchen table.

"Coffee?" Jerry asked.

"Water, please."

Jerry poured Sam a glass of water and made himself a cup of coffee, taking a seat opposite Sam.

The boy picked up the carrier bag of magazines and pushed them across the table. "Thanks for lending me these."

"No problem," Jerry replied. "I'm sorry we didn't tell you. After what happened at the gym that time, I wasn't sure if you'd want to know they were from me."

Sam looked up at Jerry. "I've been to the gym, like, fifteen times in the last month," he said bitterly. "You're never there."

"Sorry. I didn't know. I've been taking a bit of a break."

"Why?"

Jerry sighed. "Since that fight night at Walthamstow. I saw you there, didn't I?"

Sam nodded.

"You didn't get hung up in the fighting afterward, did you?" Jerry asked urgently.

"Not really," Sam replied, looking away guiltily.

Jerry grimaced. "Well. I'm sorry about what you witnessed there."

"Sorry? You were brilliant," Sam said. "I watched everything. Your instructions to your boxers won at least three fights that were going the other way."

"I meant what happened at the end."

"That was the best part," Sam continued. "Those were the fastest three punches I saw all night. You would have taken him out no trouble if everyone hadn't jumped on you."

Jerry winced inwardly. "That wasn't what I meant. I meant losing my temper."

"You used to be a boxer yourself, didn't you?"

Jerry held Sam's gaze for several seconds before eventually nodding.

Sam grinned. "You were good as well, weren't you? Better than that Walthamstow rubbish."

Jerry remained silent, disturbed by the conversation. But the boy held out for an answer.

"Quite good," Jerry finally confirmed. There was a long pause as they studied one another.

"I think I could be quite good too," Sam said shyly.

Jerry studied the young man. Sam's face fell at Jerry's silence, and he looked away. Jerry saw the discouragement and determined to stop messing around. While he was normally cautious about assessing young boxers in their presence for fear they might get bigheaded or complacent, he knew that would never be a danger with this young man.

"Sam," Jerry said seriously, causing Sam to look up. "I don't think you could be . . . quite good. I think you could be the best."

A faint smile crossed Sam's lips, but he forced it away. "I'm sorry how I was before," the boy said. "I want you . . . I need you . . . to train me. Please."

Jerry's heart thumped in his chest, and he suddenly felt breathless. This was the moment he had dreamed of. Now, finally, it was happening. As ridiculous as it seemed—the kid had never even had a proper practice bout—Jerry knew. Sam was a champion in the making. Jerry's making.

"I have three rules," Jerry said as calmly as he could. "Number one: no fighting outside the ring. Ever."

Sam nodded earnestly.

"Number two: you finish your education."

Sam looked surprised but nodded once again.

"You still going to school?" Jerry questioned.

"Mostly," Sam said, nodding.

"Is it O-level exams this summer?"

"It's called the GCSE now. They want me to take ten subjects, even though most of the other kids are only doing four or five," Sam said, a hint of bitterness in his tone.

"You'll do them all," Jerry said, pointing at Sam. "And you work hard for them. I'll explain how later, but it will help you with your boxing."

"Okay," Sam said.

"Good lad," Jerry replied. "And finally, rule three."

Jerry paused, remembering what the third rule was. In recent weeks it had become so much less important to him that if "rule three" hadn't instinctively tripped off his tongue, he might have abandoned it. But it was too late now.

"I pray for all my boxers before their fights," Jerry continued, cringing at how strange it sounded.

Sam suppressed a quizzical look and nodded again.

"Deal?" Jerry asked, holding out his hand.

"Deal." Sam shook Jerry's hand firmly.

"Right, then." Jerry picked up a piece of paper and a pen from the table. "We've got some work to do. Tell me what you've been doing training-wise."

Sam described his daily regimen of running and exercises. Jerry wrote it down in a type of code, grouping activities in different sections and asking specific questions that Sam quickly answered. By the time Sam finished, three sheets of paper were covered in Jerry's scrawl. Jerry put his pen down and looked at his scribbles. He would normally be skeptical if one of his fighters claimed to keep such a schedule, but the encyclopedic way Sam relayed his timings and progress over the last few months eliminated all doubt from Jerry's mind. This boy was seriously self-motivated.

"And what about your eating?" Jerry asked, writing *Diet* on a fresh sheet of paper.

Sam shifted uncomfortably in his seat. "That's more difficult," he mumbled. "We don't really have food at home. I eat quite a lot at school, though."

"Okay. Tell me a typical week."

Sam described his weekly diet. Jerry carefully wrote it down, noting how little decent food was passing the boy's lips. To keep such a rigorous exercise regimen on an almost permanently empty stomach was extraordinary.

"Good," Jerry said. "I'll have a think about all this over the weekend. Now. Tell me what you've learned from the videos you've been watching."

For the next twenty minutes Sam talked nonstop about the intricacies of what he had seen and studied. Occasionally he stood and demonstrated a bit of footwork or posture in the middle of the kitchen. Jerry sat entranced by both the boy's passion for the subject and the mature and complex insights he communicated. It was a level way beyond anyone else at the gym, bar Mario and Jerry himself. By the time Sam finished, Jerry felt a strange sense of elation deep inside.

"Okay, Sam. I wanna see you at the gym Monday afternoon after school, and we'll talk then about your new training and exercise regimen. We'll also see what we can do about your diet."

Sam nodded and smiled in a way Jerry had never seen before.

"Good," Jerry replied. "Now we need to get going. Where do you live?"

"Romford."

"Whereabouts?"

Sam frowned. "You can drop me anywhere."

"Okay," Jerry said, not pushing the point. "I'll drop you back at the library. I've got to pick up my wife, and then I've got to go somewhere else. Stay here while I wake the girl."

23

Jerry climbed the stairs to the gym. He had climbed these steps a thousand times but had never felt as nervous as he did now.

It had been a crazy day. Asleep in front of the TV four hours earlier, his wildest dreams could never have predicted how his afternoon would pan out. Earl, Ella, Sam . . . and then his family.

After dropping Sam off and collecting Gloria from the library, Jerry and Ella had picked the children up from school. They had stopped at a local park, where the children played happily together in the late spring sunshine. Jerry had apologized. Gloria had forgiven him. While his own faith might be shaky, his wife's grace astounded him. His children, too, had hugged him tightly when he apologized to them for how he'd been behaving.

There was only one more relationship that needed

addressing. "Go before me, Lord," Jerry said under his breath. He lifted his head and pushed through the gym door.

To his relief, the room was quiet and nobody noticed his arrival. He looked to the left and saw Bert's office light on and his boss sitting at his desk reading some papers.

Jerry walked over. "Hi," he said, standing in the office doorway.

Bert looked up and stared at Jerry before gesturing for him to sit down.

Jerry settled nervously on the edge of the chair. "Bert, I'm really sorry. I've screwed up. I've let you down. I've let the gym down. I've let myself down."

"Yeah. You have."

Jerry swallowed. He knew his boss had no reason to forgive him. Bert hadn't promised to love him like his wife had—through good times and bad, in sickness and in health. Jerry didn't even have an employment contract.

"I'm sorry," Jerry repeated quietly. There was nothing more to say.

Bert stared at him without blinking. He then lifted a finger and pointed it at Jerry. "Jerry, I want you back here first thing Monday morning. I want you to work your butt off. I want you to lift the mood around here, 'cause it's depressing. And I don't want any more trouble. Okay?"

"Okay," Jerry said, relieved. "Thank you." He reached across the desk.

Bert looked at Jerry's hand suspiciously before he finally reached up and shook it. "Are you doing all right?" Bert asked almost compassionately.

"Much better now," Jerry replied.

"Good. Now get lost."

Jerry rose, smiling. "I'm going. See you Monday." He shut the door behind him before turning and opening it again. "Oh, I forgot to say, I'm going to give you a British champion in eighteen months."

"Not Earl, I take it."

"No. Not Earl. I found the boy I told you about. Sam. Or rather he found me. Well, maybe we were led to one another," Jerry said, getting lost in thought. "Anyway, I've told him we're starting Monday afternoon."

"You cocky git," Bert growled. "As of this afternoon, I had decided to sack you." Jerry was relieved to see Bert break into a grin. "He better be as good as you say he is."

"I think he's better. We'll see on Monday."

24

Jerry pulled out onto the main road and turned toward Dagenham. Traffic was light this Sunday morning, and he enjoyed the drive.

The morning sunshine streaming through the windscreen reflected Jerry's mood. The previous day he and Gloria had taken Ella and their children to the swimming pool in Romford. Although dated now, it had been one of the first pools in the country to have a wave machine and a slide, which the children loved. It turned out Ella had never been swimming, and she was almost speechless with excitement. They had played for over an hour in the shallows and on the children's slide, only persuading Ella it was time to leave by pointing out her wrinkly fingers.

Over a messy hamburger lunch, Gloria had reached out and stroked Jerry's hair. That night, instead of switching on the TV, Jerry had bathed the children and cooked Gloria a curry. They had even spent time praying before making love. They had then slept deeply for the first time in weeks.

By Sunday morning, however, Earl still hadn't turned up, and Jerry and Gloria were concerned about what to do with Ella. So, as his family headed to church with Ella, Jerry set out to find Earl. His flat was empty, so Jerry drove toward the high-rise where he had left the big man thirty-six hours earlier.

Jerry pulled into the road leading to the block of flats. Unease gripped him immediately as he saw the blue and white tape. Fifty yards ahead, a police cordon had been strung up around the tower block beyond. Jerry parked the car and walked toward a policeman standing by the cordon. Beyond him, Jerry saw two police marksmen running toward the flat, carrying guns.

"What's going on?" Jerry asked. The young police constable glanced at Jerry and then eyed his nearest colleague several yards away.

"Got a siege situation," he said quietly. "There's a prostitute lives at the top of that tower block. A neighbor says she's been screaming at a man to let her out for the last two days. He's barricaded himself in there with her. Looks like a trick gone wrong." The policeman gazed up at the flat, smirking unpleasantly.

"Why the guns?" Jerry asked, trying to hide his anger at the policeman's inappropriate behavior.

"We traced the guy's car," he said, nodding at Earl's battered old car. "He's got previous firearm offenses, and he says he's armed." The policeman checked over his shoulder again before leaning closer to Jerry. "And he's got the prostitute's little girl in there too." The policeman grimaced suggestively and grinned again.

Jerry resisted the urge to punch the man. Instead he turned and walked away.

"Hey," the policeman called out in annoyance. Jerry ignored him and tried to gather his thoughts. Why would Earl have barricaded himself into Kirsten's flat? It made no sense, but he knew the police were wrong. Whatever was happening, he knew he had to do something.

Jerry turned and walked back to the policeman. "I need to speak to your superior. Now."

"What about, sir?" the policeman said skeptically.

"About what's going on up there. It's not what you think."

"I see. What is it then?"

Jerry paused, frustrated. He really didn't want to talk to this man, but he had no choice. All the other policemen were well beyond the cordon. "Well, for a start, the little girl's not in there."

"Is that right? So where may she be then, sir?" The policeman raised his eyebrows irritatingly.

"She's with my family."

The policeman's expression changed immediately, and he began to stammer.

"As I said," Jerry restated, "I need to speak to your superior. Now."

"Er—of course," the policeman replied, fumbling with his radio.

Suddenly two loud cracks reverberated all around them.

"Oh no, Lord, no. Please," Jerry said as he ducked under the police tape.

"Stop," the policeman said, putting his hand on Jerry's arm.

"Get lost," Jerry snarled, shoving the policeman away and breaking into a sprint.

Jerry rounded the corner of the block of flats and ran straight into a whole crowd of policemen. Immediately three burly officers grabbed Jerry and forced him to the ground.

"*Stop!*" Jerry shouted desperately, struggling with the hands that pinned him. "This isn't what you think. He hasn't got the child in there."

"Sir. Calm down. Stop struggling," said a firm, authoritative voice.

"I know Earl Powell. This isn't what you think!"

Jerry was lifted to his feet, and an older policeman with stripes on his shoulders walked up to him.

"Please tell us who you are, sir."

"I'm Jerry Ambrose," he panted. "I'm a friend of Earl's. His daughter's staying with us."

"Who's his daughter?"

"Ella—the little girl you think is in there. Well, I guess she's not his blood daughter." Jerry sighed. "It's complicated."

"Well, try telling me, sir. Calmly and clearly," the senior policeman said.

But before Jerry could start, another policeman interrupted. "Sir, can I have a word?"

The inspector backed away with his colleague, but Jerry could still hear their whispered conversation.

"Sir, they've searched the whole flat and they can't find the child anywhere. The mother's okay. Bruises and cuts on her hands, but that's all."

"On her hands?"

"Yes, sir. Sir, I know it sounds strange, but the man's injuries seem to indicate that . . . she's been hitting him."

The inspector screwed up his face. "What is going on here?"

"The paramedics are bringing the suspect down now. It's bad. Chest and arm wounds."

Jerry saw the inspector's shoulders sag.

The policeman cursed under his breath, then took off his cap and wiped his forehead with a handkerchief. He turned slowly and faced Jerry, whose mind was spinning at what he had heard.

"You shot him?" Jerry shouted.

The inspector said nothing but turned and looked forlornly in the direction of the stairwell as two paramedics emerged carrying Earl on a stretcher.

"Please!" one of the paramedics shouted. "Can someone else carry him? My back's finished."

The stretcher tipped alarmingly as two policemen tried to take over from the sweaty paramedics. Once extricated, one of them reached down to lift a packet of plasma lying next to the victim and held it high above the patient's head. The tube hung down in a curling trail and attached to the back of Earl's hand.

"Earl," Jerry shouted. Earl's head shifted slightly as the stretcher was hurried away toward a waiting ambulance. Jerry turned to the inspector, who was watching the whole scene with a grim expression on his face.

"Can I go with him? Please?"

"Go," the inspector said, making a snap judgment. "But we will need to speak to you at the hospital. Especially about the child." He turned to one of the policemen who had earlier pinned Jerry to the ground. "Go with him."

"Thank you," Jerry said and sprinted after the stretcher with his minder in pursuit.

25

Jerry sat in the ambulance, holding Earl's hand as the two paramedics worked frantically to stem the flow of blood. They cut away Earl's clothing, exposing a neat round hole in his chest from which a steady pulse of blood spilled out. Jerry reached forward and pulled Earl's face toward him.

"Don't look. You're gonna be fine."

"How's Ella?" Earl asked in a strained voice.

"Good, Earl. She's a wonderful kid. Took her swimming yesterday. She loved it."

Earl smiled before coughing violently and glancing down at his chest. His smile faded, and he looked back at Jerry with fearful eyes.

"Tell her I love her," he said, forcing his words out between coughs.

"You can tell her yourself in a few days," Jerry said, trying to sound confident. Earl looked down again at his chest.

"Keep him talking," the paramedic barked at Jerry.

Jerry nodded but couldn't think of anything happy to say. So he asked the question that burned on his mind. "What were you doing, Earl?"

Earl swallowed, grimacing with pain. "Cold turkey," he whispered. "I nailed the door shut so she couldn't get out if I fell asleep. I knew if she got out she'd just start again."

"Oh no," Jerry said. He knew it was true. The injustice of Earl's being shot for trying to help the mother of his adopted child was just too painful to bear. "Why didn't you tell the police the truth?"

Earl shook his head. "I thought if I told them I had a gun, they wouldn't try to break in. And I'd have enough time to get her through it." Earl struggled to get the last words out as he coughed and then swallowed again. Jerry sensed the paramedics getting increasingly anxious.

"I think I did it," Earl whispered in a voice Jerry could hardly hear. "She slept all night and was calm this morning."

"Earl," Jerry said, his own voice breaking, "you are the best man I have ever met."

Earl swallowed painfully twice more and tried to speak.

"What? Earl, what?" Jerry said, his voice desperate. "I can't hear you."

Earl took several more painful breaths as he fought to get his words out. Jerry bent over with his ear close to Earl's mouth.

"Pray . . . for . . . me."

Jerry slid to his knees and grabbed Earl by both hands, putting his mouth close to the big man's ear. He shut his eyes and began quietly singing his favorite song.

"'The Lord's my shepherd; I'll not want. He makes me lie in pastures green. He leads me by the still, still waters. His goodness restores my soul.'" Jerry opened his eyes. Earl had shut his, and for a moment peace had come over the man's face.

"'And I will trust in you alone. . . .'" As soon as Jerry began the chorus, he remembered how it ended and kicked himself. But he was committed now. "'And I will trust in you alone. For your endless mercy follows me; your goodness . . . will lead me home.'"

Earl squeezed Jerry's hand and opened his eyes. An audible breath escaped Earl's lips, and his lungs tried to suck another breath. But his body no longer had the strength. Instead Earl settled into a gentle smile. The two men held each other's gaze, and for several seconds neither breathed. Then, without any change of expression on Earl's face, a high-pitched mechanical tone sounded from the monitor above their heads.

One of the paramedics reached for a machine on the wall and pulled down two pads on curly wires. Jerry had seen such a machine used in hospital dramas on television, often with success. But as he looked into Earl's open eyes, Jerry knew his friend was gone.

Jerry leaned back, covered his ears, and hummed the same song he had sung to Earl, ignoring the commotion going on just a couple of feet away. He had no desire to watch.

He was still humming when he felt the ambulance come to a halt, reverse quickly, and stop once more. He didn't move as the rear doors were flung open and a team of hospital staff slid the stretcher out of the van.

After a minute or two, Jerry opened his eyes. He was alone. The last half hour had been the most traumatic of his life. Yet at this moment, more than at any other time in his life, he felt certain about one thing. Heaven was a reality. And Earl had arrived. He closed his eyes and asked God to take care of his friend.

When Jerry opened his eyes again, the police constable was standing by the rear door of the ambulance. He lifted his eyebrow.

Jerry shook his head.

26

"Are you ready for this?" Jerry asked.

Sam nodded slowly. A curl of a smile formed at the edges of his mouth before it quickly disappeared.

Jerry frowned. In recent weeks the young man had been lightening up and even smiling on occasion. But ever since he had told Sam that today would be his first real sparring session, the boy's demeanor had been different. He had seemed withdrawn and moody, and Jerry had begun to wonder if the lad was nervous. But seeing the concealed smile and the menace in Sam's eyes, Jerry realized the boy wasn't gripped by nerves. Jerry felt a pang of concern for his student's opponent. The trainer reached out and inspected Sam's gloves.

"Oh. Sorry, Sam. You're wearing the wrong gloves. Just give me a second."

Sam looked surprised but allowed Jerry to pull off his

gloves. Jerry jumped down from the ring, hurried toward the walk-in storage closet, and scanned the shelves. Sweeping dozens of gloves aside, he finally saw the pair he wanted. "Here we go," he said as he returned to Sam's side.

Sam eyed the gloves suspiciously and snatched one from Jerry's hand. He searched out the label sewn into the wristband where the words *Super Soft* were printed boldly. Sam frowned and began to protest, but Jerry beat him to it.

"Hey. I'm the boss," he said sternly. "Don't go losing your head. You've been perfect up to now. But if I can't trust you when you climb in the ring, then I can't work with you."

"It won't make any difference anyway."

Jerry ignored the comment and put his arms on Sam's shoulders. "This is what I want. We're concentrating on footwork and ring position. Strong defense. Use the jab, and only step inside when you've got a genuine opening. I don't want to see any lunging. I'm more interested in the punches you defend than the ones you throw today. Understand?"

Sam nodded and looked past his trainer directly at his opponent. Jerry was alarmed to see absolute hatred in the boy's eyes.

"Good. Stay here. I'm going to talk to Robbie," Jerry said, turning away toward his other boxer. *Wow,* he thought to himself as he walked toward Robbie.

"You okay?" Jerry asked.

Robbie nodded, but Jerry could see he was apprehensive. He wasn't surprised. Jerry himself felt nervous about what might happen, and he wasn't fighting. But he had to build Robbie's confidence.

"Right. We know he's strong and he punches hard. But you've got years of experience behind you and a great technique. That will shine through if you don't forget it. You remember that Tobin guy you fought last year at the London Championships? He was a strong nugget too, but you maneuvered him around and beat him easily. So don't get involved in a brawl. And try and enjoy it. You might face someone like Sam at the nationals."

Robbie nodded and banged his gloves together. "Let's go," he said through his gum shield, looking past Jerry to his opponent, who stood motionless, scowling back at him.

"Okay," Jerry said, backing toward the neutral corner and loudly clapping his hands. "Ding-a-ling!"

The two boxers advanced. With relief, Jerry realized that Sam had listened to his instructions, and he watched with pride as the boxers engaged one another skillfully, throwing long-range jabs while they studied each other's defense. Sam's balance and posture were just about perfect, showing a close resemblance to those of Sugar Ray Leonard. Jerry was still amazed at the way Sam had learned and copied so much from a handful of old videos. He had only had to tweak one or two things. Now was a moment of truth, though. Could he deliver in a real contest?

Robbie threw a jab that was easily absorbed by Sam's gloves. He threw another. Blocked again. Robbie was shocked that he hadn't yet seen an opening. He feinted left and fired out a jab, which again was deflected by Sam's gloves. More alarmingly, Robbie kept finding himself pressed backward with hard jabs that thudded into his own gloves and head. With mild panic, he realized his less-experienced opponent was easily marshaling him around the ring.

Robbie knew he had to fight for the ring center, so he tried to move inside, throwing his favorite combination in the process. But Sam was far too quick for him. All Robbie's punches missed the mark, and he received a stinging counter-jab to the nose that he hadn't even seen coming. As he tried to blink the punch away, Sam was instantly on top of him, and Robbie only just managed to spin away. He was in imminent danger of being smashed and was relieved when Jerry called for the end of the round. The two boxers returned to their corners.

/ / /

Jerry went to Robbie first. "You all right?"

Robbie nodded, but Jerry could see his confidence had drained away. This was the time he needed to encourage this lad, but for the first time in ages he didn't really know what to suggest. Unbelievably, this was already a mismatch.

"What do you think?" Jerry finally asked Robbie.

"Dunno," Robbie replied forlornly. "I haven't seen a single opening yet."

Neither had Jerry, but he couldn't tell Robbie that.

"I think you've got to keep spinning and hope an opening presents itself. Your defense has been spot-on. Keep it up. Don't step inside again unless you see a real opportunity. Just keep feinting and hope he makes a mistake. Okay?"

Robbie nodded and punched his gloves together again.

"Good lad," Jerry said. "Give me a second." He turned and walked toward Sam, who looked right through him as he approached. The boy still had a dangerous glare in his eyes, but Jerry was impressed with his control.

"Sam, that was fantastic. You look like you've been doing this all your life. Well done. Any thoughts?"

Sam glared at Robbie with cold, mean eyes. "Can I hit him now?"

"Yeah," Jerry said reluctantly. "But I want it clean. You got that?"

This time Sam didn't even reply. Jerry stepped from between his boxers and indicated to them to engage once more.

This time Sam advanced at pace. Robbie tried to stop him with a firm jab. Sam didn't even bother to defend it. He threw a hook with his right hand, followed in the same motion by an overhand left. Robbie's left glove took the full force of the hook. His own glove slammed into his face, knocking it backward into the path of the second punch. Sam's gloved fist slammed squarely into Robbie's face, knocking him back against the ropes. Before Robbie knew what was happening, a frenzy of punches was raining down on him. Thudding hammer blows smashed into his face, while his ribs were also pummeled. Robbie was helpless. For the first time since Jerry had been training him, Robbie shut his eyes and deliberately buckled his knees, seeking the safety of the canvas floor. But ruthless uppercuts forced him upright until Robbie literally dived past his opponent to find the canvas.

"Stop, stop!" Jerry shouted, jumping into the ring.

"Get up. Get up, you idiot," Sam yelled. "That was a dive. I'm not finished yet!"

Jerry shoved Sam powerfully backward across the ring. Sam stumbled, landing on his backside in a heap in the corner.

"You *are* finished," Jerry said, pointing at Sam. "If you want me to train you, you show some respect to your opponents. Especially when they've been as good to you as Robbie has been. You wouldn't be here if it wasn't for him."

The trainer saw Sam absorb the words and emerge from his trancelike state. The angry scowl suddenly turned to concern.

"I'm sorry," Sam said, looking at Robbie, still prone on the floor. "Is he all right?"

"Go and have a shower," Jerry barked. Sam reluctantly obeyed.

Robbie was spread-eagled facedown across the ring, gripping the floor with his arms and legs.

Jerry knelt beside him. "Are you all right, Robbie?"

"The room's spinning, boss. I'm gonna fall off!"

"It's okay, son," Jerry said soothingly. "You're not gonna fall off. You're just dizzy. Shut your eyes and take some deep breaths."

The trainer reached forward and removed the padded head guard. He picked up a water bottle and squirted its contents over the boy's head and neck. "How are you doing now?"

"It's slowing down," Robbie said in a shaky voice.

"Okay. No hurry."

After a couple of minutes Robbie finally felt well enough to sit up and have a drink. It seemed to help, and with Jerry's assistance, he soon climbed to his feet. "I think I'll have a shower," he said quietly.

"Good idea," Jerry replied. He helped Robbie dip through the ropes and step down from the ring before leading him by the arm in the direction of the showers. When they got there, the changing room was full of steam, and Robbie finally released himself from Jerry's grip. Jerry stood nearby, just in case, as Robbie moved toward the shower.

Jerry could just see Sam through the steam. The young man was standing face to the wall, allowing the jets of water from the showerhead to pound down on the top of his skull. As soon as he saw Robbie, he walked straight up to him.

"I'm sorry," Jerry heard Sam say. "I forgot who you were." He held out his hand toward the taller boy. Robbie paused for only a moment before taking it.

Jerry backed away from the showers and wandered into the gym. Finding a quiet corner, he sat and pondered how to deal with the inevitable fallout of what had just taken place.

After a few minutes Sam emerged. He looked around until he spotted Jerry and walked toward him. "I'm sorry," he said quietly. "I forgot who he was."

Jerry nodded, acknowledging the apology. "Who did you think he was?"

"Don't know."

"Okay, Sam. We'll talk about this another time. Have a few days off. You've got some studying to do, haven't you?"

"GCSEs start next week."

"Well, how about you study hard this week and then come here after school on Friday?"

Sam began to protest.

"Remember my second rule," Jerry interrupted.

Sam was silenced and eventually nodded.

"I'll see you Friday."

The boy turned to walk away.

"By the way," Jerry said, reaching out to catch Sam's arm. "I almost forgot to say. Apart from the disrespect at the end, that was fantastic. I am very, very impressed."

Sam broke into a spontaneous grin.

"Well done. I'm proud," Jerry said, smiling back.

Sam blushed and turned away.

"Oh, I also forgot," Jerry added quietly, although there wasn't anyone nearby. "There's an orange carrier bag of food just inside my office door. Pasta and stuff. Try and get a few good meals in you between now and Friday."

This time Sam scowled, but he finally nodded and made for the exit via Jerry's office. Jerry felt a pang of indignation at the lack of thanks. He was not exactly flush himself. But then he remembered his friend Earl, who had carried countless shopping bags up sixteen flights of stairs without reward. Knowing the boy would enjoy a decent meal would have to be thanks enough. Jerry stood up and walked toward the changing room.

Inside, Robbie already had his trousers on and was pulling a T-shirt over his head.

"How are you feeling now?" Jerry asked.

"Fine," Robbie said without looking up.

Jerry noted the tone in the boy's voice. He wasn't sur-prised. "That was quite a session. I'm sorry you got hurt, Robbie. I didn't realize it would pan out like that."

Robbie looked up at Jerry accusingly. "Then why did you put soft gloves on him? I saw you do that."

Jerry hesitated but knew he couldn't lie. "Yeah, I did. I hadn't planned to. I just . . . I saw something in his eyes and thought it was sensible."

Robbie looked down again. Only the distant noise of steel weights chinking gently in the main hall disturbed the silence. Jerry waited, not knowing what to say.

It was Robbie who spoke next. "I'm not good enough, am I?"

The question hung in the air for several seconds as their eyes met. The trainer saw the boy brush away a tear as he searched Jerry's face. Jerry felt so sorry for this young man. He looked him straight in the eye and replied truthfully.

"Robbie, you're a class act. You're going to the British amateurs, and you won't look out of place at all."

"Yeah. But I'm not good enough to be a pro, am I?"

Jerry sighed and put his hand on Robbie's shoulder, squat-ting down so their eyes were level. "Not the kind of pro I think you want to be, Robbie. No. But let me tell you this. If a girl walked in here and asked me who here would make the best husband . . . or if a boss walked in here and asked me who would be the best, most honest worker, you would be my first recommendation. Believe me. Being a good person, being kind and loving and respecting your wife, being a good dad, a good friend, a good neighbor—that's what's important in life. You might not get the glory, but being a good man is a million times more important than being a world champion. I can promise you that."

Robbie looked back at Jerry, this time making no attempt to brush away the tears from his eyes. Eventually he looked down and grabbed his shoes, pulling them on without untying the laces. "I've gotta go."

"Training tomorrow. Same time?"

Robbie shrugged his shoulders and walked away.

Jerry stood in the empty room and sighed again. The conversation had been both inevitable and necessary, but that didn't make it any easier. His mind wandered back to the moment almost a decade earlier when, for a very different reason, he had been told his prospects as a professional boxer were at an end. Even all these years later, he could still remember the pain. Jerry looked up at the ceiling, still shrouded in a cloud of steam from the shower. Shutting his eyes, he began to pray for Robbie.

27

"What do you think, Robbie?"

"About what?"

"About how we're going to do."

"I think we're gonna win easy."

Jerry smiled at the young man. His certainty was unflinching, typical of someone untouched by the highs and lows of years in the boxing game. Normally Jerry would have stopped to warn such a young trainee of complacency and the vagaries of sport. But in this case he shared the young man's confidence. "Yeah," he said. "That's what I think too."

Jerry and Robbie stood together in the corridor, waiting to be called. They were just minutes away from the final middleweight match in the British Amateur Championships.

/ / /

It had been an amazing few months since their emotional confrontation. From the moment Robbie left the gym that day, Jerry had been praying. Indeed, Robbie had been Jerry's first thought the next morning. It was ten hours until the young man was scheduled to return to the gym, and the trainer was worried he wouldn't come.

But Robbie was already waiting outside when Jerry arrived that morning at seven. He looked tired but greeted Jerry brightly.

"What's on your mind, Robbie?" Jerry asked as he opened his office door and ushered the boy in.

Robbie took a deep breath and began. "Boss, I've been thinking. I'm bored with boxing. I don't wanna box anymore."

Jerry looked at the boy with genuine concern. "Robbie, boxing's been your life. I know yesterday was a setback, but you shouldn't make rash decisions based on one defeat in sparring."

Robbie quickly backtracked. "No, boss. I'm not bored with boxing generally. Just *me* boxing! I wondered . . ." He stammered nervously. "I wondered if you might allow me to help you train Sam instead."

Jerry paused as he considered the idea. It immediately appealed as a way of staying involved with Robbie, about whom he cared so much.

Robbie's mouth kicked into overdrive. "Boss, you wouldn't need to pay me. I'll get a part-time job so I've got enough money to support myself, or a night shift at a factory so I can be here the rest of the time. I'll be so dedicated you won't believe it. I'll—"

"Whoa!" Jerry interrupted, holding his hands up. "Slow down!"

"Sorry, boss. I've . . . I've just been thinking about it all night." Robbie stopped and held his breath as if his life depended on Jerry's answer.

"Robbie," Jerry began, "I would love you to help me train Sam. Maybe I could even persuade Bert to give you some work doing a few odd jobs here so you can stay close to the gym. Clean up and stuff. What do you think?"

Robbie didn't reply with words. Instead he sprang to his feet and whooped loudly, jumping up and down on the spot and punching the air, to the bemusement of two regulars who were just arriving at the gym.

"Thank you so much! I am gonna clean this place like you'll never believe. I'm gonna fix everything up. I'm—"

"Hold on a minute!" Jerry said, smiling. "Let me speak to Bert first. You can definitely help me with Sam, though. His next session is here after school on Friday. So if you come here Thursday night at six, we'll sit down and plan out a strategy. Sound good?"

"Good?" Robbie replied, almost exploding with excitement. "That sounds amazing! I'll be here at *five* on Thursday."

"Six will be fine. See you then."

"Six o'clock," Robbie repeated, looking around the room with wide eyes. "What should I do now?"

"Go home. Get some sleep. I'll see you Thursday."

Robbie nodded, pumped Jerry's hand up and down, and bounded away.

"Oh," Jerry called after Robbie. "What about the amateur championships? They're in three months. You don't want to miss that opportunity."

Robbie turned slowly and looked back at Jerry.

"Oh yeah," he said solemnly. "I've thought about that." Robbie paused and took a deep breath. "I think Sam should take my place."

Jerry looked at the young man, stunned by his sacrifice. Robbie, misreading the trainer, suddenly appeared alarmed. "Sorry, boss. Only if you think that's a good idea."

Jerry smiled reassuringly as he realized how well it could work. "I think that might be perfect."

/ / /

As Jerry stood beside Robbie now, he marveled again at how everything had fallen into place. Here they were at the national championships with Sam holding a 7–0 record. All Sam's wins except one had been by knockout in the first round. Sam had breezed through the four rounds of the southern region qualifying competition in Bognor Regis six weeks earlier. The three bouts here had lasted only seconds too.

Even in the semifinal, facing an opponent who was an experienced old campaigner, Sam had completely overwhelmed his adversary, putting him away in under a minute. That performance had raised eyebrows from the boxing press present, who otherwise had been underwhelmed by the talent on display.

The man who now stood between Sam and instant success had nearly qualified to represent Great Britain at the upcoming Olympics. Tommy Boyd had missed his chance when he lost to a hairy-backed Ukrainian in the final of the Olympic-qualifying competition in Germany. While commentators agreed that the Glaswegian would have been unlikely to medal even if he had qualified, he was still an excellent fighter. Now, with this unknown sixteen-year-old called Pennington blitzing his way through the competition, the middleweight final had become the most eagerly awaited matchup of the last day at the British Amateur Championships.

Jerry looked up as an overweight official approached from the direction of the hall. "Are you with Pennington?"

"Uh-huh. He's in here," Jerry said, nodding over his shoulder at the changing room door behind him.

"You're on in two minutes."

"Here we go." Jerry took a deep breath and rapped his knuckles on the door before quietly letting himself in. Ever since his second amateur fight, Sam had asked to be on his own for the last ten minutes before a bout. By the end of it Jerry had never seen a boxer so menacingly pumped up.

Jerry walked up to Sam and looked into his fighter's eyes. He knew right away this final would be no different from the fights that had gone before.

"Are you ready?" Jerry asked, already knowing the answer.

Sam nodded and pushed to his feet.

"Okay," Jerry said, clapping his hands. "Let me pray." Sam and Robbie looked at the ground as Jerry prayed as usual, laying his hand on Sam's shoulder. When he had finished, he turned and looked at his young assistant. "Robbie. Show us the way."

///

Seconds later they were in the corridor beside Sam's opponent and his entourage. Neither boxer acknowledged the other as they stood at the closed door of the arena, waiting for their match to be called. The doors opened and the steward beckoned. Both teams obediently moved forward into the hall.

There were only a few hundred spectators, but they were making quite a din as the fighters entered the arena. The announcer started up the moment they reached the ring.

To an impartial observer just coming into the hall, comparing the records of the two men would have indicated a mismatch in prospect. On one side, a twenty-eight-year-old Glaswegian—twice British amateur champion and a Commonwealth Games bronze medalist—with eighty-six amateur bouts, including seventy-one wins with thirty-four stoppages, to his credit. Against him, a sixteen-year-old lad with just seven fights to his name and fewer than nine rounds of competitive boxing under his belt.

But those who had watched the semifinal suspected it would not be a foregone conclusion. All eyes were fixed on the ring as the two men glared at each other. The referee laid out the rules and standards he expected. Then he ordered the two boxers to touch gloves, and they backed away to their corners.

"Same as last time," Jerry said calmly, popping Sam's gum

shield into his mouth. "He'll probably try and rush you, so the first round's going to be rough. But fight for the middle of the ring, keep your hands up, and wait for your opportunity. Okay?"

Sam nodded. The moment the bell rang, he spun around and made for his opponent.

For the first time Sam experienced a boxer coming at him from the start—the Scotsman was determined to put the youngster in his place. There was an immediate flurry of punches, and the boxers clinched in a tangle of arms. A brief wrestling match ensued, which the referee swiftly broke up. Again the boxers launched into each other, throwing fearsome punches. Jerry watched confidently. Boyd was only doing what any experienced boxer would try against such a young opponent. By roughing him up, he no doubt hoped to throw his opponent off his technique.

But Jerry was delighted with what he was seeing. Sam was not yielding the middle of the ring, but he wasn't getting ragged in defending it either.

"Yes!" Jerry breathed to himself as Sam threw a beautiful jab that landed flush on Boyd's nose.

There followed a period of jabbing at a distance as Boyd realized he wasn't going to win by shoving Sam over. With the experience of a veteran, he quickly adapted his style to a more patient approach, waiting for the opening he reasoned would surely come eventually. Jerry was confident, though, and after another thirty seconds Sam landed a sharp jab and then a crushing right cross that sent the Scotsman shuddering backward. Sam waited for his opponent to reengage before forcing him backward again with a powerful body shot. For the first time Jerry could see fear in the Scotsman's eyes as he lowered his guard a touch to protect his sore midriff.

Sam backed away slightly, encouraging Boyd to step forward and throw a jab. Boyd obliged, and Jerry saw Sam throw out another body shot that landed on exactly the same rib. While most in the hall missed the punch and applauded Boyd's first scoring blow of the bout, Jerry blinked with amazement. Sam's instinct had been to target that rib again, even at the calculated expense of taking a hit himself. It was perfect. As they tangled together again, Jerry saw Sam throw another short punch to the same rib area. The Scotsman flinched in pain and grabbed Sam to prevent another punch. When the referee separated the fighters, Jerry could see immediately that Tommy Boyd had lowered his guard even more.

Sam stepped forward and feigned another body punch, causing Boyd to drop his elbow farther. In one movement Sam changed the trajectory of his fist, lifting his glove upward and forward. The punch caught Boyd's head with a heavy thud, sending him reeling backward. Instantly Sam was on him, throwing a flurry of punches that ended only when the referee forced himself between the two men. The referee pushed Sam backward and then turned toward Boyd, who was breathing heavily. The Scotsman was given a standing count before assuring the referee, a little unconvincingly to Jerry's mind, that he wanted to continue.

The moment the ref opened his arms to usher the boxers together, Sam was on his opponent again, unleashing an unanswered volley of punches. As Jerry watched with morbid fascination, he noticed that, although Sam was throwing several punches a second, none were wild. Nearly every shot was thrown with power and balance, landing heavily on his opponent, who was now cowering in a corner. In that moment Jerry knew—Sam was the real deal.

A crescendo of sound filled the hall as four more savage blows found their mark. The referee fought his way between the two men and waved his hands above the Scotsman's head. The fight was over.

/ / /

Sam dropped his fists to his sides and scowled at the referee, frustrated that another contest was over so quickly. He turned back with disappointment to his corner and was engulfed by Robbie, screaming with joy.

"We won it! We won it!" the assistant trainer cried, hoisting Sam unsteadily skyward. Sam gripped Robbie's shoulders to secure his balance and tried to grin down at his friend. But he just couldn't share in Robbie's joy. Instead he felt a strange emptiness. Robbie put him down as Jerry approached.

"Well done," Jerry said, reaching up to remove Sam's gum shield. "That was very impressive."

"Thanks."

"Feel good?" Jerry said, smiling.

Sam nodded, hoping to hide the confusion that was swirling around inside him. He was rescued by the referee, who took Sam by the wrist and pulled him toward Tommy Boyd. Without looking at one another, the boxers embraced as convention required. The referee led them both to the center of the ring. Lining up in front of the three judges who sat at a trestle table five yards from the ring, the referee thrust Sam's hand into the air.

Samuel Pennington, after just eight fights, was the British Amateur Boxing Association middleweight champion.

28

Jerry breathed a quiet sigh of relief as he turned off the M25 to join the A12 dual carriageway. While there had still been a bit of late-night traffic on the London orbital motorway, the familiar road near his home was virtually deserted. Half an hour more and he would be in bed. He couldn't wait. The emotion of the day, followed by the four-hour drive back from Birmingham, had completely worn him out.

Jerry looked in the rearview mirror as he joined the new road and was not surprised to see an empty road behind them. His eyes lingered for a moment on the two boys sitting in the backseat. On the left Robbie was fast asleep with his mouth wide open and his head resting against the glass. Jerry grinned. Robbie had talked incessantly all the way down the M1 until Mario, sitting next to Jerry in the front, had finally told him to quiet down with a few choice Italian expletives. After that, Mario and Robbie had both fallen asleep.

Jerry shifted his head slightly to try to see Sam sitting behind him. The boy had finally succumbed to sleep too, and Jerry watched for a moment as light and darkness pulsed across the young man's face as they passed the halogen street-lights. For the first time Jerry saw Sam's face truly relaxed, a stark contrast to his normal demeanor.

After Sam had been presented with a medal and a garish trophy, a small semicircle of journalists surrounded Jerry and Sam as they climbed down from the ring. Four days earlier Samuel Pennington had walked into the championships as a complete unknown. When he left the hall that evening, he was the talk of the competition.

Jerry had no doubt this was just the start. Even though it was amateur level, the manner in which Sam had dismantled his opponents ensured he would never again be anonymous in the tight British boxing fraternity. Indeed, nearly all the postfight questions had centered upon Sam's future plans and specifically whether he would remain an amateur or turn professional. Jerry had batted away the questions while Sam remained silent beside him. It was a conversation they would have to have soon.

But Jerry had already made up his mind. Had there been an Olympic Games in the next year or two, he might have been tempted to hold off. But it would be four years before Sam could even qualify for the next showcase amateur event. On the evidence of this tournament and the hours they had spent in the gym, Jerry expected Sam would be a professional world champion by then. In his mind, there was no dilemma. Sam would turn pro straightaway, before some do-gooder tried to enroll him in college or pull him in some other direction.

Jerry glanced in the mirror again as he slowed down for some traffic lights. Sam shifted slightly in response to the vehicle's slowing but remained asleep. The same nagging doubt rose in Jerry's mind once more. It had taken him the entire journey to work it out. Sam had taken no enjoyment in actually winning.

There had been no celebrations or waving to the audience. Later Jerry had seen Sam casually throw his medal into the bottom of his kit bag, and they had almost left his trophy behind before Robbie remembered and ran off to find it.

Jerry frowned. How could a sixteen-year-old who had just become the youngest-ever British champion leave his first trophy behind? Did Sam really not enjoy winning? If not, surely he would tire of boxing. And Jerry's dream of training a world champion would be at an end. Jerry grimaced at the irony. He had a gym full of boxers who dreamed of glory but lacked the talent to match it. Now he had a boxer who really had the talent to be the best in the world and yet seemed indifferent to the glory.

Stop worrying, Jerry vowed as he pressed on the accelerator. There was no evidence Sam was losing motivation. And today he had shown his true potential. The kid was on his way. Jerry was going to train a world champion. He, Jerry Ambrose, was going to be a world-champion trainer.

Jerry enjoyed how good that sounded. But a nagging word

entered his head. *Pride.* Jerry automatically began to pray an apology for getting carried away. But as he did so, another thought came to mind. Maybe this was God's will. Why not? Maybe being the trainer of a world champion would give him a platform to tell people about God. In fact, maybe this was God's reward for Jerry after all the years of hard work and the unfair way he had missed out on riches in his own career.

"I deserve it," Jerry whispered.

His mind flitted to another of the benefits of training a world champion. The trainer's cut. Typically it was 20 percent. If Sam was as good as Jerry thought, and if he could hold on to him, 20 percent could amount to hundreds of thousands of pounds—perhaps even millions if the boy had a long career.

Jerry focused his mind on the week ahead and the now-pressing priority. The next day he and Bert would start working on a professional contract for Sam. Of course this would be to protect Sam first and foremost, but it would also protect the gym as well as Jerry and his family. After all, he was investing a lot in Sam's future. Twenty percent was the least he deserved.

Half an hour later Jerry climbed into bed next to his sleeping wife and fell into a deep, satisfied sleep.

29

"Sorry I'm late," Bob said as he entered the school foyer.

Norman put his newspaper down on the reception desk and stood to shake his friend's hand. "No problem. Trouble?"

"One of my clients," Bob said grimly. "Domestic bust-up. Got a call first thing, and I had to call an ambulance and then take the girl's kids to her sister's house in Peckham. Normal kind of thing."

Norman grimaced. "I don't know how you do it."

"Nah. Wouldn't swap with you," Bob countered. "At least I don't have fifty miserable teachers backbiting and blaming me for everything."

"Okay, it's a draw!" Norman said, laughing. "We've both got equally lousy jobs."

"So how can I help you?" Bob said, turning to business.

"Sounds serious if you couldn't tell me on the phone. Who is it this time? And aren't you supposed to be on summer holiday?"

"Actually," Norman said with a grin, "it's good news."

Bob staggered theatrically, grabbing the corner of the reception desk as if to steady himself. "Wow, Norman. I don't think I've ever been called out for good news before."

"I'm in today because the kids were collecting their exam results. Fairly normal bunch of substandard grades—" Norman pushed a small square envelope across the desk—"except one set. Take a look."

Bob pulled on glasses that were hanging from a string around his neck and peered at the name on the envelope. "Samuel Pennington!" Bob broke into a grin and looked up at his friend. He turned the envelope over and then frowned. "Are you sure I should open this?"

"Don't worry. I'll stick it back in a new envelope."

Bob hesitated before curiosity took over.

"Whoa!" he said as he scanned down the letters, then looked up at his friend. "Seven As and three Bs. That's pretty good, isn't it?"

"Best results we've ever had."

"Well!" Bob said, scratching his chin. "He is a dark horse!"

The headmaster took the results slip back from his friend and placed it carefully in a fresh envelope. "Best results at this school ever, and he didn't even turn up to collect them."

"What about us delivering them?" Bob suggested. "I'm finished for the day. And we can go for a drink afterward. What do you say?"

"Do you know where he lives?" Norman asked.

"Nelson Mandela complex. I've been to his flat lots of times."

"Great. You can drive."

Bob grinned. "I guess I walked into that one."

///

Five minutes later they turned off the main road and came to a halt behind a long line of cars waiting at a red light. Britain may have been in a recession, but there were still thousands of automobiles crawling out of London at the end of another workday.

Bob sighed and looked over at his friend, who was picking at a bit of dirt on the dashboard with his fingernail as they waited for the light to change.

Norman looked up. "You know, I can't really claim any credit for his results. He's just naturally clever."

"That's rubbish," Bob stated forcefully. "You might not have taught him yourself, but you saved him from oblivion by not expelling him when you had every justification."

"Well, I guess. I hadn't thought about it like that. By the way, how's his mum doing?" Norman asked.

"No different. At least not last time I saw her, anyway."

The light finally turned green, and after a few hundred yards Bob steered the car into the Mandela housing complex. He looked out his window at the concrete blocks of flats, a number of which were boarded up with plywood that had obscenities and racist taunts spray-painted across them. He looked back at the road and had to stop to let an old man shuffle across in front of them. Off to the side he glimpsed a mangy-looking cat eating vomit off the pavement.

"Argh," Norman said with disgust. "I've heard about this place. But I've never been here before."

"Lucky you," Bob replied.

They pulled up to Sam's flat, and Bob parked behind the forlorn-looking Land Rover that he had watched over the years gently rusting into the road.

The two men climbed out of the car and were moving toward the concrete stairwell when Bob's attention was caught by a familiar figure. Sam rounded the corner a hundred yards up the path and sprinted toward them. Bob grabbed Norman's arm and nodded in Sam's direction. They both stepped back and waited as the boy rushed down the pavement with legs and arms pumping.

/ / /

Sam glanced at his watch as he came in sight of his flat and nodded with satisfaction. He was going to beat his time again. He put his head down and broke into a sprint finish. Sam crashed across the line and came to a halt, acknowledging for the first time the pain burning in his lungs. He bent down with his hands on his knees, panting. Then, resisting the urge to collapse to the ground, he straightened up and lifted his wristwatch to his face. As he did, he recognized the two men waiting for him and frowned.

"Hi, Sam. How are you doing?" Bob asked, stepping forward and offering his hand. Sam scowled slightly but took the hand and shook it firmly.

Norman stepped forward too. "Hi, Sam," he echoed warmly. "Missed you at school today."

"I've finished there. Haven't I?"

Norman reached into his pocket and removed the envelope, which he then held out to Sam. "Exam results."

For the first time in two months, Sam thought about school. He had studied hard and sat his exams as part of his obligation to Jerry. He had forgotten they would end in results. Sam reached out and took the envelope, aware the two men watching him were smiling.

"Well! Are you going to open it?" Bob asked impatiently.

Sam blushed and turned away as he opened the envelope and scanned the thin paper slip inside. He looked back at the two men, who were now grinning broadly.

"Well done, Sam. They're the best results we've ever had. In fact, best at any of the schools I've taught at."

Sam frowned again as Bob joined in. "Yeah. Well done, Sam. Fantastic."

The young man nodded.

"Have you thought what you're going to do?" Norman asked. "You should definitely be going on to study for university. Any of the next-stage schools around here would snap you up with those grades."

Sam shook his head firmly. "No. I'm going to be a boxer. I've just turned pro." A flicker of disappointment crossed Norman's face, but Bob quickly interjected.

"Good on you, Sam. I look forward to seeing you on TV!"

Sam smiled shyly before reaching up with his arm and wiping his upper sleeve across his forehead, leaving a wet sweat patch on his T-shirt. There was an awkward silence. Sam wiped his face again. "I need to have a shower."

Bob and Norman nodded.

"Good to see you, Sam," the headmaster said, holding his hand out again. "And well done. You can always do A-levels later. If you need any advice, just come and see me. Okay?"

Sam nodded and they shook hands.

"Yeah. Well done, Sam," Bob said. "You deserve it."

/ / /

As Bob shook Sam's hand, he realized it might be for the last time. The boy was now off his books.

Sam stood for a moment and faced the men. "Thanks," he said, nodding to each of them. He then turned away and climbed the steps to his flat.

Bob and Norman looked at one another and smiled. As thank-yous went, it hadn't been much, but it was something. In their worlds they took every vote of thanks they could. They turned and walked back to the car.

"That was nice," Bob said as he climbed behind the wheel. As he leaned across to pop the passenger-door lock so Norman could get in too, he saw a man sitting in a parked car twenty yards away, watching them. The man wore a look of pure hatred.

Bob started the engine and performed a three-point turn in front of the parked car, where the man continued to glare at him. He gratefully pulled away, disturbed by the momentary encounter. As he drove off, he glanced in his rearview mirror to check if the car was following. It didn't move, and Bob relaxed again. "I'm glad we did that."

"Agreed," Norman replied. "Real shame he's not interested in staying at school, though."

Bob shook his head. "He'll be fine. I've got a good feeling about him."

"Yeah," Norman agreed eventually. "So have I."

"King's Arms at Warley?"

"You're buying."

"I'm driving!"

"Okay. King's Arms it is."

30

Jerry watched the car turn out of the road and once again found himself sitting alone in the street. "What was that?" he said angrily as his mind tried to make sense of what he had just witnessed.

Half an hour earlier, he had been on his way home when he felt a strange prompting that led him to be seated here outside Sam's flat. It had happened before—an odd sense that he needed to stop and pray for someone or go visit an old acquaintance. Nothing dramatic had ever come of it, but he had always felt better afterward, confident he had been obedient to God's leading. And once an old friend he had visited unexpectedly had called later to thank him and said how Jerry's visit had lifted him from a very low place.

But Sam wasn't an old friend. He was a client. Besides, Jerry had seen the boy only half an hour earlier at the gym for an epic training session. Jerry was still buzzing from the combination of ferocity, skill, and stamina that his young boxer had delivered. So why had Jerry felt led here? And what on earth had he just seen?

Five minutes earlier he had been debating whether to knock on Sam's door or give up his strange feeling as a mistake and drive away. But the arrival of the two middle-aged men had piqued his curiosity. Then Sam had arrived, sprinting at full tilt, his gym bag strapped to his back. Only then had it dawned on Jerry with both awe and concern that his fighter had run home from the gym rather than catch a bus as Jerry vaguely assumed he did each day. However, Jerry's pride had turned to fear as he watched the exchange. One of the men handed Sam a piece of paper, which he studied carefully. Words were exchanged, and Jerry watched in disbelief as Sam nodded at the two men and then shook hands. It could have been only one thing. A boxing contract.

Jerry shouted a curse and punched the middle of his steering wheel. He had just been mugged in broad daylight. Rage welled up inside him against the two men who had just driven away. Jerry hadn't recognized them, but all sorts of new people were entering boxing these days. Nothing surprised him anymore. Up to now, he had always been pretty philosophical when such things had happened to him. Even the Frank McCullough episode hadn't upset him much. But Sam's leaving him was a totally different matter.

"How could he betray me like this? After all the effort I've put in for him." Jerry swore again loudly. He had been denied the chance to be world champion himself. And now someone was trying to steal his opportunity to train a world champion as well.

///

Inside the flat, Sam stood at the kitchen sink, repeatedly filling a glass from the tap and downing the contents. When he had drunk enough, he set the glass down and reached into his pocket again. As he held the envelope between his fingers, he recalled a long-forgotten memory.

It was a teacher at Sam's primary school who had suggested the Common Entrance exam in the hope of attracting a scholarship to a private school. Sam had done well in the exam, and he and his parents had been invited to visit a well-regarded school an hour away.

From the moment he had seen the amazing sports fields on his school tour and heard an hour every day was reserved for outdoor activities, Sam had been determined this was the place for him. He had sailed through the headmaster's interview with charm and confidence while his parents hovered uncomfortably outside, intimidated by the grand buildings and other parents' cars that contrasted with their shabby old Land Rover.

A week later Sam had returned home from school to find his parents sitting in the kitchen. A white envelope with the crest of the private school embossed upon it lay on the table. Sam reached forward with trembling hands.

"Well done, Sam!" his father said as Sam studied the contents. "It means you start in September." Sam had buried himself in his father's arms before breaking free and hugging his mother, too.

"We're so proud of you, sweetheart," she had said through tears.

Sam sighed. So much had changed in the five years since then. But as he held the envelope in front of him, he felt an overwhelming urge to be that little boy again and proudly show his parents his achievement. He looked across the room at his mother's bedroom door.

"Be awake," he said as he walked over and grasped the door handle. The door swung open, casting some light into the darkened room. A pungent smell of sweat and alcohol immediately filled his nostrils. Sam screwed up his face as he saw his mother's form under the covers. For once she wasn't snoring, and he allowed himself to hope she was awake.

Walking to the window, Sam drew back the curtains, allowing more light into the room. He turned and this time spotted a writing pad that he had stepped over in the gloom. He picked it up.

My dear Sam,

I can't cope anymore. I'm so sorry. Please forgive me one day.

Love, Mummy xx

Sam looked up, confused. Why would his mother write him a note like that? He moved around the bed to see his mother's face, but she had her eyes closed. Only then did Sam see the brown bottle of tablets on the bedside table with the cap off. Sam reached out and picked it up. It was empty.

31

"Are you mocking me?" Jerry railed at God. "Why did you want me here? To show me I'm losing my best boxer?"

He fell silent. He knew in his heart that he couldn't blame God, but his emotions demanded he lash out at someone. He hadn't had the courage to confront the two men and Sam earlier. God was an easier target.

Jerry took a deep breath and finally got his mind and heart aligned. He was ashamed. In the last couple of weeks he had felt closer to God than he had in a long time. His faith had almost returned to its previous assurance following the severe shaking it had suffered during his depression and the immediate aftermath of Earl's death. He still couldn't see the sense in his friend's death, but he had to acknowledge that Earl would have been pleased with what had followed. Social services had broken protocol and allowed little Ella to stay with Jerry's family for three weeks while her mother, Kirsten, had been rehoused in Upminster. The mother had also been assigned plenty of support from a special medical unit for people who had suffered trauma. The two weeks in a rehabilitation center had seen her through the end of the cold-turkey process that Earl had started. In the meantime, Jerry's family had spoiled Ella rotten as she came to terms with what had happened.

Jerry had been hugely skeptical when social services informed them that Kirsten was ready to have Ella back. But they had prayed about it, and Gloria, at least, had peace that it was the right thing to do. And even Jerry had admitted, when they drove with Ella and the social worker to Kirsten's new flat across town, that Ella's mother seemed much improved from their first encounter. Indeed, at the suggestion of the social worker, Jerry, Gloria, and Kirsten had agreed the Ambroses should stay involved for a while. Since then, every Saturday morning Jerry's family had picked Ella up and taken her swimming while Kirsten had some time to herself. While the first week had been tense, the relationship between the adults had improved week after week to a point of warmth, if not yet friendship.

But what encouraged Jerry most was the sweet and attentive way mother and daughter now interacted. It was as if, free from the influence of heroin, the girl's mother was suddenly on a mission to give her daughter the loving home she had never had. And as much as Ella enjoyed the swimming, she never seemed sad to be returned home to a hug from her mum. It warmed Jerry's heart and rebuilt some of the foundations of his faith.

In fact, the only area of his life where he was struggling faith-wise, although he hated to admit it, was with Sam. He found himself continually daydreaming about Sam's future career and the glory and riches it might bring. And now, as Jerry sat in the car, he tried to give it back to God.

"I'm sorry, Lord," he said, shutting his eyes. "I'm sorry. What do you want me to do now?" He tried to clear his mind in the hope of hearing God and sat silently for a while. Hearing no answer, he finally opened his eyes, subconsciously glancing through the windscreen to check that no one had seen him praying. The sight and the sound struck Jerry simultaneously.

"Help me!" Jerry heard as he saw Sam stagger out of the stairwell, carrying a woman in his arms.

Jerry jumped out of the car and sprinted as Sam lost his grip on the woman and she slithered to the strip of grass in front of his flat. "What happened?" Jerry demanded as he grabbed the woman's arm and pressed his finger into her wrist.

Sam didn't reply.

"What's wrong with her?" Jerry shouted this time, shaking the boy from his trance.

"Pills," Sam blurted. "Lots. Mum, wake up!"

Jerry lifted the woman's eyelids. The eyeballs had rolled back into their sockets.

"Mrs. Pennington, can you hear me?" Jerry placed his ear near the woman's mouth and was relieved to hear a faint sound. She was alive. But the memory of Earl's weakening final breaths immediately came to mind.

"We need an ambulance right now. Have you got a phone in the flat, Sam?"

Sam slowly shook his head, eyes still fixed on his mother's face. The boy was behaving in the faraway manner of a punch-drunk boxer. They needed help. Jerry looked around the empty street with desperation.

"Where is everyone?" he said angrily, seeing a curtain flutter in a ground-floor flat nearby as the resident inside backed away from the window.

"Sam, is there a pay phone around here?"

Sam didn't answer, and Jerry grabbed the boy's shoulder and shook him roughly. "Sam," he repeated. "Is there a pay phone near here?"

Sam looked at Jerry with wide eyes, eventually nodding. He pointed over his shoulder down the street.

"Go now. Phone 999. Tell them we need an ambulance straightaway. Give them your address."

With relief, Jerry saw consciousness return to Sam's eyes.

"Jerry?" he said, confused.

Jerry nodded. "Yes, Sam, it's me. Now go. Run!"

Sam jumped up and sprinted down the street. Jerry watched him run away before Sam suddenly stopped and turned.

"I haven't got any coins."

"You don't need any for 999. Just dial it!"

Sam nodded and sprinted away.

"Please, Lord," Jerry said, turning back to the unconscious woman lying on the grass in front of him. "Please, God. Not again. Save her. Heal her."

As Jerry prayed, he continued trying to rouse the woman from her comatose state, beginning to panic now. Sam hadn't returned, and Jerry imagined the boy running desperately from one vandalized phone booth to another. Adrenaline coursed through his body.

Abruptly Jerry felt a sense of calm come over him. The woman wasn't going to die today, he felt. Good was going to come from this.

Jerry heard the siren. "Thank you!" he said aloud as he saw Sam turn the corner at full sprint, beckoning over his shoulder at an ambulance trying hard to keep up. Both boy and vehicle accelerated up the final stretch of road toward where Jerry knelt over the unconscious woman.

Within a minute two paramedics had lifted Mrs. Pennington onto a stretcher, and they were all speeding toward the hospital.

32

"I'm not leaving her," Sam insisted, shaking his head.

"Okay," the nurse said, glancing around the emergency room. "Let's just move over here to give the doctors some space."

Sam relented, and Jerry followed him and the nurse to a quieter corner of the room. Sam confirmed his mother's name and date of birth, all the time keeping his eyes fixed on the activity around her bed.

"And has your mother got a husband or partner?" the nurse asked gently. Jerry saw the boy shake his head.

"Dead."

"Are there any other relatives we should call?"

"No. No one."

Jerry sighed. He had always assumed from Sam's manner that his father was no longer on the scene, but Jerry had no idea the man was dead.

"Has she ever taken an overdose before?" the nurse continued.

Sam shook his head again.

"Do you know what the pills were?"

"No. They were in a brown bottle."

"Does she drink alcohol?"

"Half a bottle of gin a day. Sometimes more."

"And was her skin yellow before?" the nurse probed.

"Yeah. For a while."

"Has she got any other medical conditions?"

"Not that I know of."

The nurse dropped her clipboard and squeezed Sam's arm. "Thank you. We're going to do our very best for your mum."

Sam opened his mouth to reply but stopped. His eyes welled up with tears, and he looked away toward his mother.

The nurse gave his arm another squeeze and exchanged a look with Jerry before turning back to the boy. "Sam, I need to go and give this information to the doctor. But if you need anything—somewhere quiet to wait, a cup of tea, anything—just let one of the nurses know. Okay?"

Sam nodded without removing his eyes from his mother's bed. But the moment the nurse walked away, his shoulders began shaking, and he broke down. Jerry stepped forward and took the boy in his arms.

/ / /

"I'm afraid your mother is very ill," the doctor said quietly.

They had been standing for an hour in the corridor, watching the emergency room through an internal window.

The frenetic activity around Janet's bed had eventually died down, and a doctor had finally come across to them.

"We have stabilized her. Her heart stopped a couple of times, but we were able to get it going again. I'm afraid it was too late to stop the pills' getting into her bloodstream. We're trying to clean her blood and protect her liver, but it's clear from the color of her skin that her liver's been failing already. It may be that the overdose has put it beyond repair. Time will tell. We can only wait and see over the next twenty-four hours. I'm sorry."

Jerry watched Sam as the doctor relayed this grim news. The boy's face gave nothing away. The doctor expressed his sympathies again and excused himself.

Sam pushed through the door and walked to his mother's bedside. Jerry followed, unsure of what to do. Sam took hold of his mother's hand, careful not to disturb the tubes that were protruding from her veins.

Jerry, standing behind, prayed again.

33

Jerry pulled his car to a halt outside Sam's flat. Climbing out, he glanced at the patch of grass where he had cradled Sam's mother the day before. The afternoon sun had just dipped beneath the roof opposite, plunging the square of grass into a gloomy shade. Jerry took a deep, weary breath. The last twenty-four hours had been exhausting.

He had sat up all night with Sam as the boy kept a vigil by his mother's side. Despite the depressing prognosis, Janet Pennington had made it through the night, and by that morning the doctors were starting to sound cautiously optimistic. Although her liver function was massively impaired, it had not stopped working altogether. Thus, for the time being at least, she might survive. The next test, they said, was whether she would recover consciousness, but there was no way of telling how long that could take. Jerry had eventually gone home to bed, taking Sam's key and promising to pick him up a change of clothes.

Jerry climbed the stairs, reaching into his pocket for the key. But it wasn't needed. The door was ajar. Jerry sighed as he concluded Sam must have left it open when he carried his mum out of the flat. But as he gently pushed the door, it was immediately clear that Jerry wasn't the only one who had discovered it unlocked.

The flat was trashed. Much had been stolen and the rest smashed to bits. A dust-free square of carpet in the corner showed where the television had once stood, and bare surfaces betrayed the theft of more belongings. Even the kitchen cupboards were open and the crockery shattered on the floor. Filthy pictures had been spray-painted on the walls, and the settee had been slashed with a knife, the foam stuffing protruding through the cut fabric.

Jerry walked into the bedrooms. The mess there was just as bad. The wardrobes were empty, and clothes were strewn across the floor. In the smaller bedroom, Sam's belongings had been ground underfoot, and ripped pages from Jerry's boxing magazines covered the floor.

"What is this, God?" Jerry shouted with his eyes lifted toward the ceiling. "Couldn't you look after their flat for just one night? I'm trying to show him your love, and you're letting him be screwed over left, right, and center."

Jerry fell silent and tried to gather his thoughts. He left the flat and drove around the housing complex until he found the pay phone. A female operator answered and asked what service was required.

"Police," Jerry said wearily.

34

"She hasn't changed," Sam said quietly. "I thought she opened her eyes at one point, but I'm not sure."

Jerry had found Sam still at his mother's bedside and had finally persuaded him to join him for a meal in the hospital cafeteria. He had already resolved not to tell Sam about the burgled flat. There was nothing to be gained from it now.

"I've been asleep," the boy said guiltily, looking down at the plate of food in front of him.

"You need sleep. Don't feel bad about that. Now eat."

Jerry watched the boy devour the meal before him, waiting until he had finished before asking another question. "So, what did the doctor say?"

Sam swigged from a milk carton and took a deep breath before speaking. "He said her liver's only just working. They've got her rigged up to this thing underneath her bed." He didn't elaborate further, and Jerry didn't push it.

Sam took another swig of milk and looked back up at Jerry. "Thanks for your help yesterday," he said, wiping his mouth on his sleeve.

Jerry shook his head. "You don't need to thank me. I'm just so sorry you're going through this."

"How come you were outside my flat?"

Sam's tone was curious rather than suspicious. Jerry coughed nervously. He had known the question would surely come at some stage. "I, um . . ." Jerry paused, aware Sam was studying him carefully. "I just had a feeling I should go home via your flat."

"What do you mean?"

Jerry took a deep breath. He used to welcome the opportunity to talk about his faith. But that was before. Before Walthamstow and Ray Butcher. Before his depression. Before Earl's death. Even discovering Sam's trashed flat had knocked Jerry's confidence in the faith that had defined him for so many years. Ever since the first of those incidents, he had declined nearly every opportunity to speak about God. But he didn't want to hide now.

"It's part of my faith in God, Sam. Occasionally I get a strong feeling that God is telling me to do something."

Sam frowned. "You think God talks to you?"

Jerry winced at how it sounded but didn't detect any mockery in Sam's tone. "Yeah. But not with a voice. I mean, not aloud. Normally through thoughts and feelings, or just through reading something in the Bible."

Jerry watched Sam frown, but again there was no ridicule in the boy's expression. Jerry reached out and took a sip of his tea as he watched the boy processing what he had heard. Many times Jerry had prayed that his relationship with Sam would move beyond the superficial boxing level. Now, in the midst of another tragedy, here they were, talking about faith.

"How do you know it's God?"

"I don't know for sure," Jerry replied honestly. "Over the years I've seen good stuff come when I've followed those feelings. I guess I'm pretty glad I was there to help yesterday. You could say it was a coincidence. Or luck. Fair enough. But . . ." Jerry shrugged. "I think it was God."

"How long were you sitting there?"

"About ten minutes, I guess," Jerry said, recalling the elapsed time before Sam had emerged from the flat carrying his mother. It was good they were talking about God, but here was his opportunity to ask Sam what exactly he was doing meeting with other boxing managers. The words slipped out quickly.

"Just before you met with those two guys. . . ." Jerry trailed off, leaving the words lingering as a slight question. He saw Sam recall the sequence of events in his head and suddenly look down and blush. *Yeah,* Jerry thought to himself. *I've caught you, you little git. Explain that.*

/ / /

Sam looked down at his empty plate, hoping the implied question would pass. Part of him wanted to share his exam results with Jerry, especially as it had been one of Jerry's three rules that had motivated Sam to study harder than he would have done otherwise. But the last thing he wanted now was congratulations. He didn't deserve any. Not when, by ignoring his mum over so many years, he had driven her to try and kill herself.

The thought that his behavior was the cause of his mother's suicide attempt had been plaguing him all day. And now those thoughts had become a tidal wave of condemnation. He was her only family. Yet he had ignored her. Been rude to her. Refused to stop and talk when she so desperately wanted to. He hadn't smiled at her for years. Hadn't thanked her for anything. *He* was the only one to blame.

Sam could hold back no longer. A sob grew deep in his stomach, and he couldn't stop it from forcing its way out. Jerry circled the table and squatted down in front of him. Sam didn't resist as Jerry hugged him.

"It's all right, Sam. It's going to be all right."

"I'm sorry," Sam said, wiping his tears away with embarrassment.

"Don't worry," Jerry said reassuringly. "We'll get it sorted out with Bert when your mum's better. She's all that's important now."

Sam blew his nose on a paper napkin. He felt completely exhausted. He didn't know what Jerry meant about sorting it out with Bert, but just now he felt too tired to ask. He shrugged Jerry's arms away, suddenly self-conscious of how sweaty he felt and smelled. He was also aware of how long they had been in the cafeteria.

"I need to see my mum," he said, standing up abruptly. "I've been away too long."

/ / /

Back on the ward, Jerry watched as Sam took his seat at his mother's bedside and reached for her hand. She lay motionless. Jerry debated whether to stay or leave. He decided to leave but then remembered the clothes he had bought for Sam on the way over. He leaned to the side and picked them up.

"Sam, I bought you some clothes. I need to go in a minute, but do you want me to stay here with your mum while you go and have a shower and get changed? I'll call you right away if anything changes."

Sam frowned but then stood and nodded. "Yeah, that would be good. Thanks."

Jerry watched the young man walk away and then turned back toward Sam's mother. She looked peaceful as she lay with her eyes shut and her face muscles relaxed. Although her features were softer than Sam's, Jerry could see a family likeness in the shape and position of her eyes and the line of the woman's jaw. Compassion welled up in Jerry, and he immediately knew what he should do.

He cast a quick glance over both shoulders, seeing with relief that the ward was quiet. Then he held his hands out over the woman, closed his eyes, and began to pray.

35

The thirst struck Janet Pennington first. Instinctively she tried to stimulate her salivary glands but couldn't. She felt such an overwhelming tiredness that it was beyond her strength even to run her tongue around her parched mouth. Confusion swirled around her mind before giving way to panic. What was wrong with her?

The fog in her mind began to clear, but the clarity only prompted more questions. Where was she? And why was it so dark? She tried to reach out but couldn't. The only sense seemingly available to her was her hearing. She stopped trying to move and concentrated all her efforts on listening in the darkness.

The sound just reached her ears—a strange whispering that she couldn't decipher. It stopped and then started again, and the noise began to torment her. Was she dead? And if so, where was this? Was this hell? Was this punishment for trying to kill herself?

Kill herself. The realization of what had gotten her here forced its way to the forefront of her mind. She had tried to kill herself. As she lay paralyzed, the memory of that last day flooded back.

/ / /

The gentle knock on the door came soon after Janet had emerged from bed. Sam had already gone off to wherever he went now that he was finished at school.

As soon as Janet heard it, she froze. *Dwayne.* Every Thursday afternoon for six months he had knocked on the door. The gentle knock now haunted her life. Ten times a day, the small sound of a chair moving across the floor upstairs or a car door being slammed outside would send Janet's heart into palpitations.

She glanced up at the clock. It was at least three hours before Dwayne normally called for the money. She looked at the door in panic. The gentle knocking sounded again. It was unmistakably him. She shuddered and walked toward the door, dropped to her knees, and lifted the letter box flap.

The familiar form filled the narrow slit. The face moved downward, and Dwayne's cold eyes appeared, glaring through the gap. "I need thirty pounds today. In fact, thirty pounds from now on. You got that?"

Janet closed her eyes and clenched her teeth. Her mind tried to focus on the arithmetic, but she knew it was im-

possible. She was now buying virtually no food except breakfast cereal, milk, bread, and sharp-tasting cheap-brand gin.

"I . . . I can't," she stammered. There was silence, and
Janet opened her eyes in hope Dwayne might understand
that thirty pounds was just too much.

Her answer was instant. A gob of saliva splattered Janet's
face. She recoiled away from the door, pawing at her eyes in
shock.

"It's not a choice. Thirty pounds by three o'clock or I'll
send my boys round for a bit of action." With that, a punch
sounded against the door, and she heard his footsteps fade
away.

/ / /

Janet had not planned suicide. But from that moment on,
she had been on autopilot. Benefit money from the post
office. The supermarket—for food and just the one bottle.
Note to Sam. Gin. Pills. Bed.

It was only when Janet could no longer feel her limbs that
the fear and realization of what she had done gripped her. She
tried to call out for help, but she couldn't form words. Only
a pitiful moan escaped her mouth—a sound so faint that
someone standing at her front door would struggle to hear
it. And the only person coming to her door that afternoon
would be Dwayne.

Janet shut her eyes as one clear thought pressed down
upon her. How could she have done this to her son? She
was filled with guilt as she thought about Sam and how he
would be the one to find her. Just like she had been the one

who found Robert after the accident. The recognition that she would be inflicting the same experience on Sam was her last conscious thought.

But now she was awake again. Janet's mind was clearer now. She wasn't dead! She must still be in her flat, she thought. If only she could open her eyes. . . .

Concentrating all her remaining energy, Janet forced her eyelids open. As she did so, she heard the same muffled whisper again. She was immediately aware of someone standing over her, and she fought to focus her eyes on the face above.

Slowly the blur came into view.

Fear gripped her as she saw the black skin of the man leaning over her. *Dwayne.* He was here. Somehow. To finish her off.

Janet wanted to scream, but she had not an ounce of energy left. Already she could feel her eyes shutting again, and the last thing she saw were the eyes in the face above her flickering open. The inevitable blows would surely follow. She was finished. Her fight was gone. Tiredness engulfed her, and she let her mind slip away.

Jerry paused. Was it his imagination, or had her eyes been open when he had opened his own after praying? He studied the woman's face. It was completely still, yet he was sure he had not imagined it. Had God answered his prayer? Was she emerging from her coma?

He stood and watched for another minute, but there were no further signs of movement.

Jerry looked up to see Sam approaching, wearing the new clothes Jerry had brought him.

"Any change?" Sam asked, looking past Jerry to his mother.

Jerry paused for a second and backed away from the bed. He didn't want to give false hope but was quite confident of what he had seen. "Well, she's still now. But I thought I saw her eyes open for a moment," he said.

Sam looked up at Jerry and smiled excitedly as he hurried closer. "I saw her eyes move earlier too, I swear! But the doctor wouldn't believe me." Sam knelt down on the floor and grasped his mother's hand. "Mum. It's me, Sam. Can you hear me?"

Jerry watched the scene in silence. It was amazing to see the normally gruff Sam hold his mother with such tenderness.

He knew it was time for him to go. Telling Sam about the burglary would have to wait for another time. He picked up Sam's bag of clothes. "I'll take these home and wash them and bring them back tomorrow. Okay?"

"Thanks," Sam replied quietly.

Jerry put his hand on Sam's shoulder. "I'll see you tomorrow. We'll be praying for your mum."

36

"How is she?" Gloria asked as she stirred the contents of the pan.

"She's alive," Jerry concluded eventually. "But she's still in a coma. Although I was praying over her when Sam had gone for a shower, and . . ." Jerry paused. An hour later he was still confused about what he had or hadn't seen.

Gloria turned and looked at him. "Yes?"

"Well," Jerry continued, "I thought she opened her eyes for a second."

"Hey, that's great."

Jerry scratched his head. "I can't be sure, though. It was like when you glance up at a window and think you just saw someone walk past it. Although Sam did say he thought he had seen the same thing earlier too."

"Well, maybe she did open them," Gloria said confidently.

Jerry looked up at her, unconvinced. "Yeah. Maybe. Either way, she doesn't look well at all. She's yellow. I've never seen anyone that color. The doctor said her liver's only just working."

"How's Sam?"

"He seems okay, considering," Jerry said. "Really tender with his mum. I've never seen that side of him before."

Gloria turned and wagged her finger at her husband. "He is a sweet boy, I tell you. He's got manners. He's just had an incredibly tough few years."

Jerry sighed. "Well, that's true. You're never going to believe what I found at their flat today. I went over there earlier to get Sam some spare clothes."

By the time Jerry had finished describing the state of the flat, Gloria had quietly dished up dinner. It was only when she sat down opposite that he noticed the tears in her eyes.

"Sweetheart . . ." Jerry reached out to grab her hand. "I'm sorry. I didn't mean to upset you."

"You didn't upset me. I'm just so angry." She reached across the table. "Let's pray," she said, determined. "Let's pray something good happens for Sam really soon."

"Okay," Jerry agreed, glancing down at his steaming meal. When his wife got angry at injustice, the prayers that followed were normally not short. *There's always the microwave,* he thought as he shut his eyes.

///

By the time they had prayed and eaten, all Jerry could think about was his bed. He wandered into the corridor toward the stairs and saw the carrier bag containing Sam's clothes that he had dropped when his children had welcomed him home.

"Blast it."

"What's the matter?" Gloria asked, appearing from the kitchen.

"I forgot about Sam's clothes. I said we'd wash 'em."

"Bring them here. I'll put them in now."

Jerry carried the bag into the kitchen and handed it to her. She pulled out a T-shirt and held it up in front of her, frowning at its condition.

"Oh," Jerry said a little guiltily. "I know we're trying to save money, but I bought Sam a new change of clothes today. I could hardly find anything at his flat. I don't know if they had all been nicked or he just hasn't got any." He nodded at the garment Gloria was holding. "I think I've only ever seen him wear that one T-shirt."

"That's fine," Gloria said, shaking her head. "Never worry about spending money on things like that. In fact, we should buy him some more. He's worn this so much there's hardly anything left of it."

"Well," Jerry said wistfully, "if we can get him boxing again soon, he'll be able to buy all the clothes he wants."

"Hmm," Gloria said, her voice hinting at a thought she wasn't sure whether to share or not.

Jerry chose to ignore it. He was tired, but more than that, he wasn't sure if he wanted to hear it. Whenever he talked to Gloria about Sam's career, she was irritatingly cool on the subject. Instead he watched his wife check through Sam's pockets. Jerry was notorious for leaving things in his pockets.

More than once, five-pound notes had been through a wash cycle.

Jerry froze as he watched Gloria retrieve a slip of paper from Sam's pocket and open it to assess its importance. It was the piece of paper the two strangers had handed Sam the day before. Jerry watched as his wife's eyes suddenly opened wide and she lifted her hand to her mouth. He held his breath.

Gloria held the piece of paper toward him, and Jerry's heart thumped as he reached out and took it.

A few seconds later he looked up in confusion at his smiling wife. He had so convinced himself as to what the piece of paper contained that when instead it showed two columns of words and letters, his brain couldn't compute their meaning.

Gloria rolled her eyes at him, grabbed the paper, and pointed to the title at the top. "Look. General Certificate of Secondary Education results. GCSEs," Gloria said excitedly.

Still Jerry was confused.

"Come on, Einstein! They're exam results."

Her finger moved from the title to the column on the right. "Look at these grades. They're amazing! English—A. Math—A. History—another A. There's like—" she quickly counted down the list—"seven As and three Bs. That's seriously good!"

"Wow," Jerry said, finally processing the information. *Exam results. Not a boxing contract!* He remembered back to the two men outside Sam's flat. Now he thought about it, they did look more like teachers than boxing people. Jerry immediately felt embarrassed and ashamed at having jumped to conclusions. But the shame was overshadowed by a happier thought—Sam was still his boxer! A broad smile broke out across his face.

Gloria engulfed him in a hug. But as he squeezed her back, he knew they were happy for different reasons.

"Praise God! Thank you, Lord!" Gloria said, releasing Jerry and dancing around the kitchen. "Jerry! We prayed just half an hour ago that Sam would get some good news. He had already received it!"

"Yeah." Jerry smiled as convincingly as he could. "That's great."

Despite her excitement, Gloria noticed her husband's manner. She tilted her head and looked quizzically at him. "Are you okay?"

"Sorry, sweetheart. Just miles away. It's fantastic."

/ / /

Gloria frowned. Different thoughts sprang to mind as she realized the difficult conversation she had been anticipating was now imminent. She dreaded her husband's reaction and had been fighting her feelings, trying to convince herself she was wrong. But these exam results just gave her further proof. She silently prayed and then spoke in the gentlest voice she could.

"You know, Jerry, with grades like these, maybe he shouldn't be pursuing boxing. He should be going to university. He's obviously very smart. He could have a proper career. Be a doctor. Or an architect or something."

"What's wrong with a boxing career?" Jerry bristled defensively. "He could make more money boxing than he ever could as a doctor or a stupid architect." By the end of the sentence Jerry was shouting.

Gloria and Jerry stared at one another, both shocked by the force of his reaction.

"Sorry," he barked, not sounding sorry at all. "You're just meddling in something you don't understand."

Gloria glared at her husband. He had never shouted at her like that before. Even when he was going through his depression, while he might have been sullen and sarcastic, he had never, ever shouted at her. How dare he, after all he had put her through? Anger bubbled up, and she opened her mouth to let him have it.

But just as she began to unleash her temper, she saw something else in her husband's angry demeanor: fear. Her feelings softened, and she prayed for grace. Quickly her anger subsided, replaced by a conviction that at the heart of this lay something a long way in the past.

"Is this about New York?" Gloria asked quietly.

Despite the gentleness of her voice, the words visibly affected Jerry. He looked like he'd just gotten a sword through the gut, and for a moment Gloria wondered whether he was actually about to hit her.

She watched him suppress the physical urge and begin to form a denial. But he couldn't find the words. They both knew there was truth in her question.

Gloria was the first to speak. She reached up and took his face in her hands, tilting it gently until they looked into each other's eyes. "It's okay, sweetheart. We'll work through this. I might be wrong! Carry on training him. Take him to the top.

But promise me this: We're going to love him while you do it, okay? Him and his mum, if she makes it. And God will work out the rest. Deal?"

Gloria saw the fear and anger begin to drop away in her husband. Eventually he nodded.

"Okay," she said, kissing him on the forehead. "You need to sleep. Let's get you to bed."

▰ ▰ ▰

Sam sat still, watching his mother's face.

The ward was virtually silent. All the main lights had been switched off, leaving a faint glow from the corridor, where the nurses' station was thinly manned. He glanced up at the figures on the machine by her bed. They hadn't changed much, which was a good sign, the nurse had said. A steady high-pitched beep sounded from the heart monitor, reassuring Sam that his mother was still alive. She was stable at least, and he could hear an occasional sucking of liquid through the tube to the small tank beneath her bed. Another good sign, the nurse had assured him. But how he wished she would wake up. How he wished they could talk. He wanted just one chance. One chance to say sorry. One chance to tell her he loved her.

As he sat studying her, his mind returned, as it had done throughout the day, to memories of happier times. Times when they had been a family—Sam, Mum, and Dad. Holidays in the old caravan in Suffolk. Day trips to nearby rivers, Dad and Sam absorbed in fishing while Mum sat on a blanket, reading a book. But most of the memories revolved around the farm—his dad stopping the combine harvester so they could all sit together and eat sandwiches and drink tea out of white tin billycans; Sam and Dad daring each other to jump in the duck pond after a particularly hot and dusty day in the field; racing the dog with the tractor, bouncing over the bumps and sprayer marks.

Sam had rarely allowed himself to reminisce like this in the past several years. In fact, after being caught there, he had neither been to nor hardly thought about the farm. But since he had found his mother in the flat two days before, he had thought of little else.

Suddenly Sam saw the movement. He stood out of his seat, all his attention focused on his mother's face. There it was again! Her eyes flickered, and he gave her hand a squeeze of encouragement.

"Mum! Can you hear me? It's me, Sam!" The muscles around the eyes flickered again. Then, with almost torturous effort, the eyelids opened, and the pupils of his mother's eyes contracted as she attempted to focus. Sam knelt on the edge of the bed with his face directly above hers.

"Mum, can you see me? Can you hear me?" As he stared at her eyes, Sam suddenly felt his mother's fingers curl around his own and give his hand a gentle squeeze. He looked down in amazement. "You're alive—you're alive!"

The edges of his mother's mouth moved, and a slight smile formed across her lips.

"Mum, I'm so sorry. I'm so sorry about everything."

PART
THREE

37

"Here we go again," Jerry said under his breath. His heart was thumping with anticipation as he stood alone outside the changing room door. The corridor was quiet except for the distant hum of the audience in the arena. Jerry savored the peace and calm and allowed his mind to wander back to everything that had happened in the last year.

Eleven months had passed since Sam's mother had emerged from the coma. She had spent another three weeks in intensive care with her liver function not recovering above critical. But slowly and surely, she had improved.

Jerry's first meeting with Janet had been a difficult one. He and Gloria had visited the hospital together. As they approached the bed, they saw Sam leaning toward his mother, holding her hand. Sam jumped up and greeted them warmly, giving Gloria a spontaneous hug. But as soon as he turned to introduce his mother, all their smiles fell away.

Janet was eyeing Jerry in terror, cowering into the bed and scrunching up the sheets in her fists. She stammered that she needed rest and turned away. Sam, confused and embarrassed, had apologized as Jerry and Gloria walked away.

"Now don't get all haughty," Gloria had said when Jerry began sounding off as they took the elevator to the lobby. "There's more to that than racism. Let's pray." There and then, his wife had prayed for God to reveal what lay behind the fear so clearly gripping Janet.

And while they hadn't received an answer, Gloria had persisted, visiting Janet every day with gifts of fresh fruit and other treats. Slowly she had gained Janet's trust, and after a few visits they had begun to build a friendship. Eventually Jerry had been able to join Gloria, and Janet's fear of him gradually subsided. Gloria had been amazing, and it was no surprise to Jerry when Janet asked Gloria to be with her when the doctor came to talk.

It wasn't good news. The doctor had reported there was no sign of Janet's liver recovering. It had survived the overdose, but the previous abuse had already done too much damage. If anything, Janet's liver function was deteriorating, and although the strong medication would help for a while, eventually the liver would stop working altogether.

Gloria reported that Janet had gripped her hand so hard it hurt.

"Surely something can be done," Gloria said.

The doctor shook his head. "The only hope is a liver transplant. But they're very rare. There's a shortage of donors, and . . . priority is given to non-self-inflicted cases.

"There is some good news, though," the doctor added. "Your current condition can be maintained with medication. As long as you can attend outpatient appointments with me and the psychiatric department, there is no reason why you can't return home in a week or so."

Gloria said the look on Janet's face had been one of total horror.

"I'd rather die in the hospital," she had said as tears streamed down her face. But she wouldn't elaborate any further.

Jerry and Gloria had a long conversation that evening. Jerry was skeptical, but Gloria reminded Jerry of their deal, and the very next day they invited Janet and Sam to move in with them.

Jerry and Sam had collected the Penningtons' few belongings from the flat. Jerry still remembered the anger in Sam's eyes as he surveyed the damage. It was the same look as before fights, and as ever, Jerry was struck by its ferocity.

They packed the borrowed van quickly. None of the furniture was salvageable except the two bed frames. Apart from those, Sam and Janet's remaining possessions fit into seven large cardboard boxes.

A week later they brought Janet home from the hospital. Jerry was still unsure about inviting a terminally ill and suicidal alcoholic into their home, not to mention Sam with all of his problems. But Gloria was convinced it was the right thing to do.

And despite his misgivings, Jerry had to admit things had turned out well. Janet was a blessing rather than a hindrance, even helping around the house, much to Gloria's distress.

"You should be resting!" Gloria said when she first caught Janet vacuuming.

"Please don't stop me," Janet replied. "It's the only way I can thank you for everything you've done for us."

Gloria had leaned forward and hugged the older woman. After a few awkward moments, Janet had hugged her back. From then on, she had become like one of the family.

And week by week Janet had seemed better. Not physically. Her skin continued to be an alarming yellow color, and weekly tests at the hospital showed a persistent deterioration in her liver function. But in her mind, in herself, in her spirit, she was stronger.

But Gloria wasn't satisfied. She prayed daily for Janet's complete restoration with a faith that amazed and humbled Jerry, who battled with old doubts about healing. He had always attended churches where altar calls for healing were commonplace. Indeed, he had seen a few healings that seemed divine, or at the very least unexplainable. But he had also seen the same people going forward, month after month, year after year, with illnesses and injuries that God didn't seem to heal. It was the apparent randomness that he struggled with most. That and his own bitter experience.

///

Robbie suddenly appeared through a swing door and shook his head at Jerry.

"It looks like it's going the distance," he said. "It's terrible. They're just circling each other, throwing the odd jab."

"What round are they in?" Jerry asked.

"End of the seventh." Robbie nodded at the door behind Jerry. "Sam's had a good long time to psych himself up. Do you think we left him on his own too early?"

Jerry bit his lip. "Maybe. But I'm not going to go in and change the routine now. I think he'll be all right."

Robbie nodded. "Okay. I'm gonna go back to the fight then. Watch the end in case it finishes early."

"Go for it."

Robbie pushed back through the door just as the bell rang. Jerry heard a single frustrated shout of "Come on—hit him!" before the door swung closed again.

Jerry smiled. If Sam continued his recent form, the crowd would see some aggression soon enough.

/ / /

Alongside loving Sam and his mum, as he had agreed with Gloria, Jerry had continued to train his star boxer. He had been concerned that living under the same roof might strain their professional relationship. But this hadn't been a problem yet. Sam was polite but self-contained—more like a lodger than a member of the family.

The training and boxing had gone better than Jerry could ever have hoped. As soon as Janet was discharged from the hospital and settled at home, Sam had returned to the gym. Jerry marveled at how quickly Sam got his sharpness back, and his aggression was undiminished. Indeed, anger at his mother's deteriorating health seemed to spur him on even more. Twice, after particularly discouraging test results, Jerry had canceled sparring sessions for fear Sam's opponents would get seriously hurt. Instead Jerry let the young boxer pound away on the heavy bag with frightening ferocity until he finally fell down exhausted. As a trainer, it was thrilling. As a friend, it was deeply disturbing.

Sam's first year as a professional had been a whirlwind. He had ended up fighting nearly every month, which would normally be considered an excessive workload. However, each fight was so short and clinical that recovery time was hardly necessary. Six fights ended in knockouts or stoppages in the first round, while three stretched to the second as Jerry made Sam concentrate on practicing specific skills. In one of the bouts, Sam had won using only his left jab after Jerry had nagged him about not overlooking the punch's importance.

The only fight that had gone beyond two rounds had been extraordinary. Lee Saunders, a young whippet of a lad from Coventry, had virtually bounced around the ring, bending away from punches with an almost rubberlike elasticity. Jerry had never seen anything quite like it, and for a moment in the second round, Sam had become ragged in frustration at not being able to land his punches. But Jerry formed a plan to trap the opponent in a corner and communicated the strategy to Sam during one of their chats between rounds. The plan took half the next round to execute, but the finish was brutal and decisive when Sam finally nailed him.

Ten minutes later Jerry guiltily observed the distinct lack of elasticity in Saunders's legs as he was helped from the ring. While the lad's skill in punch avoidance was not matched by his punching power, there was no doubt that the boy had real talent. Boxing could be a hard game.

Sam's exploits quickly began to attract attention, and a sense of excitement was growing. Fight by fight, Sam's contests had moved further back in the evening schedules. The purses got bigger, and Sam was building a vociferous little fan club. But most important, the boxing press was increasingly taking an interest, with a profile of Sam appearing in the regular One to Watch column in *Boxing News*. While there had been plenty who had disappeared over the years following a heavy defeat or two, the list of previously featured fighters was pretty impressive. It included Carl Froch, Joe Calzaghe, Lennox Lewis, Naseem Hamed, Chris Eubank, Nigel Benn, Frank Bruno, and, further back, Barry McGuigan and Lloyd Honeyghan. All world champions.

Jerry looked down at his watch impatiently. He was desperate for the fight to start and to see his decision vindicated. Tonight was to be Sam's first outing at the top of the bill. From the moment the fight was announced, the boxing press questioned the wisdom of the matchup. One journalist had even written a piece about the ethics and safety of a seventeen-year-old fighting a former British and Commonwealth champion. Even Bert, who was both loving and profiting from Sam's rise through the ranks, had been concerned about taking the fight. But Jerry was insistent and Sam unquestioning. So Bert signed the contract, and now here they were, just a few minutes from the biggest fight of Sam's career.

Yet a persistent doubt was nagging at Jerry's mind. Ever since Sam's first amateur win, Jerry had been troubled by the boy's demeanor after fights. Beforehand he was brutally focused. Afterward, while others celebrated, he seemed . . . depressed. It was the only way to describe it. Jerry even thought he had seen a tear in Sam's eye after one particular contest. Jerry had lost sleep about it, but Sam had not been forthcoming, and Jerry had no desire to push it.

/ / /

Robbie suddenly rushed back through the door along with a couple of other people who hurried past and disappeared into the other changing room.

"Over?" Jerry inquired.

Robbie nodded. "Just adding up the scorecards now. Neither of them deserves to win. That was rubbish."

A man in a blazer appeared and gestured at Jerry. "Ten minutes," he called before continuing down the corridor to the other dressing room.

"Here we go!" Jerry said, backing through the door behind him.

Twelve minutes later they were standing in the ring. The entrance music died down.

"That's the last time we let you choose the music, Robbie," Jerry hissed at his assistant, only partly in jest. "Not exactly low-key."

Robbie grinned broadly. "Best boxing anthem ever!"

Jerry couldn't help smiling back at Robbie, who was clearly loving the razzmatazz of his first big fight night. And while it might have been corny, "Eye of the Tiger" had certainly got the crowd going after the slumber of the previous fight.

Jerry looked out into the packed arena just as the lights were extinguished. Everyone in the room turned toward the double doors, now lit up by two spotlights. A Bruce Springsteen number blared, and Sam's opponent swaggered in.

Chris Johnson stood for a moment, an arrogant leer on his face as he tensed the muscles on display through his gaping dressing gown. His shorts rode halfway up his stomach, with his nickname, Boom Boom, emblazoned across the front. Jerry looked away. Bert had been insisting for weeks that they needed to develop a nickname, persona, and appropriate boxing attire for Sam if they were going to make the most of his marketability. But Jerry was not one for showiness and had been quietly pleased when Sam had shown equally little interest.

"Relax, Sam. Nice and loose," Jerry said as he massaged Sam's shoulders while the opponent's elaborate entrance routine carried on behind them. He pressed his thumbs into the slabs of muscle, noticeably thicker than the first time Jerry had seen them. At nearly eighteen years of age, Sam was now almost fully developed physically. He still lifted heavy weights but worked more on conditioning and stamina nowadays, careful not to add further muscle bulk and so push him above the middleweight threshold. Already Jerry was convinced there wasn't a fitter boxer in England.

The trainer studied his fighter's face. Sam returned his gaze. Silent communication flowed between the two, although neither could have translated it exactly. Just a confidence. A trust. A kinship. But just before Sam looked away, Jerry caught sight of something else. The sadness was there again. The trainer's stomach fluttered nervously. Was it fear? Uncertainty? Or something else?

Chris Johnson finally reached the ring. Climbing in, he immediately came toward Sam, shoving against Jerry in the process.

"You're dead!" he said to Sam with a snarl.

Jerry shoved him back, holding his ground.

"I'm going to chew you up and spit you out," Johnson snarled again.

Sam gave his opponent a contemptuous glare, the sadness replaced by aggression. Jerry breathed a sigh of relief. That was Johnson's first mistake. Jerry was confident it wouldn't be his last.

The referee came across and remonstrated with Chris Johnson. The boxer backed toward his own corner, chanting his "You're dead!" mantra all the way. Seconds later the referee called them both to the center of the ring and set out the rules of the fight. The fighters touched gloves at the referee's command and returned to their corners.

The bell rang. Sam raised his gloves and advanced toward his opponent.

38

Within twenty seconds the crowd was cheering loudly. All hangover from the previous tepid contest was forgotten as the two men went for each other with total commitment. Chris Johnson swarmed forward in a way Jerry knew Sam had never encountered before. For a few seconds Sam struggled to cope.

The first round was marginally Johnson's as both boxers traded punches. But the pace proved too much for the older boxer in a brutal second round as Sam found his range. By the time the bell rang at the end of the round, Chris Johnson had already stopped advancing. His left eyebrow was swelling, and although Sam was breathing heavily too, in comparison he was relatively unmarked.

In the third round Chris Johnson changed tactics. He had realized he wasn't going to overpower Sam, so he settled down to try and box him out of the ring. He was a talented boxer with a tight defense, and the change in tactic meant far fewer of Sam's punches found their mark. But, equally, not a single punishing punch landed upon Sam. By the end of the round he was looking fresher than ever. Sam had matched Chris Johnson's boxing skills throughout and, just on the bell, landed a shuddering inside punch to the chin that rocked Johnson onto his heels. Only those closest to the ring actually saw the punch and the wobbly walk as Johnson returned to his corner and sat down heavily on his stool.

Even fewer could see the emotion in Johnson's eyes as he looked at Sam across the ring while his cut man attended to his bruising. But Jerry did. To a trained eye it was unmistakable. Resignation.

Chris Johnson's last throw of the dice arrived early in the fourth. In the first close exchange of the round, the older boxer grabbed his opponent around the waist and thrust his forehead into Sam's face. Bright-red blood spurted from Sam's eyebrow, spilling down his chest and onto the blue canvas floor. Sam staggered backward in shock. The referee jumped in immediately.

"That was deliberate!" Jerry shouted furiously at the referee as Mario led a still-dazed Sam back to the corner.

"No, it wasn't!" Johnson's trainer yelled as he, too, entered the ring. "Accidental."

"Rubbish!" Jerry screamed at the referee, pointing at Chris Johnson, who was suddenly holding his own head, pretending to be hurt. "He was losing, and he butted my boxer."

"No way! Your boxer was off balance and stumbled into mine."

"That's crap and you know it!" Jerry said, moving toward his opposite number. The two men began to square off, and the referee jumped between them.

"That's enough!" he screamed. "Get back to your corners. NOW!"

The two trainers glared at each other as they backed away. Loud jeering filled the room, the crowd frustrated at the lull in action after such an explosive first few rounds. It was the first decent fight of the evening, and they seemed determined to get a tasty finish.

Jerry returned to his corner, where Mario was working frantically on Sam's face.

"Talk to me, Mario," Jerry shouted above the noise of the crowd.

"Bad, bad," Mario said, shaking his head. "I can probably stop the blood for a minute or two, but the first time he is hit there, it will just . . . I won't be able to stop it. It needs stitching."

"Cheating git!" Jerry shouted in frustration before turning to Sam. "Are you okay?"

Sam, obscured by a chilled towel that Mario was pressing against the wound, said nothing.

The referee came across. "How is he?" he asked before turning and yelling at Johnson's trainer, who had once again rushed across the ring. Finally the ref turned back to the huddle of men around Sam. Mario slowly removed the towel, and four sets of eyes focused on Sam's head.

The cut was severe, almost a centimeter long and dissecting Sam's right eyebrow vertically. The skin was gaping open, and the gap was filled with welling blood. Mario dipped a cotton bud into a small jar of chemical solution and prodded it into the center of the cut. For a moment, as he removed it, they could see virgin pink flesh that had never previously seen the light of day. All four men watched closely as tiny pinpricks of blood appeared as if from nowhere. Mario immediately dipped another bud into a different glass bottle and pushed it gently into the newly formed blob of blood. The cut man removed the bud, and they all studied the wound once again. As if by magic, the globule began to harden.

"It's stopped!" Robbie said excitedly. Jerry gave him a severe glare.

"I can Vaseline it up," Mario said, shaking his head again. "But as soon as he gets hit there, it will start pouring all over again."

Jerry pleaded with the referee beside him. "You've got to stop it and give us the fight. That was blatant!"

"I know. I'm going to dock him points."

"Points!" Jerry exploded. "You've got to stop the fight. Otherwise we're gonna lose on a stoppage because the blood's pouring out of him."

"If he's bleeding badly at the end of the round, I'm gonna give it to your man."

"Then why not stop it now?" Jerry shouted. "It's going to put Sam out for three months if that cut opens up any farther."

"ENOUGH!" Sam shouted.

All four men fell silent and looked down at the boxer.

"I just need twenty seconds," Sam said quietly. The words were expressed with such menace and certainty that there was nothing more to be said. The referee nodded curtly and backed away. Mario liberally smeared Vaseline over the cut.

"You don't need to do this," Jerry said.

"Twenty seconds," Sam replied. Jerry gave him a long, hard look before nodding and climbing wearily down from the ring.

The crowd cheered as Sam stood. The referee lectured Chris Johnson, animating a head-butt to make clear to the crowd and the ringside judges what the conversation was about. Neither Chris Johnson nor his trainer raised another objection. They had taken a gamble that deserved immediate disqualification and had seemingly gotten away with it. Now they had a chance to turn the fight.

The referee faced the officials below the ring and held up three fingers to indicate the points to be deducted. He then turned back and gestured to the boxers to engage again.

Johnson stepped forward and threw an overhand right at the onrushing Sam. It was the last punch the man threw.

The next fifteen seconds saw the most savage assault many in the crowd had ever witnessed. Sam connected on his very first punch and followed it with a sequence of perfectly executed blows. Within three seconds Chris Johnson was completely on the defensive. Within six he was battling to reach the floor. By nine he had lost consciousness. The twelfth second saw Johnson's body finally reach the canvas. It was fifteen before a combination of

Jerry and the referee finally prevented Sam from landing any more punches on the unconscious man below him.

The room was eerily silent. Finally a murmur of awe and wonder began to grow, turning into a sustained cheer as drunken men celebrated the savagery of what they had seen.

The ring was devoid of celebration. The ringside doctor jumped up and immediately began tending the stricken man, instinctively feeling for his pulse. Mario joined him, sliding to his knees alongside Johnson's trainer and cut man. On the other side of the ring, Jerry still held Sam in a bear hug on the canvas while the referee sat beside them, stunned.

The referee climbed to his feet and stood shaking his head as he watched the four men frantically tending the injured man.

"Are you okay?" Jerry whispered to Sam.

"Can we get out of here, please?" the boxer replied quietly.

Jerry breathed out heavily. "Yeah. We just need to see he's all right," he said, finally releasing Sam. Both men pushed to their feet and walked over to Chris Johnson. Jerry deduced from the doctor's behavior that he had found a pulse, but the man was still unconscious and desperately pale.

The referee looked across at Jerry. "I should have stopped it," he said, his eyes returning to the prone boxer. "Bottled it."

"Yeah." Jerry looked at the referee, then at Sam. "So did I."

A hush descended over the hall as two paramedics pushed through the crowd toward the ring, carrying a stretcher above their heads.

Jerry put his hand on Sam's shoulder. "Let's go. There's nothing we can do here."

/ / /

When Sam finally emerged from the shower cubicle, a white towel tied around his waist, Jerry saw his eyebrow had swelled to the size of a small egg. The cut sat upon it like a cake decoration.

"How are you doing?" Jerry asked.

Sam seemed lost for words. He shrugged and began drying himself in silence.

Jerry quietly prayed as he wandered around the room, picking up equipment and stuffing it into a kit bag.

Suddenly Robbie bounded in. "It's all right. Johnson's come round, and he's talking okay. He can move his hands and feet. He's going to be fine. They've just taken him to hospital as a precaution."

Jerry let out a sigh of relief and ran his fingers across his scalp. "Thank you, God."

He looked up to see Sam turn, pretending to dry his toes. But the boy's whole body was shaking uncontrollably. Jerry instinctively glanced up at Robbie and saw that he, too, had seen Sam's reaction.

"That's great news," Jerry said, standing between the two youths. "Will you give us a bit of time, Robbie? We'll come and find you when we're done."

Robbie got the hint and left, stealing one last concerned glance at Sam.

The moment the door shut, Sam slumped to the bench, sobbing.

Jerry hurried over and squatted down next to him, putting his arm around the boy's shoulder.

"He's going to be all right, Sam. You did nothing wrong. You did brilliantly, in fact. That head-butt was filthy, but you kept your form and won the fight. You've just taken apart a former British and Commonwealth champion."

"Yeah," Sam said between sobs. "But that doesn't make me feel any better."

The statement stopped Jerry in his tracks. Conflicting emotions battled for control of his mind. As a boxing trainer, it scared him that his protégé, who had the boxing world at his feet, was crying, declaring he took no enjoyment in winning. On the other hand, as someone who loved and cared for this kid, he wanted to reach out and say, *"Of course it doesn't. Fighting isn't going to give you true, lasting happiness. Only knowing that God loves you can really do that."*

The battle continued to rage in Jerry's mind as he squatted in silence next to Sam.

39

Robbie climbed on his old chopper bicycle and set off on the long ride to North Woolwich. The month since Sam's fight had been, without a doubt, the best month of Robbie's life. The big fight night had been a good start. To be able to choose the music for their fighter's entrance! To be assistant trainer to the fighter who topped the bill! To be next to the ring when their fighter beat—or, rather, *smashed*—a former British and Commonwealth champion! That night had been amazing. But it wasn't the fight that had made this month the best so far. It was the journey home afterward.

There was silence in Bert's Mercedes on the way home from York Hall in Bethnal Green, where the fight had taken place. Sam and Jerry had sat in the back emotionless, as they had been since they finally emerged from the changing room an hour earlier. Robbie, on the other hand, was still buzzing and could only just control his excitement, grinning to himself as Bert accelerated along.

When Bert pulled into a petrol station, Robbie jumped out and wandered toward the shop to buy some bubble gum, having nervously chewed through his whole supply during the evening. He was greeted by a warm Australian accent.

"G'day, how are ya this evening?" said the chirpy salesgirl.

Robbie was frozen to the spot, finally stammering a hello in reply. She was the first Australian he had ever met, she had a lovely smile, and he was awestruck.

Robbie had idolized Australia since he was a small child. All the old Australian soaps had been avidly followed in his household—*The Flying Doctors*, *Home and Away*, *Neighbours*. Charlene Robinson had been the first and most enduring love of his life.

As Robbie approached the counter where the slightly plump blonde girl sat, his heart thumped so loudly he thought she might hear it. "Are you from Australia?" he said, failing to hide the admiration in his voice.

"I am. Melbourne in Victoria."

"Melbourne!" Robbie said a little too excitedly. The setting for *Neighbours*! He quickly suppressed a smile.

"You been there?" she asked with a curious grin.

"N-no," Robbie stuttered. "I've just . . . heard about it."

"It's beautiful. And warm. Not like here!"

"Sounds amazing," Robbie said, awe once more in his voice as he listened to her accent.

The girl giggled this time before nodding out the window. "Are you paying for fuel?"

Robbie followed her eyes out to the sleek black car, which

shimmered under the neon lights of the garage forecourt. Bert was just returning the nozzle to the pump.

"No. Not my car," Robbie said before panicking that she probably saw a lot of boys in nice cars. "I do have a car, though," he blurted. "Well. Kind of. It's broken down at the moment."

"I'm not that interested in cars," she said nonchalantly. Robbie's heart thumped again.

"What are you interested in?" he said, shocked at his forwardness. But before the girl could respond, Bert pushed through the glass door behind him.

"G'day," she greeted him brightly. Bert grunted in reply, grabbing a Mars bar and throwing it on the counter.

"How much?" he said, fishing a wad of notes from his pocket.

"Eighty-seven pounds, fifty-two pence, please, sir."

Bert peeled five notes off the wad and handed them over. The girl counted out his change.

"Twelve pounds, forty-eight. Thank you very much."

Bert grunted again and walked away, giving Robbie a sideways glance.

"Come on, Robbie. You got what you wanted?"

"Er, not yet."

"Well, hurry up!" Bert said impatiently, walking out of the shop.

Robbie turned in embarrassment back to the girl.

"What would you like?" she said, smiling again. Robbie thought about picking up a chocolate bar instead as a more mature purchase. But he realized he only had enough cash for one packet of bubble gum. Nothing else on the stand was in his price range. He reached out and nervously picked up a packet of Hubba Bubba and placed it on the counter, along with a ten-pence piece from his pocket.

"We don't get that in Australia," she said, picking up the coin and putting it in the till.

"You want one?" Robbie replied immediately, tearing the top off the packet and handing her a chunk.

"Aw. Thanks!"

"No worries!" Robbie said loudly, then froze as he heard his exaggerated Australian accent. His face went crimson and he wanted to die.

But the girl smiled and rescued him. "You're so kind," she replied in a posh English accent.

Robbie's cheeks now burned with another emotion.

"I'm Shelley," she said, holding her hand out across the counter.

Robbie wiped his clammy palm on his side before lifting it and shaking her hand warmly.

"Robbie."

Bert's angry car horn destroyed the moment. Robbie released his grip and walked toward the exit.

"Bye," he said forlornly.

"Bye," Shelley replied with yet another smile.

/ / /

Robbie had been in another world ever since that night. He knew for sure he had met the girl of his dreams. Winning her, however, had not been straightforward.

The following Monday evening he had cycled for an hour to reach the garage in Stratford, only to find a middle-aged Asian man standing behind the counter.

Robbie had hung around in the shop for an hour, reading magazines and continually glancing over at the counter area and the office behind, hoping against hope that Shelley would appear.

"Can I help you?" the man behind the till eventually asked.

"Is, um, Shelley on duty tonight?"

"She just works weekends."

Robbie cycled home deflated.

But the next Saturday evening he was back and thrilled to see Shelley at the desk.

"Hi, Robbie!" she said when she looked up and saw him. Robbie's stomach leaped—she remembered his name—and this time they chatted freely without Bert leaning on the horn.

"And how come you pass through here every Saturday night?" she asked.

Blushing, Robbie had admitted that this time he'd come on his bike.

"All the way from Ilford?"

"Yeah."

"Wow! To see me?"

Robbie blushed even redder. But by the time he left two hours later, they had made a date to go to the bowling alley the next night she was free.

Robbie had never been bowling before, and he was

worried. Shelley had said she played every week when she lived in Australia. So Robbie spent all Sunday afternoon at the bowling alley, practicing with a whole lane to himself. By the end of his third game, his best score had risen to sixty-two. It would have to do. If he spent any more money, he wouldn't have enough to take Shelley to Pizza Hut afterward. Robbie wanted to show her he was a classy bloke.

Unfortunately the practice hadn't helped. Robbie was useless, while Shelley rolled ball after ball down the middle, knocking pins everywhere. As his sixth successive ball went down the gully without scoring, Robbie wanted to curl up with embarrassment. But Shelley started giggling uncontrollably.

"Don't worry, darl. You've got other gifts, I'm sure," she said, hugging his arm.

Buoyed by the fact that she seemed to like him despite his poor bowling, he relaxed and began goofing around. As he delivered the next ball, he did a little dance, and as he grew more confident, he started throwing in "Muhammad Ali shuffles" and other boxing steps. Shelley was reduced to hysterics, to the bemusement of bowlers in the neighboring lanes.

On his final bowl, Robbie shuffled a dozen times and finally delivered the ball between his legs. Miraculously the ball stayed on line and knocked down eight pins, bringing his final score up to thirty-one. He held his arms up in triumph, and Shelley ran into them and gave him a hug, which led to a first kiss.

They walked out of the bowling alley arm in arm, and Robbie had never felt happier or prouder in his entire life.

/ / /

Robbie finally reached North Woolwich, where Shelley's family lived. He steered his bike down a side street full of drab Victorian houses and came to a halt next to a small blue gate. He climbed off and pushed down the now-familiar front path.

Robbie heard the raised voices immediately. It was clear Shelley was having a full-blown row with her dad. Robbie stood on the doorstep, unsure what to do. Thankfully the argument soon came to an end, and after waiting a couple more minutes Robbie knocked nervously. Shelley answered almost immediately, and his heart sank when he saw her tearstained face.

"What's wrong, Shell?" Robbie asked, concern clear in his voice.

"Can we go down to the river on your bike, Robbie? I've got something to tell you."

Robbie stood on his pedals with Shelley on the saddle behind him, and they freewheeled most of the way to the Thames.

"Let's walk," Shelley said when they had reached the riverbank. Fresh tears ran down her face as she clung to Robbie's arm.

"What's wrong? Tell me." Shelley buried her face in Robbie's jacket and hugged him tight.

"Dad's quit his job. We're going back to Australia."

40

Jerry leaned on the ropes and watched. Robbie stood with pads on his hands, lifting them high and low and tilting them toward the punches. Opposite him, Sam threw jabs, hooks, and uppercuts at Robbie's instruction.

Jerry frowned. Something wasn't right. Not right at all. The whole thing lacked snap. Jerry scratched his head in irritation, glaring from one to the other. Robbie had been wandering about in a dreamworld for four weeks, wearing a dopey smile—at least until yesterday. Now he had a face as long as a donkey's. Sam, meanwhile, had returned from his postfight break as flat as Jerry had ever seen him.

"Okay!" Jerry said, clapping. "Come over here."

Sam and Robbie sauntered over.

"Can either of you tell me *what is going on*? Robbie, you're asking for the whole range of punches. Fine. Sam, you're delivering them. Fine. But, gentlemen," Jerry growled, "'fine' is *not good enough*. From *either* of you! You're flat. 'Fine' will win us twelve fights but then get you knocked on your *backside*."

Neither boy said a word, and both looked down at the floor.

"From tomorrow," Jerry continued, "I want a whole lot more passion. More commitment. More intensity. You hear? I never want to say 'fine' to either of you again. Okay, Robbie?"

Robbie nodded. "Sorry, boss."

"Okay, Sam?" Jerry repeated. Sam nodded slowly too.

There was silence as Jerry searched their eyes, not wholly convinced by what he saw.

"Okay," Jerry said finally. "Get lost."

The two boys climbed down from the ring and dragged themselves toward the showers, dodging Bert, who was standing outside his office. The promoter had clearly heard some of the exchange, as he also glared at the boys filing past. He then looked up at Jerry.

"You got a minute?"

"Sure," Jerry replied, stepping down from the ring.

"Trouble?" Bert asked as he ushered the trainer into his office and shut the door.

"Dunno," Jerry replied. "They're both just really flat. Robbie's got girlfriend problems, I think. Sam . . . I don't know."

"Well," Bert replied, his eyes twinkling, "I've hopefully got something to brighten them both up." The promoter broke into a broad smile. "I've just had Ron Donovan on the phone."

Jerry whistled with mock awe. "We are moving in exalted circles nowadays."

"Tell me about it," Bert said, still beaming. "He rang me!"

Jerry smiled. He was happy for Bert. Ron Donovan was the biggest boxing promoter in the UK, with some of the biggest names in British boxing on his books, not to mention numerous British and European champions.

"So what did good old Ron want?" Jerry asked casually, even though his curiosity was piqued too.

"He saw film of Sam's fight with Chris Johnson and said he was really impressed."

"Quite right too," Jerry said. "I bet it had him salivating into his champagne."

"Yeah. Good thing we've got Sam on a tight contract." Bert bit his lip as a flicker of anxiety crossed his face.

"Don't worry, Bert. Sam's not going anywhere. I promise."

"Well, Donovan's got Darren Spencer putting up his British middleweight title against some Welsh guy next month. It's two down the bill from the heavyweight title fight."

"Geraint Thomas," Jerry offered. He had watched him fight on satellite television and had seen the proposed matchup in *Boxing News*.

"That's it! Well, apparently our Welsh friend broke his hand in training yesterday. Donovan's offered for Sam to step in."

"You're kidding!"

"I know!" Bert said excitedly. "Wembley Stadium. This is the biggest British fight card in years."

"Why is he offering us that, Bert? What's the catch?"

"He promises me there's no catch. He's offered us nine

grand. Only condition is a compulsory rematch for Spencer if Sam wins."

"Nine thousand quid?" Jerry said, shaking his head. "It's a different world, isn't it?"

"It certainly is!" Bert smiled before doubt furrowed his brow. "Am I missing something?"

Jerry rubbed his head, pondering the question. "Spencer's good, but not fantastic. I think Sam can have him fairly comfortably. And if Donovan watched Sam's fight at York Hall, I'm sure he knows that. Spencer's thirty-three now, I think. Maybe even thirty-four. So I imagine Ron thinks he's coming to the end."

Jerry paused to think. Bert was hanging on every word.

"I don't think Donovan's got anyone else decent at middleweight at the moment," Jerry continued. "Except his top guys, of course, but they're in a different league. So maybe he thinks if he gets in with us, he'll have some access to Sam."

"Yeah," Bert agreed. "That's what I reckon. I told Donovan our contract with Sam was so watertight, you couldn't get a pressure hose through it."

Jerry grinned. "What did he say to that?"

"He told me to relax. But he did say if Sam won, maybe he could help set up a world title shot a bit further down the line."

"Did he now?" Jerry said, shaking his head. "I bet Darren Spencer wasn't in the room to hear his manager say that! Still, if we're being offered nine thousand, I suspect Spencer's probably getting three times that. Maybe it will be enough for him to retire on."

"And to be honest," Bert said, lowering his voice even

though the office door was closed, "if Sam goes much further, we'll probably need help from someone like Donovan. 'Cause I haven't got the financial clout at that level."

Jerry nodded thoughtfully.

"So what do you think?" Bert asked at last. "It seems a no-brainer to me."

Jerry was silent. Normally when a newcomer won a bout in the manner Sam had destroyed Chris Johnson, other fighters holding belts and titles tended to shy away unless offered a massive financial inducement. This fight, on the other hand, was coming to them on a plate. From a boxing perspective it *was* a no-brainer. But Sam was worrying him. Jerry had never needed to dress him down like he had ten minutes earlier. "How long have we got?" he asked.

"We need to let Donovan know today."

"Today!"

"Yeah," Bert said quickly. "That was his other condition. Because it's a level-one televised bout, he has to submit the whole lineup to the board of control a month beforehand. That's tomorrow. He's sending the contract over now. If we want the fight, we've got to check it, sign it, and send it back with the same courier."

"Okay," Jerry said. "I better have a word with Sam."

Jerry inched his car forward in the traffic, grimacing as he smelled the clutch. The struggling vehicle was on an incline, forcing him to do repeated hill starts as the traffic shuffled along.

Jerry turned and glanced at Sam, who was staring through the windscreen with a vacant expression, and frowned. It had been a funny conversation just an hour earlier. Jerry had explained to Sam the pros and cons of the fight on offer. He had described Spencer and his style. He had described what a fight night at Wembley would be like. And as he had spoken, he had studied Sam carefully, looking for excitement or fear. He had seen neither. Instead Sam had simply shrugged and nodded before signing the eighteen-page contract with a bored, almost resigned expression.

Jerry glanced at Sam again. The boy finished a yawn, leaned back against the headrest, and shut his eyes. Sweat broke through on Jerry's palms. Something was desperately wrong. Sam had just signed a contract to fight for a British title and pocket the lion's share of nine thousand pounds. Yet an hour later he couldn't even stay awake.

Jerry shivered as he realized the truth. He had ignored his concerns about Sam and had encouraged the boy to take the fight. He had stood over him as he signed it. Sam hadn't taken the fight. Jerry had.

"Oh my God!" Jerry whispered under his breath. *God.* The word hit him like a slap in the face. He hadn't asked God whether this was right for Sam or for himself. He had just done it.

Jerry's mind raced. He should cancel the fight—chase down the courier. Ring Bert at least. He grimaced. He knew what Bert would say. Jerry remembered the penalty clause for canceling spelled out in the contract. "Can you afford that?" he had asked Bert, pointing at the five-figure cancellation fee.

Bert had answered nervously, "Let's just not cancel."

The club would be ruined. He, *Jerry*, would ruin Ilford Boxing Club. Beads of sweat formed on his forehead.

"Calm down, Jerry," he said aloud, glancing across as Sam opened his eyes and looked at him curiously.

"Sorry," Jerry muttered. "How are you doing?"

"Fine," Sam replied, giving nothing away.

"Hey, Sam. Look at me a second," Jerry said.

Sam met his trainer's eyes.

"This time next month, you could be British champion. Two fights after that, if all goes well, you could be fighting for a world title. How does that feel?"

Sam looked away. "It feels good."

Jerry's smile felt empty. Sam's answer had been a second too late to be convincing.

"Proper training starts tomorrow," Jerry said.

Sam nodded and shut his eyes once more.

The rest of the journey took place in silence. The congestion finally gave way to open roads, and a few minutes later Jerry pulled into their street.

His heart raced. An ambulance with blue lights blazing stood in front of the house. Jerry accelerated forward and screeched to a halt on the pavement behind it. They jumped out of the car and sprinted toward the house. Gloria appeared in the doorway, stopping them in their tracks.

"What's going on, sweetheart?"

"It's Janet," she said, looking up at her husband in shock. "She just vomited blood everywhere and then collapsed."

Jerry glanced at Sam. The rage was back.

41

Gloria still felt the shock a week later. The doctor had predicted it could happen, but nothing could quite prepare a person for seeing her friend clutch her stomach and vomit blood all over the kitchen floor.

It had also changed her outlook, Gloria reflected as she walked toward the front entrance of the hospital. Until last week she had been convinced Janet would be healed. She had prayed hour after hour. She had fasted. She had petitioned God every night. And Janet had indeed lasted much longer than the doctors had predicted. But there had been no miraculous healing, and the sight of all that blood finally brought home to Gloria that physical healing for Janet might not be part of God's plan.

Instead Gloria was now praying that Janet would know God was close to her, whatever happened. And of God's will for that, Gloria had no doubts. But every time Gloria visited, Janet had been asleep, and Gloria was devastated that she might have missed her opportunity to talk with Janet.

"Please let her be awake, Lord," Gloria pleaded as she entered the elevator and pressed the button for the fourth floor.

When the doors opened, she walked to the nurses' station on the ward, where a familiar nurse looked up at her. "Hi there."

"Hi. How is she?" Gloria asked anxiously.

"She's quite alert today."

"Wow!" Gloria exclaimed. "That's wonderful! I thought she was only going to get worse."

The nurse frowned. "It's likely to be only temporary, I'm afraid. The doctor will explain when he comes around. He's due soon. In the meantime, why don't you go through?"

"Thanks."

Gloria's spirit leaped as she saw Janet awake and sitting up in bed. The two women embraced.

"How are you doing, sweetheart?" Gloria asked, perching on the bed next to Janet and taking her hand.

"I feel a lot better, thank you."

"Good. Jerry and the girls send their love. The girls painted you a picture." Gloria bent down to her bag and retrieved a large card. Janet held it up in front of her, trying to make sense of the swirling brushstrokes.

"It's you on a sailing boat, apparently," Gloria said, grinning. "But I couldn't see it either!"

"Tell them it's beautiful." The woman propped the picture

up on the side table next to her bed. "Tell them it's the last thing I'll look at before I go to sleep, and it will give me happy dreams."

"I'll tell them." Gloria smiled and squeezed Janet's hand. "Jerry's going to try to call in and see you after work today."

Janet's eyes welled up. "Gloria, I just can't say how grateful I am for everything you've done for us. You are wonderful people."

Gloria shrugged. "It's nothing."

"It's not nothing," Janet said firmly. "You have been a gift from God."

Gloria's heart thumped. She had never heard Janet refer to God before. She and Jerry hadn't hidden their faith. They had still prayed at mealtimes and gone to church on Sundays. Janet had even gone with them a few times before she got very weak. But they had never actually talked with Janet about their beliefs.

"Well, we think you're pretty special," Gloria said, smiling.

"What's special about me?" Janet whispered, her voice suddenly breaking.

Gloria reached out and took Janet's hand again. "You are special in so many ways. You are kind. And you're so sweet with our children. You always put others first." Gloria took a deep breath. "But the most important reason is that God made you special, and he loves you so much."

"Why would God love me?" Janet blurted, her eyes welling up once more. "I tried to kill myself. I almost left Sam an orphan. I still am going to leave him an orphan. How could God love me after that?"

Gloria sighed and sandwiched Janet's hand between hers.

"Sam will never be alone. We love him—just like we love you. He can live with us as long as he wants to."

Janet mouthed a silent thank-you, her eyes full of gratitude.

"But most importantly," Gloria said urgently, "even when we're gone, Sam won't be alone. God's with him. Just like he's with you."

"But I tried to kill myself. . . ."

"It doesn't matter. God forgives you!"

"But why? And how do you know?"

Gloria took a deep breath. "I know . . . because I believe what it says in the Bible. . . ."

/ / /

Sam chained his bike to a railing in the car park, then turned and glanced up at the hospital. The whole place was horribly familiar now, and he braced himself for what he might face today.

When his mum had relapsed a week earlier, he had stayed up all night at her bedside, holding bowls to her mouth as she vomited. The doctors had finally stopped the internal bleeding. But the drugs had knocked her out. She had hardly been awake since.

So Sam had returned to Jerry's house for the night, done his morning shift at a factory down by the river, and then cycled here to the hospital. Every lunchtime he'd sat next to his unconscious mother, watching her die. By the time he arrived at the gym an hour later, he was ready to kill. As he walked through the entrance of the hospital, he was already looking forward to pounding the punching bags later that afternoon.

/ / /

"Hi there," the nurse said sweetly as he reached the desk.

"Hi," Sam replied.

"She's awake this morning," she said encouragingly. "In fact, she's got your friend with her."

"Thanks," Sam said and walked down the corridor. He peeked shyly around the corner of the bay to see Gloria sitting next to his mum. They were deep in conversation, and Sam instinctively stopped out of sight and listened.

"I still can't believe he'd forgive me," Sam heard his mother say. "After what I did."

"Why did you do it, Janet?" Gloria's voice was only just audible. "What drove you to that?"

Sam held his breath as his mother nervously cleared her throat.

"It was more than a year ago. I was coming home from the shops when I walked into these three—" Janet paused, struggling to find the word—"youths. They took my shopping bags and pretended to carry them home for me. Then, when I got there, they threatened me and stole my money."

Sam's heart began to pound as his mother continued.

"After that, the ringleader came to my flat every week for my money."

"Did you tell the police?" Gloria asked.

"No. He threatened me. He was taking half our money every week. Every week for over six months."

"You must have been terrified."

"I was."

Sam shook with anger as he heard the emotion in his mother's voice. Rage welled up within him as he fought the urge to sprint around the corner and demand that his mother tell him who the man was.

"But more than the fear," Janet continued, "my biggest feeling was guilt."

"Guilt? From what? It wasn't your fault those thugs were threatening you."

"It was my drinking. I just couldn't stop. With that man taking half my money, once I had bought my gin, I didn't have enough to feed Sam."

"Oh, sweetheart," Gloria said with compassion.

Sam heard his mother sobbing quietly.

"So what happened in the end?" Gloria asked. Sam could barely wait for the answer as he heard his mother blow her nose on a tissue.

"He came to the door the day I took the overdose and asked for even more. He said if I didn't pay up, his friends would come and . . . rape me."

Sam's hands balled into fists.

"He was black, wasn't he?" Gloria said next.

Sam held his breath, remembering his mother's reaction the first time Jerry had visited.

"Yes," his mother said. "He's called Dwayne."

Sam didn't need to hear any more. He stepped back without making a sound and strode past the nurses' station.

By the time he reached the stairs, he was sprinting.

42

Gloria and Janet looked up from their conversation as the doctor approached.

"Stay with me," Janet pleaded, gripping Gloria's hand.

"Of course."

The doctor smiled at them both as he reached the bed. "Hi, Janet. How are you feeling today?"

"A little better, thank you," Janet said with an optimistic smile.

Gloria saw a sadness flicker in the doctor's eyes as he turned sideways and dragged the cubicle curtain around the bed. He sat down and leaned forward earnestly. "Janet, I'm afraid the situation is very serious. Your liver has basically stopped working. The liver cleans the blood and flushes the waste away. If it's not working, the waste poisons your whole system. You'll continue to bleed internally, and we won't be able to keep stopping it." The doctor paused. "We took a blood sample from you yesterday, and we've detected an infection in your blood. I'm afraid this is the beginning of the end."

Both women leaned toward each other, gripping one another tightly.

"So why do I feel better today?" Janet whispered.

"We've reduced your medication so you'll feel less drowsy, but as soon as you start experiencing pain or vomiting again, we'll need to increase the dosage."

"How long have I got?" Janet whispered again. "And what will happen in the end?"

"It's difficult to predict," the doctor replied, biting his bottom lip. "We'll make you as comfortable as possible, of course. But you need to focus on the time you have. This is the time to say what you need to say to your family. You really need to do it today."

/ / /

Sam cycled his bike crazily, switching from the road to the sidewalk whenever slowed or stopped vehicles threatened to slow him down. Pedestrians stepped fearfully aside as Sam powered by, pounding on the pedals.

When he reached the A12 roundabout, he careered straight across it without slowing, forcing a truck to slam on its brakes. A volley of angry car horns sounded, but Sam was already across the roundabout and cycling down the dual carriageway as fast as his bike would carry him.

/ / /

"How are you doing, precious?" Gloria asked gently, handing a tissue to Janet.

The woman took the tissue, dabbed her eyes, and blew her nose loudly. "I'm scared."

"I know. So am I. Do you want me to go and find Sam?"

"In a bit." Janet lifted the tissue and blew her nose once more. She then turned and fixed her eyes on Gloria. "Tell me again why God might forgive me."

Gloria shut her eyes and prayed. From nowhere, a dark, painful memory made its way into her mind. She tried to dismiss it, but as the recollection came flooding back, she realized she could offer no better example of God's forgiveness. She took a deep breath and opened her eyes to see Janet watching her desperately.

"Janet. I'm going to tell you something that I've only ever told Jerry."

Janet nodded and squeezed her hand in encouragement. Gloria took another deep breath and continued. "When I was sixteen years old, long before I met Jerry, I slept with my boyfriend. We had gotten drunk, and one thing led to another. We were just kids. We hadn't meant to. I was a Christian and had wanted to wait. Anyway, two weeks later I missed my period." Gloria paused as the painful emotions came flooding back.

"I was so scared and ashamed. My parents were really proud of me. I was doing well at school. And my dad was a lay preacher at our local church. I sang in the choir, was a leader in our youth group. I'm sure I was looked upon as the shining example of young godly behavior." Gloria grimaced and looked up at Janet, who was listening intently.

"To admit that I was pregnant would have made things so hard. Looking back, I know I should have told my parents. As a parent now myself, I can see that while they might have been angry and upset at first, they would have stood by me."

Gloria shook her head painfully. "I just couldn't face it. Couldn't face the shame that I felt. The pain and embarrassment I thought I was going to put everyone through. So my boyfriend and I put our savings together, and I went and got an abortion."

This time Gloria reached for the tissues and blew her nose. "It was only after I had the abortion that I thought about what God might think. Up to then, I had only thought about what my parents might think, my teachers and my friends. But suddenly it hit me. What I had done. I called myself a Christian. Yet I had aborted my baby."

Gloria shook her head again. "I had been okay with forgiveness before. Forgiving my brother for calling me names. Asking for forgiveness for being mean to someone at school or being rude to my mum. But as I saw it, this was something totally different. And I figured God could never forgive me for something like that."

Gloria stretched her hands in front of her and then looked up and smiled at Janet. There were tears of compassion in the older woman's eyes.

"You poor thing," Janet said gently and waited for Gloria to continue.

/ / /

Sam finally came to a halt. He climbed off his bicycle and tucked it behind a stairwell, pointed in the direction he'd be cycling to get away. He then walked toward Dwayne's ground-floor flat. Although he had never crossed swords with Dwayne, he knew exactly who he was. And where he lived.

Sam crept up to the window of the flat and peered in. Right away he saw his quarry slumped on a sofa, holding a remote control. Sam fought the urge to smash through the window and tear Dwayne apart there and then. But Dwayne wasn't alone. Sam could see at least three other young men in the room, leering at the television, which was showing some hip-hop video with seminaked girls shaking their backsides at the camera.

Sam ducked and shuffled to the other end of the window to look from another angle. There was one more youth lying on a beanbag on the floor. That made five. Sam contemplated the odds for a moment but then backed away. He would wait.

43

"So anyway," Gloria continued, "I turned my back on my faith."

She thumped her chest with her hand. "Inside, anyway. I still went to church and youth group. Still sang in the choir. But I didn't pray by myself anymore. Didn't read my Bible. And I still went with my boyfriend. Although we were much, much more careful after what happened."

Gloria sighed. "But I wasn't happy. I got obsessed with how I looked and what my friends thought of me. And my life felt pretty empty. This went on for months, and I slowly began to realize that my friends in my church youth group seemed different. Happier. Less fixated on themselves and boys and makeup and stuff. And I started missing feeling close to God like they did."

Gloria shook her head at the memory. "But I didn't know what to do. I thought after the abortion there was no way back to God. No way he'd forgive me for what I'd done. After a few months more, Christmas came around. I went to church with my family as I always did. And the minister told us all to shut our eyes and try to imagine what that stable where Jesus was born was really like. Not the romantic scene of fluffy, warm straw and friendly animals all gathered round. But the cold. Israel in winter. The filth and manure of a dirty stable. The dark. And the screams and crying of Mary in labor." Gloria smiled. "We had a minister who was always trying to shake us out of our preconceptions about things.

"But as I shut my eyes," she continued, aware Janet was listening to every word, "I didn't see that picture. Instead I saw someone holding a baby. I couldn't see who it was—thought it was maybe Mary holding baby Jesus. But when I got closer and looked at the baby, it was black. It was a black baby. And then, in my vision, I looked up at the person holding the baby. And it was Jesus. I don't know how, but I just knew it was him. He was smiling down at the baby he was holding, and then he suddenly turned to me and smiled. And he said, 'Don't worry, Gloria. He's safe. I'll look after him until you get here. Now go. And live for me.'"

Gloria looked up at Janet, who was listening wide-eyed. "Then he was gone. I was sitting in church next to my brother and parents.

"Now," Gloria said in a determined tone, "some people might say it was just my imagination. But I don't care. That moment changed my relationship with God forever. It was the first time I really understood what Jesus did for me on the cross."

Gloria reached forward and looked deep into her friend's

eyes. "Janet, that's why I know for sure that God can forgive you for trying to kill yourself. Because God forgave me, too."

///

Sam saw movement in the room. The front door abruptly opened inward, and Dwayne stood in the doorway, looking back at his friends. Rage coursed through Sam's body as he crouched behind the concrete wall twenty yards away. Dwayne put his knuckles up against his friends' clenched fists one by one as they stepped past him through the doorway. Sam's stomach jumped when he realized Dwayne was staying behind. Dwayne shouted friendly insults at the four men as they walked away; then he retreated back into his flat and shut the door.

Sam waited until the others were out of sight before emerging from his hiding place. He walked slowly toward Dwayne's door, stretching his wrists and fingers as he went. He reached up and rapped quietly on the door.

"What you forget, you losers?" Dwayne's mocking voice said from within. A moment later the door opened.

Sam slammed into the man, sending him flying back into his flat. Sam calmly stepped inside and shut the door behind him.

///

"I want what you've got," Janet said with quiet determination. "I want to follow God."

Gloria's heart thumped, and she squeezed Janet's hand. But before she could say anything, Janet spoke again, desperation clear in her voice.

"But I can't do anything for God! I can't live for him as he asked you to do. I've just been told I'm going to die any day. So why would he have me?"

"It's not about what we can do for him!" Gloria said. "Not at all. It's about us. He just wants us. Wants to have a relationship with us."

Janet looked confused, and Gloria prayed for inspiration. Immediately a Scripture came to mind.

"Do you remember the story of when Jesus was on the cross?"

"I think so," Janet answered tentatively.

"Well, do you recall there were two criminals crucified beside him?"

"Yeah," Janet replied. "They shouted insults at him."

"Only one of them did! The other recognized Jesus for who he truly was. And he said to Jesus, as they were both hanging there, 'Please remember me when you enter your kingdom.' Now that guy was a criminal. Probably a murderer and a thief. That's why they were crucifying him. So in the world's eyes, he didn't deserve to go to heaven. But do you remember what Jesus said to him?"

Janet shook her head, and Gloria smiled. "Jesus said, 'Today you will be with me in paradise!'"

Janet said nothing as she reflected on Gloria's words.

"So you see, Janet. It's not about being good or living a good life. It's about believing that God is God, that *he's* good and *he loves us*, and that we need his forgiveness. That's it!"

"That's it?" Janet said skeptically.

"That's it."

"I want that," Janet said.

Gloria reached forward and hugged Janet. The two women swayed gently from side to side, clinging to one another. Eventually they let go but still gripped hands.

"Let's pray," Gloria said. "Listen to what I say, and if you feel happy with it and able to say it, then repeat it. Or use your own words if you want."

Janet nodded her agreement and scrunched up her eyes in prayer like a child. Gloria felt utter joy.

"Thank you, Lord," Gloria began.

/ / /

"Who are you?" Dwayne growled, pushing off the sofa where he had tumbled and jumping back to his feet.

Sam stood in front of the door. Every sinew in his body screamed to jump on Dwayne and kill him, but he was determined that Dwayne should know first why he was about to die.

"A year ago you were taking cash from a woman in Soweto Rise. That was my mum."

Shock flickered across Dwayne's face before he thrust his hands in his pockets and snickered nervously. "Your mum, eh? She kept you quiet."

The two boys glared at one another.

"So how is Mum?" Dwayne smirked. "I heard she tried to kill herself."

"She's alive."

"Oh," Dwayne said. A nasty grin formed on his face. "Well, tell her she owes me a lot of money now. And two of my boys wanna give her somethin' else, too."

That was it. Sam stepped forward and raised his fists.

Immediately Dwayne whipped his own fist from his pocket. He held a five-inch blade up before him. "You're screwed now."

Sam stopped and studied the knife as Dwayne swished it menacingly in front of him. But it changed nothing for Sam. He looked up without fear. "You're gonna die," Sam said calmly and stepped forward again.

"Lord, thank you that you have been with me from the moment I was born," Gloria said.

Without hesitation Janet repeated Gloria's words.

The younger woman continued. "Thank you for loving me even when I haven't acknowledged you."

Again Janet repeated the words.

"Lord, I recognize that I have done wrong."

As Janet repeated it, Gloria prayed for God to inspire her with the words to speak. But there was no need. Janet didn't wait for Gloria to speak again. Instead words burst out of her mouth.

"Lord, I'm sorry I tried to kill myself. I'm sorry about my drinking. I'm sorry for how I've failed to look after Sam. I'm sorry for . . ."

Sam crouched and then exploded upward and forward with his fist just as Dwayne lifted his knife and plunged it toward his attacker. The two blows landed simultaneously. The power of Sam's punch sent Dwayne hurtling backward onto the sofa, and Sam jumped on him, raining down punches. Dwayne continued slashing and kicking desperately, but Sam's attack was overwhelming. As if through a haze, Sam felt Dwayne gather himself for one last upward lunge with the knife.

/ / /

"Thank you, Lord, that you've forgiven me by your Son dying on the cross. Thank you that . . ."

Gloria listened in silence, a golf-ball-sized lump lodged in her throat. It was the most beautiful, heartfelt prayer she had ever heard. And she thanked God for the privilege of just being able to hear it.

Janet continued freely. "Thank you, Lord, that I can feel you right now as I pray. And thank you that I'm soon going to be with you in paradise."

There was a change of tone in Janet's voice as thanks turned to petition. "But, Lord, I pray for Sam. Please help him. Please protect him. Please let him feel you too. . . ."

44

Sam was vaguely aware that Dwayne had stopped lunging. But Sam didn't stop punching. The voice chanting in his head drove him on and on.

"Kill him. Kill him. Kill him."

Sam felt cold to the core. Somewhere deep in his being, he knew he should stop. He knew in another thirty seconds Dwayne would be dead. He was scared, but the rage and the voice had overtaken him, controlling his every punch. It was the same rage he felt in the boxing ring. But now there was no referee—nor Jerry—to stop it. And he was out of control. The voice continued to beat out its frenzied rhythm as Sam's fists pounded down on Dwayne's face.

"Kill him. Kill him. Kill him."

"Help me," Sam called out from deep within.

Suddenly he heard a voice behind him. "Stop, my son. Stop."

Sam froze. Immediately he had control of his arms again, and he lifted them away from Dwayne. Sam wheeled around to see who had spoken.

There was no one there. Sam jumped up and searched through the flat. It was empty. As Sam ran back into the living room he noticed that he no longer felt cold. The rage and the chant were also gone.

Sam's eyes fell on Dwayne. The boy's face was a mangled mess of blood and broken teeth. The bridge of his nose was squashed flat to his face, and his lips were swelling grotesquely.

"Oh no. Oh no." Sam started panicking. "What've I done?" He leaned down and put his ear next to Dwayne's mouth. All Sam could hear was his own heart beating through his chest. But then he heard a shallow breath escape the boy's mouth. He turned Dwayne onto his side, propping a cushion from the sofa under his head. Sam's eyes fell upon the knife lying next to Dwayne's body. The blade was smeared with blood. Sam flicked it away and leaned close again to listen to Dwayne's breathing. To Sam's relief, it was now stronger and more even. He climbed to his feet and rushed to the telephone. He punched 999 into the keypad, leaving a smear of blood across the pale-cream telephone.

"Ambulance," he barked as soon as someone answered. "Someone's been beaten up. Badly. He needs help right now."

The operator asked his location.

"Mandela complex. Erm. Biko Avenue. Hold on." Sam slammed the receiver down on the sideboard and ran to the door. Flinging it open, he looked at the front of the door and then ran back to the telephone. "Thirty-six." He paused, listening, running his fingers through his hair in agitation. "Me?" he answered hesitantly to another question from the operator. "I'm no one."

/ / /

"How do you feel?" Gloria asked when Janet finally stopped praying.

"Peaceful," Janet replied. "Like everything's going to be all right."

"Praise God." Gloria smiled, amazed at how God had led and blessed their conversation.

"Thank you so much." Janet smiled back at her and then yawned. "I'm sorry. I think I need to sleep."

"You sleep, sweetheart," Gloria said, leaning forward and kissing Janet on the forehead. "I'm going to try and find Sam. Is there anyone else you want me to contact?"

Janet had already shut her eyes but opened them again in response to the question. "No," she said, shaking her head. "Just Sam. But can you send him this evening? I want some time to think."

/ / /

Sam wiped away the persistent leak of blood trailing from Dwayne's mouth. The youth hadn't recovered consciousness, but at least he was breathing.

Finally Sam heard a siren in the distance. He stood and looked down at Dwayne. The siren got louder, and Sam reluctantly stepped away. He went to the front door and jammed it open with a cushion. He looked up and saw the ambulance pull into the end of the road, blue lights flashing. He ran to his bicycle. By the time the ambulance pulled up outside the flat, Sam was gone.

45

The kettle boiled, and Gloria poured water into three mugs. Swirling the tea bags around, she glanced up at the clock. Half past six. Jerry and Sam should be home any moment. She prayed again about what she would say.

A minute later Gloria heard the familiar sound of Jerry's key in the lock. She wandered into the hallway to see her husband push through the door. Gloria walked forward and gave him a kiss before looking anxiously behind him. "No Sam?"

Jerry shook his head and frowned as he shut the door. "He didn't come to training this afternoon. First time he's ever missed a session. He's not here?"

"I haven't seen him either," Gloria replied, panic rising within.

Jerry noticed her agitation and his brow furrowed. "What's going on?"

"We've got to find him," Gloria said urgently. "He has to see his mother."

"Calm down," Jerry said gently, taking Gloria by the arms. "We'll find him. But tell me what's going on first."

/ / /

"Wow," Jerry concluded when Gloria finally finished recounting her morning with Janet. "That's fantastic. And terrible. What are we going to say to Sam?"

"We've got to tell him the truth. And quickly."

Jerry frowned. "Have you checked his room?"

"No. But I would've heard him."

Jerry pushed his chair back and walked to the kitchen door. Just as he did so, he heard a floorboard creak on the stairs. He stepped out of the kitchen to see Sam trying to open the front door as quietly as he could.

"Sam," Jerry called.

The boy froze.

"Where are you going?"

"Out," Sam replied without turning. "Sorry about this afternoon. Something came up."

"Don't worry about that. Can you come through to the kitchen? We've got something we need to tell you."

Sam didn't move.

Jerry stepped forward, both concerned and suspicious. "What's going on?" He put his hand on Sam's shoulder to turn him around.

Sam flinched and yelped in pain, lifting his hand to his chest just inside his shoulder.

"Oh no!" Jerry said when he saw Sam's severely bruised hand. He forced the boy to turn and kicked the front door closed. "What happened?"

"Nothing," Sam replied, tucking his hand behind him.

"Look at your hand!" Jerry exclaimed, pulling Sam's arm to reveal the damage. "What have you been up to?"

Sam was silent as they both looked down at his bloodied left hand.

"And what's wrong with your shoulder?" Jerry demanded.

Sam glanced up at Gloria, who had just appeared behind Jerry. "I've got a bit of a cut."

"Come through here. Sit down," Jerry ordered, leading Sam into the kitchen. He pulled the open coat from Sam's shoulders and dropped it on the floor. "Take your shirt off."

Sam gingerly removed his shirt. A square of poorly secured cotton dressing came away from his pale torso, revealing an ugly gash that had penetrated both the skin and underlying muscle.

"Whoa! What is that?" Jerry said, rubbing his head.

Sam remained silent.

"That's serious, Sam. We need to get you to the hospital."

Sam shook his head. "I'm not going to any hospital."

"Sam," Jerry said angrily. "That needs stitches. Internal ones too. That's gone right through your muscle."

"I'm *not* going to hospital," Sam repeated.

Jerry stood back and glared at the boy, struggling to

contain his anger. For a shocking moment he wondered if he was going to hit Sam.

"That's a knife! That's a knife wound. What are you doing?" Jerry looked down at Sam's hands and pointed at the bloodied, swollen knuckles. "You idiot! You've got a British championship fight in three weeks."

"Jerry," Gloria barked at her husband, sounding angry herself now. "That is not what's important here. Now pull yourself together."

Jerry backed away, muttering under his breath as he rubbed his scalp.

Gloria squatted next to Sam so her eyes were level with his. "Have you got any other injuries?" she asked gently.

Sam slowly lifted his left arm to reveal a long cut from his armpit to the bottom of his rib cage. It was a nasty gash, longer than Gloria's hand but not as deep as the other one. Jerry, still rubbing his scalp and muttering noisily, watched from the other side of the kitchen as Gloria turned her attention to the boy's hands.

"Can you move all your fingers?"

Sam nodded and wiggled his fingers to demonstrate.

Gloria went to the freezer and removed two bags of frozen vegetables, tying them to Sam's hands with tea towels. "Who was this, Sam?" she asked.

Sam shrugged.

"Why don't you want to go to the hospital? Is the other boy dead?"

The question hung in the air. Jerry stopped scratching his head and held his breath, awaiting an answer that might change everything. Sam shook his head, and Jerry breathed again.

"Could Mario stitch this?" Gloria asked, turning to her husband.

Jerry hurried over to the telephone on the wall and dialed a number, glaring back at Sam as he held the receiver to his ear. "Mario? It's me, Jerry. Can you come over to my house? . . . Right now. Bring your medical kit. All of it. . . . Yeah. Thanks. See you soon."

/ / /

Ten minutes later there was a knock on the door. Gloria sat with Sam as Jerry answered it. He returned after a few seconds with Mario behind him. The Italian smiled at Gloria before his eyes settled on Sam and the smile fell from his face.

"Idiota, cosa ti sei fatto?" Mario clipped Sam gently around the crown of his head. He put his bag down on the table and undid the knots attaching the bags of frozen vegetables. He winced when he saw Sam's hands and unleashed another volley of Italian. He began prodding the knuckles and hands, flexing the fingers as he did so.

"Lucky boy," Mario concluded when he had finished. Next he turned his attention to the other wounds. He applied a row of butterfly bandages to the cut underneath Sam's armpit and then addressed the wound on Sam's chest. He studied it for a minute and looked up at Jerry. "This should be done in a hospital. I'm used to doing faces."

"I'm not going to the hospital," Sam said forcefully. Mario looked at him and then at Jerry, who shrugged.

"I don't know where to put anesthetic for this. I can stitch, but . . ." He paused and stared hard at Sam. "It's gonna hurt."

Gloria hurried toward the door. "I'm going to put the kids to bed."

Behind her she heard Jerry say, "Your choice, Sam. I think you should go to the hospital."

Sam didn't hesitate. "Just stitch it."

/ / /

"Thanks, Mario," Jerry said as he showed his friend to the door. "Do you think he'll heal in time?"

Mario considered the question for a moment. "Chest? Skin? Yes. Muscle—not sure. Might be down on power. Hands? Yes. As long as he does no punching before then. Sparring is out."

Jerry nodded and put his hand on Mario's shoulder.

"What is he doing?" the Italian asked quietly.

"I don't know, Mario."

Mario grimaced. "That boy's never been straight in the head. It's what makes him so good at fighting. But it might be what gets him killed too."

Jerry patted Mario again on the shoulder. "Thanks."

Mario nodded and stepped out.

Jerry shut the door and turned slowly, taking a deep breath. Gloria was there, standing on the stairs.

"Kids down?" Jerry asked.

Gloria nodded and tiptoed down the remaining steps. "We have to tell him," she whispered.

He took her hand, giving it a squeeze. "God, be with us. Please."

They both shut their eyes for a moment in prayer and then went into the kitchen, where Sam was carefully pulling on his shirt.

"Sam," Jerry said, sitting down opposite him, "I'm afraid we've got some bad news."

PART
FOUR

46

Jerry woke in a panic, his legs tangled in the bedclothes.

"Jerry, it's okay," he heard Gloria say, but he continued to thrash around the bed for a few more seconds.

"It's okay, sweetheart."

Jerry took several deep breaths as he got his bearings and tried to control the fear that engulfed him.

Gloria found the bedside lamp switch, and the room was thrown into light. Both shielded their eyes from the sudden glare.

"I'll get you some water," Gloria said, swinging her feet out of bed and padding to the door.

Jerry looked down at his hand. It was clamped tightly around a fistful of bedsheet. It had been that same dream again. Camera bulbs flashing. The woman in the red dress. And Bert smoking cigars with . . . Ron Donovan!

Ron Donovan had never been in the dream before. Or had he? Jerry grimaced. Bert had always been sitting next to someone vaguely familiar. Jerry had never been able to place him before. That's who it was. Ron flippin' Donovan.

The rest of it had been the same. Two boxers, deep into the fight. One beating the other. And Jerry standing just below the ring with towel in hand, poised and able to save his fighter. But as always, he just couldn't throw it.

Gloria came back into the room, carrying a glass of water, which Jerry gratefully drank. "What's the time?" he asked.

"Five thirty," Gloria replied wearily, climbing into bed. "Try and get some more sleep. A long day ahead." She reached across and switched the light off before settling down with her back to him.

"Yeah. Okay," Jerry said. He shut his eyes and tried to settle. But the images flashed back. Ron Donovan. Why did it have to be him? Tonight Bert and Ron probably would be sitting together at ringside as promoters tended to do. There *would* be cameras and flashbulbs. The nagging thought persisted, and he could no longer casually dismiss it. What if it were more than a dream? What if it were some kind of weird premonition?

Jerry's heart quickened, and he felt his body flush with sweat. He pushed off the duvet, eliciting a moan of protest from Gloria.

"Sorry. I'm awake now. I'll go downstairs."

Jerry made himself a cup of tea and sat down on the sofa, reflecting on the absurdity of his situation. The dream might not matter anyway. At lunchtime today he was supposed to be taking Sam to a London hotel for the weigh-in before going on to Wembley Stadium to fight for the British title. Yet he had no idea whether the boy would even turn up, let alone whether he'd be fit and healed. What could be Jerry's greatest professional triumph could just as likely turn out to be the most humiliating episode of his life.

Jerry cursed his luck and sank deeper into the sofa.

/ / /

Sam watched his breath cloud above him in the cold dawn air as the first shaft of sunlight shone through the dirty window of the straw shed. All was quiet except for the ever-present traffic noise of the London–Southend dual carriageway that droned across the flat countryside. Sam lay still, enjoying the warmth of the sleeping bag and trying to ignore his bursting bladder. He looked up at the cobwebbed elm crossbeams and trusses that he had climbed through as a child, when the shed had been full of straw bales.

Sam hadn't been back to Copse Farm in years—not since being whacked on the head by the fat farm manager. But as Jerry drove him slowly past the farm a fortnight earlier to his mother's funeral in the village church, Sam had known that afterward this was the only place he wanted to be.

"Shall I cancel the fight?" Jerry had asked when Sam told him after the funeral that he was disappearing for a fortnight.

"No," Sam had replied. "I'll be at your place the morning of the fight."

Sam had packed a bag and left. Since then he had been here, peaceful and undisturbed. And he had been thinking.

Thinking about his parents. His life. And that voice he had
heard.

/ / /

Jerry sat on the sofa, stewing over the disastrous month of
preparation since they'd signed the fight contract. One month
for a fight of this magnitude would have been tight anyway,
even if all had gone perfectly. But it hadn't. Far from it.

The first week had been good. Great, in fact. Sam had
been brutal in training, driven on, Jerry suspected, by his
mother's deteriorating health. But then Sam had gotten in
whatever scrape it was that had resulted in smashed-up hands
and a nasty stab wound. Mario had dealt with the injuries as
best he could, but a few days later Janet had died peacefully
with Sam beside her, and the next week was taken up with
arrangements for the funeral. The service had taken forever
to organize, while Jerry couldn't help thinking of the wasted
tactical training days ticking by. Still, he'd comforted himself
that once it was over, he would have Sam's full and angry
attention. Even during the funeral service Jerry had found
himself plotting the accelerated tactical training he would
do with Sam. But then Sam had dropped his bombshell and
disappeared.

Bert and Jerry had talked a dozen times about whether
they should cancel the fight and whether the unusual circumstances would excuse them from the penalty clause. But they
hadn't. The contract they had signed was horribly perfect. All
they could do was hope against hope that Sam would turn
up. Fit. And angry.

/ / /

The doorbell rang, and Jerry's stomach leaped. It was now late morning, and he had been pacing the house in such agitation that Gloria had taken the children out to the park to get away from him. Not for the first time in the last few weeks.

Jerry ran into the hallway and opened the door. Sam stood on the front step.

"How are you doing?" Jerry asked as tenderly as he could, despite the surge of adrenaline he felt.

"I'm okay."

"How are your hands?"

"They're fine," Sam answered, holding them up for Jerry to see. Jerry nodded with relief as he saw that the grazing and bruising had healed.

"Are you hungry? Do you want some breakfast?"

Sam shook his head. "I could do with a shower, though."

"Go for it," Jerry said, stepping aside for Sam to enter. "We need to leave in twenty minutes for the weigh-in. I've gathered your kit, so you just need to get into a club track-suit. It's on your bed."

Sam nodded and climbed the stairs. Jerry watched him go and then ran into the kitchen and shut the door. Grabbing the telephone, he dialed Bert's number. The call was answered immediately.

"Hi. It's me. He just turned up. . . . Yeah. . . . Don't know yet. He looks okay, apart from being filthy. He's having a shower, and then we'll be over. . . . Yeah. See you soon."

47

Sam stepped onto the scale. Jerry held his breath. The operator pushed a few weights across the rack until the indicator balanced in midair.

The announcer looked over the operator's shoulder at the scale. "One hundred fifty-six and a half pounds."

Jerry breathed again but couldn't help hearing the murmur of surprise among those gathered. Sam's opponent had weighed in as a boxer always should—a couple of ounces under the limit. But Sam was almost four pounds under the middleweight limit he normally had to diet hard to make. Jerry wondered what the boy had eaten over the last fortnight.

Bert moved alongside.

"Not good," Jerry whispered to his boss. "He looks thin."

"At least he's not over the weight. It means he can fight," Bert replied.

The conversation was halted by the announcer speaking again into his microphone. "The boxers and their trainers will now take a few questions."

Jerry stepped forward to join Sam on the stage. A handful of journalists were perched among the dozens of empty seats. The weigh-in for the heavyweight title bout had taken place the day before, and the huge number of chairs showed the interest in that fight. But for the undercard fights, the weigh-in and press conference took place on the same day, and there were only a few hard-core boxing journalists present.

The first few questions were directed at the champion, Darren Spencer. He spewed the normal stuff about how he was going to put Sam in his place, how his experience would tell, and how Sam had never met anyone in his class before.

Sam and Jerry listened silently. Sam had never had a press conference like this before. Indeed, it had been years since Jerry had faced a similar situation, and he was grateful there were only a few journalists present.

Finally the announcer welcomed questions for Sam. A balding journalist at the back raised his hand.

"Go ahead," the announcer instructed.

"Sam, is it true that your mother died recently?"

Jerry winced at the question. He had hoped and assumed no one knew. He looked sideways at Sam. To Jerry's concern, there was no anger in Sam's eyes.

"Yeah," Sam said quietly into the microphone in front of him.

"Has that affected you mentally ahead of this fight?" the journalist continued.

Sam wore a curious soft expression as he pondered the question. It filled Jerry with fear, and he jumped in, not trusting Sam's response. "Sam is ready. He'll be fine," Jerry said sharply.

The journalist scowled, aware he had been denied what, for a moment, looked like it might have been an interesting answer.

"How's training been going then?" he persisted.

"Good," Jerry lied, determined to field all the questions now.

"How come Sam's underweight?" another journalist asked, cutting in from the side of the room.

Jerry paused for a moment as he tried to think up a story. He was glad Gloria wasn't there to hear him. "Sam's never struggled with punching power. We've been working on his speed even more. He's so light he's moving like a dream. Mr. Spencer won't be able to lay a glove on him."

It was lame, and Jerry knew it. But it was the best he could do under the circumstances.

"The scar on Sam's chest?" another journalist asked. "It looks fairly fresh."

"Just a small accident," Jerry lied again. "Nothing to worry about."

"What did he do?"

"Nothing. Just a mishap at the gym." It felt a bigger lie than the first two.

There was silence again, and the announcer finally spoke up. "Okay. Thank you, gentlemen."

/ / /

"You've been gone for hours. I was worried sick!"

"Sam came back. We went to the weigh-in," Jerry said without apology.

"You couldn't just leave me a note to say he had come back safely? I didn't know what had happened." Gloria shook her head as Jerry looked away. "Where is he?"

"At Bert's house, resting. I just came home to get something. I've got to go back in a minute."

"How is he?" Gloria asked, her tone softening for the first time since Jerry had returned.

"He's going to be all right. His hands are healed."

Gloria looked at her husband in disbelief. "Argh! I don't care about his *hands*. I wanna know how *he's* doing. Inside! How he is, considering his *mum's just died*! Have you thought about that, Jerry?" Gloria said, raw frustration clear in her tone. "Have you thought about anything, apart from yourself and this stupid fight?"

Jerry said nothing. He knew his wife was right. He had been expecting this outburst for days. He had just hoped it would come one day later.

"I'm scared," Gloria said, emotion rising in her voice. "I'm scared that you've lost it altogether. Lost sight of what's important. You've hardly even talked to me or the kids for weeks. You're grumpy. You shout at the children when they're just being kids. All you can think of is Sam's fight. But you're not even thinking about *him*, or what he really needs. You're not even considering whether a fight might actually be the last thing in the world he needs. Maybe what *he* actually wants and needs is just a friend."

Jerry remained silent, watching as his wife poured out her frustrations.

"What about your faith, Jerry? Have you thought about where God is in all this? You're not reading your Bible. Not praying. You sit in church like a zombie. Everything about you is wrong at the moment. You're eating badly, snacking on rubbish. You're staying up late, watching trash on TV. You're not looking after yourself at all! I want . . . my . . . husband . . . back."

She turned and sat down dejectedly.

"I'm sorry, sweetheart. I'm sorry. I know I've been behaving badly." He sighed heavily before continuing. "And I know I'm not in a good place with God. I'll sort it out—I promise. I just need to get this fight out of the way. It's important."

"Why is it important?" Gloria demanded as she looked up at her husband. "Who for? Sam? Or you?"

"Please, sweetheart," Jerry pleaded, irritation rising in his voice. "I promise after tonight I'll get myself sorted. I'll go and see Pastor Mike. I'll take next week off and make it up to you and the kids. I just need to get tonight out of the way."

"I've tried," Gloria said, shaking her head. "I've tried and tried not to say anything until after tonight. But I just can't. You taking off like that today was the final straw."

"Just one more day. Please."

"Tomorrow might be too late."

"What's that supposed to mean?" Jerry snapped. "Are you saying you're going to leave me or something?"

Gloria stared at him, and then her face softened. "Of course not. I've just been praying and praying and praying. And . . . I don't know how. But I've just got this feeling God wants this dealt with tonight."

Jerry recoiled, assaulted by the words. He stood up and looked down at his wife. He turned, picked up a bag, and opened the front door.

"I've gotta go. I'll be late."

He slammed the door behind him, leaving Gloria alone.

/ / /

There was silence in the car. Jerry sat in the backseat, looking forlornly forward as Bert glided the vehicle through the traffic toward Wembley Stadium.

Jerry felt wretched. His Christian lifestyle had gone to pot. Impatience. Pride. Telling untruths at the press conference in front of all four men who sat in the car now. What was he doing?

Jerry looked across at Mario, who was sleeping, and then at Robbie. Robbie had been miserable for weeks, but Jerry hadn't even asked him what was up. He had just snapped at him constantly. Jerry glanced diagonally at Bert. He felt bad as he recalled the thoughts he had been entertaining about his boss, contemplating abandoning him as Sam's career progressed. But Bert had never abandoned Jerry—not even after the Walthamstow incident.

And Sam. Jerry stared through the headrest at the back of Sam's head. Where did he start? Gloria was right, for sure. He had lost sight of the person.

Just one more night, he reasoned to himself. After tonight he would sort out all these broken relationships.

But immediately Jerry heard his wife's words echoing in his ears. *"Tomorrow might be too late."*

48

"Are you ready to be left alone?" Jerry asked. "Do your thing?"

Sam shook his head. "No. I'd like you to stay."

Jerry nodded and smiled unconvincingly. "No problem." The trainer glanced up at Mario, who shifted uncomfortably. *Not good. Sam's changing the routine.* Jerry rubbed his scalp.

Everything had gone okay up to now. They had arrived in good time and had explored the stadium, looking out from the ring upon the thousands of empty seats. They had been allocated a changing room, where Sam had listened carefully as Jerry spent an hour running through a series of sparring scenarios. Jerry mimicked Darren Spencer's style, which he had studied endlessly on video, and Sam had thrown the punches Jerry plotted. But so far Jerry hadn't seen the rage they needed.

Mario grunted and tapped Robbie's shoulder. "Come on, Robbie. Let's have a look at the other fight."

The moment Robbie and Mario had left the room, Sam turned to Jerry.

"What's up?" Jerry said, alarmed at the boy's sudden agitation.

"I think God spoke to me."

Oh no, Jerry thought silently. *Here we go.*

"What do you mean?" he asked, trying to sound interested. "When?"

"You know the day I got this?" Sam said, reaching up to touch the scar on his chest. "It was then."

Jerry was quiet. A sinking feeling gripped his stomach. Gloria was right. God wasn't going to wait until tomorrow.

"Tell me what happened," the trainer said wearily, pulling up a plastic chair.

The moment Jerry was seated, Sam stood and spoke in a way Jerry had never seen before. All Sam's reserve was gone, replaced by an extraordinary urgency to communicate. Jerry sat back and listened, stunned as Sam recalled his story.

". . . and my mum said Dwayne. Well, I knew exactly who Dwayne was. So I cycled to his flat and confronted him."

"He pulled a knife, I take it."

Sam nodded. "But I didn't care if I got hurt. I was just gonna make sure I killed him."

Jerry took a nervous breath. "Did you? Kill him?"

Sam shook his head. "No. I was going to. I had him down here. . . ." The young man simulated swinging his fists at a body below him. "And I was smashing him. Bang. Bang.

Bang. I was totally out of control. I always get it when I fight—this kind of rage. But this time it was worse. It was like I was possessed. I was just smashing him and smashing him. You know."

Jerry nodded miserably. That was the rage they needed tonight! He didn't want to hear Sam renouncing it. On the other hand, hearing Sam describe himself as feeling "possessed" shook Jerry to the core. A scramble of emotions crowded Jerry's mind as Sam continued.

"And then suddenly this rage had a voice. It was in my head. And it was chanting, 'Kill him. Kill him. Kill him.' And I couldn't resist it. I couldn't stop. The rage and the voice were, like, controlling me."

"And you think that was God's voice?" Jerry asked dubiously.

Sam shook his head. "No. I don't. That was the next voice I heard."

Jerry's heart began to pound as it always did when he heard about encounters with God. For a moment the impending fight was forgotten.

"Suddenly," Sam continued, "I hear this deep, beautiful voice directly behind me in the flat."

"What did it say?"

"It just said, 'Stop, my son. Stop.'"

Sam paused as he watched Jerry absorb the words. "I did stop," he continued. "I was freaked out. I jumped up and searched the whole flat. But no one was there. I didn't hear it again. But then I realized that the other voice in my head was gone too. Completely. And it hasn't been back."

"That's great," Jerry said, almost in a whisper.

"Jerry, I don't feel the anger I used to feel. The anger I used to live with. It's gone." Sam lifted his open palms and then did something Jerry had rarely seen. He smiled.

"I don't need to fight anymore. I don't want to."

Jerry took a deep breath and fought the urge to scream in frustration.

"That's a bit of a problem," he said instead, looking up at Sam. "Considering you've got a fight in about—" he looked down at his watch—"fifteen minutes."

Sam breathed out and grimaced. "I know."

They both fell silent, unsure of what to say.

/ / /

Gloria finally got the children to sleep and came down the stairs. She paused at the bottom. Her first thought was to go into the kitchen and fix herself some dinner. But she wasn't hungry. Her stomach flitted with butterflies, and she wandered instead into the living room.

Then, without warning, she burst into tears. Gloria allowed her knees to buckle, and she sank to the floor, crying into the carpet. Her heart hurt so much it felt like it was going to explode. But as she cried, she realized her tears were not for herself. They were for the two men in her life. Jerry. And Sam. Two men she loved so much. And she knew that they needed her tonight. She wiped her eyes and began to pray.

49

"So, why did *you* start believing in God? Did you hear his voice too?"

Jerry shook his head. "Not like that."

"Tell me," Sam said with pleading eyes.

Jerry took a deep breath and looked at his watch again. Almost nine o'clock. His mind cried out at the timing of this conversation. A year earlier he knew he would have been jumping for joy at sharing his story with a boxer. But not now. Not at this moment. Sam needed to focus, not hear about God. He needed to be in this room. On his own. Getting mad, as he always did. Why did God have to get in the way?

"Look, Sam. Why don't we go out for some food, straight after this fight? And I'll talk to you all night if you want me to! But let's just get this fight out of the way first. You need to focus."

"I don't care about the fight," Sam said vehemently. "I wanna hear about you. Right from the beginning."

Jerry cursed under his breath. "Okay. I had a crappy upbringing. My mum was a good woman. But my dad was a drunk."

"Where did you live?" Sam interrupted. "Around here?"

Jerry frowned. It was clear Sam wanted the long version. He finally conceded. He took a deep breath and began.

"Yeah. East Ham. I was born in Jamaica, but my mum and dad came across here for work when I was four years old. I don't think they wanted to come, but my father got into some kind of trouble back home, and they came here in a hurry. Dad took a job on the railways. But after a few years he got into a fight over something and they sacked him. After that he picked up a bit of casual work from time to time, but when he didn't have any, he started going to the pub instead."

Jerry frowned again. He hadn't trawled up these memories in a long time.

"He started drinking a lot. And when he got drunk, he used to hit me. And he used to hit my mum. We were always terrified when he got back from the pub 'cause he used to stumble into our rooms, turn on the lights, and start arguments over nothing. It was terrible. He never hurt me too badly, but he would beat my mum to a pulp. My dad was huge, and my mum was tiny. But that didn't stop him."

Jerry looked at his watch again. Sam nodded for him to continue.

"I grew up very angry. I hated him. So I started to train myself to fight. I'd stand in front of the mirror at home, throwing punches as fast as I could. All so that one day I could defend my mum and he could feel what it was like to be beaten up for once.

"When I was about twelve, I began getting into fights at school with bigger kids and pretending they were him. But I'd normally lose. I didn't know what I was doing, and I gave up hope I could ever defend my mum. But then one day I saw on a TV somewhere a recording of Muhammad Ali. He was Cassius Clay then. It was the fight where he beat Sonny Liston to become heavyweight champion. Liston was a big, mean old lump who looked just like my dad. He was much bigger than Ali, who was only a youngster at the time. But Ali thrashed him. He danced around, and Liston couldn't land a punch. And I remember deciding, there and then, that I was going to be a boxer.

"So I joined this boxing club run by a church mission just around the corner from where I lived. I didn't listen to any of the God stuff they went on about, but I did learn to box. And I was good. I got to the stage when I was about fifteen when I reckoned I could take my dad out. His drinking had gotten really bad by then, and once he almost killed my mum.

"So I decided the time had come. I sat up one night and waited for him to come back from the pub drunk." Jerry paused and looked up at Sam.

The boy was transfixed. "So what happened when he got home?"

Jerry breathed out deeply. "He never got home. He was

so drunk he stumbled in front of a car on his way back and was killed."

Sam's eyes widened. "Did you feel like justice had been done?"

"No," Jerry said with a sad smile. "I felt like I had been cheated of the chance to kill him myself."

Sam's next question was disturbed by a knock on the door. Robbie poked his head in. "We've just had a ten-minute warning," he said, looking nervously at Sam.

"Okay. Thanks, Robbie," Jerry said. "Just give us a bit longer."

Robbie retreated, and Jerry got up and retrieved Sam's boxing gloves. He stood in front of Sam and began working them onto his hands. "Right. That's it," Jerry said firmly. "We can talk about the rest after. We need to focus on the fight now."

"I know what I have to do," Sam said impatiently. "Keep going forward. Press him. Mind his overhand right. Target the ribs. Draw his hands down and then look for the big opening." Sam reeled off the instructions like a list. "Keep my hands up. Keep the tempo high. Watch for when he drops his right hand when he's tired. So. What happened after your dad died?"

Jerry grimaced in frustration but couldn't dispute the fact that Sam had remembered every instruction. Reluctantly he continued.

"I left school and threw my life into boxing. I turned professional at sixteen and won every fight I fought. I was very skillful and moved well. But I was also mean as heck.

Every time I fought, I just imagined it was my dad opposite. I visualized him coming at me and my mum. And then I'd hammer him. I was a middleweight like you. Most of the time."

"Were you ever British champion?" Sam asked, waving through the wall in the direction of the arena.

"Should have been." Jerry smiled ruefully. "But I couldn't get a shot at the title. It was all pretty political in those days. And racist. All the boxing promoters were white, and there were a lot of white middleweights around then. I was just some poor Jamaican-born black kid from the East End of London."

"What did you do?"

"Well, I should have been patient. I would have got my shot in the end. But I was angry and bitter. *Boxing News* offered me a small interview, and I ran my mouth off, calling all the promoters racist. I didn't get a sniff after that."

"So what happened then?"

"I needed money to live, so I started fighting bare-knuckle for cash. It was illegal, so the fights were held in secret. Mainly in nightclubs in the West End. It was weird. The nights were organized by gangsters, but we used to get politicians and bankers and loads of posh people there too. That's where I met Mario. He was doing the same, only a few weights lower."

"Was it good?"

Jerry shook his head. "I did it for a while and got a good reputation and quite a following. Made enough money not to have to work. But then the main gangster who organized it all got jailed, one of the newspapers ran a story on bare-knuckle boxing, and it stopped overnight. By then I had been off the legal fight scene for years and couldn't get back in. The boxing promoters hated the bare-knuckle boys."

Jerry finished lacing Sam's second glove and glanced up at the young man, who was listening intently.

"Then what?"

"I started drinking. Getting into bar brawls and stupid things like that. I was turning into my dad. It was all going downhill fast until one day I ran into an old boxer I had known from years before. He bought me a drink, and when I told him my woes, he told me I should go to America. He said black boxers weren't discriminated against there. Strange, really. Racism was much worse there, what with the civil-rights battles and stuff. But the whites seemed to tolerate blacks boxing. Something to do with letting us smash each other up, I guess," Jerry said wryly.

"So anyway, I told my mum about this conversation. And the next thing I know she's sold nearly everything she's got and bought me a plane ticket to New York. Said she had been praying about it. And God told her I should go to America."

Jerry smiled at the memory. "I didn't believe in God then. But I went anyway. I only got through immigration because I had the address of a distant cousin of my mum's who lived in the Bronx. They gave me a two-week tourist visa, and I was in. Of course I stayed on after the two weeks were up. I spent my last money on a one-way Greyhound bus to Chicago and finally found Vince Carlotti's Lincoln Gym."

Sam looked confused. "Sorry—Vince Car . . . ?"

"Carlotti. He was the top trainer at the time," Jerry explained, smiling at the memory of arriving at the gym so many years earlier. "They almost told me to get lost. Boxers turning up randomly caused problems. But I think because I had come all the way from England, they thought they should give me ten minutes to prove myself. So they stuck me straight in the ring with some rough Cuban guy who tried to knock my block off. But he didn't manage it, and I eventually gave him a good pasting. They had me in that ring for over an hour, fighting different guys. I was shattered by the end because I hadn't slept or eaten properly for two days on the bus. And I hadn't trained properly for a year! But I obviously did all right, because afterward Carlotti offered me a job at the gym, sparring. And they gave me a room at the back, so I had somewhere to stay, and I doubled as nighttime security."

"Vince was training up this young kid called Jimmy Levine. Because I was so good at mimicking other people's styles, I became Jimmy's main sparring partner."

"You sparred with Jimmy Boy Levine?" Sam asked with awe in his voice.

Jerry smiled. "We were good friends. I fought more with him than anyone else. We must have sparred five hundred rounds together."

"Whoa," Sam said. "Was he as good as he looked?"

"Yeah. He was fantastic," Jerry replied. "He was just a kid then. Seven years younger than me. But you could see he was going to be a star."

"Did you ever put him down?"

"Twice."

"Huh," Sam said, shaking his head in wonder. "I knew you were good." Then he frowned. "I've never been able to find you in any of the record books. Did you fight professionally out there?"

"I couldn't," Jerry said, his tone bitter. "Because I was an illegal. My tourist visa had run out, so if I had gone professional with an English accent and no paperwork, I would have been caught and deported straightaway."

"Of course," Sam said, screwing up his face. "That's rubbish."

"Tell me about it," Jerry said, a cloud coming over his face. Despite the imminent fight, he had quickly gotten lost in his career memories—something he hadn't done for many, many years. And with surprise, he realized it all still hurt. Badly.

"What happened after that?"

"Well, after four years Levine was world champion. He had beaten everyone. And then one day Jimmy's next opponent got injured. There weren't any decent replacements around at short notice. And so Vince thought of me. I think he had always felt sorry for me. He knew how talented I was, although I don't think he wanted me fighting Jimmy early on. By then Jimmy was probably better than me, yet I think Vince felt I deserved a shot."

"Wow," Sam said, amazed.

Jerry smiled at Sam's reaction, but the smile was tinged with sadness. "We were in New York by then, where the fight was to take place. So they organized for me to be smuggled into the airport so I could pretend I had just arrived from London. I still had my passport with me, but this time I had an official letter of invitation to fight Jimmy Boy Levine at Madison Square Garden two weeks later. This was before they really used computers to cross-reference names, and I guess they didn't expect illegal immigrants to present themselves at the immigration desk. So I got a month's working visa, and I was legally in America for the first time in four years!"

"So you fought Jimmy Levine at Madison Square Garden?"

Jerry shook his head sadly. "As you can imagine, even in the early days, anyone fighting Jimmy got plenty of attention in America—even an unknown from England. The press obviously got on the phone to the UK and discovered I had a 21–0 professional record but that I had also disappeared for six years." He gave a rueful smile. "I tried to keep my head down and avoid any questions. But I had to do one public sparring session before the bout. So I was hauled down to the Garden as part of the promotion and got put in the ring with some local kid from the Bronx."

"Sorry to interrupt," Sam said. "But what was the Garden like?"

"That day, apart from the twenty or so journalists and hangers-on, it was empty. But I had been there a few times to see Jimmy fight, as part of his entourage. And when that place is full, let me tell you! It is the most amazing boxing venue in the world." Jerry's eyes clouded over again. He looked up at Sam and couldn't help himself. "I had hoped you might fight there one day."

Sam said nothing.

After a few seconds Jerry continued. "So I did the customary ten minutes sparring with this lad from the Bronx. I was going easy, as I had the biggest fight of my life in a few days' time." Jerry's eyes scrunched up with anger. "But no one had told this stupid kid the etiquette of these kinds of things. So he was coming at me, throwing everything he had, trying to make a name for himself in front of the cameras. I fended him off easily enough, of course, and when the bell went, I dropped my hands and moved forward to tap gloves with him and have a quiet word in his ear."

Jerry took another deep breath. The memory was almost too painful to recount.

"The idiot threw a right hook at me just as I stepped forward. I managed to sway my head inside it, but he was hanging his thumb out. And it went straight in my eye. Bam."

"Oh no," Sam said, screwing his face up in sympathy.

"I knew I was in big trouble," Jerry said. "The pain was unbelievable. It felt like my eye had exploded. I vomited all over the ring. And I was rushed to the hospital—in the same ambulance as the kid from the Bronx. He had broken his thumb, would you believe it. If I hadn't been in so much pain, I would have smashed his head in."

"Was it bad?"

"That was it. End of career. Torn and detached retina. I never fought again," Jerry said with a wry smile that didn't reach his eyes.

"Vince paid for me to see the best eye surgeon in New York. He operated the next day. Worst he had ever seen, he said. But he did manage to sew it back together. And three weeks later I could see again. But he told me if I ever got punched in that eye again, I would probably be blinded for life."

"So what did you do?"

"There was nothing to do but get on a plane and come back to the UK. Got home to find my mum had cancer, which she hadn't told me about. And two months later—" Jerry swallowed hard—"she was dead."

Gloria was on her knees by now, elbows on the seat of the sofa. Fresh images of her husband flashed through her mind.

"Please, God," she prayed. "I love him so much, Lord. Help him turn back to you."

50

"Sorry to disturb you," Robbie said. "But I've just had the nod. It's time."

"Okay." Jerry jumped to his feet. "Come in, guys."

Robbie and Mario entered gingerly as Jerry turned back to Sam.

"That's it. No more talk until after the fight. Let's go."

Sam didn't move. "You've forgotten to pray for me," he said.

"Oh yeah." Irritation crossed Jerry's face as he leaned forward and put his hands on Sam's shoulders.

Sam ducked his head and shut his eyes.

Jerry was silent for several seconds. Then he cursed. "Sorry. Can't do it. You'll be fine. Let's get out there."

Sam opened his eyes and looked at Jerry in bewilderment. "Why are you being like this? I thought you'd be happy."

Jerry ran his hands over his scalp in agitation. He then turned to the wall and punched it violently, leaving a dent in the plasterboard. *"NOOOOO!"* The elongated scream masked the noise of the changing room door swinging open.

"'What in the world is going on?" Bert shouted, glaring at Jerry as he strode across the room. "You call this preparation?"

Robbie and Mario were silent, unsure of what to do. Jerry squatted with his face in his hands and said nothing.

Sam broke the deadlock. He stood and placed his gloved hand on Jerry's shoulder.

"Let's go," he said quietly, lifting Jerry to his feet and leading him to the door. "As long as you tell me what happened next."

In the corridor they stood and waited in front of the double doors that led to the open-air arena beyond. They could hear the voice of the announcer calling over the loudspeakers for the audience's attention. Suddenly there was a crackle of feedback from the speakers, followed by a loud bang. The announcer was silenced.

Jerry leaned toward Sam and whispered in his ear. "I'm sorry, Sam. I don't know what's wrong with me."

Sam inclined his head, accepting the apology. "So what happened next?"

Jerry took another deep breath and massaged the boxer's shoulders as they waited for the PA to be fixed. "I was a mess. A drunkard. Wandering the streets, sleeping under bridges and in doorways." He paused and reflected. "But it was my head that was really wrong. I was all over the place." He stopped, struck by his own description. That's where he was now—all over the place, a thousand thoughts colliding in his mind, threatening to drive him insane. He shut his eyes, and for the first time in days a simple prayer formed in his mind. *Help me, God.*

Jerry's panic subsided a little, and after a few seconds he was able to continue. "I spent two years like that. Begging for money, which I then spent on booze. Stealing stuff. . . ."

Sam turned, looking at Jerry in disbelief.

Jerry nodded grimly. "Oh yeah. I was rock bottom, believe me. Then one day I was pushing a shopping trolley full of my stuff down the street in Ilford. And I came across the boxing club." Jerry laughed at the memory. "I was so bitter about what had happened in New York that I had vowed never to go in one again. But something made me abandon my trolley and wander in. As soon as I got in there and saw all the young men training, I just wanted to get out. So I turned and ran away. But this bloke had seen me. And he came running after me and persuaded me to come back in. Turns out he was the head trainer."

"Huh," Sam said.

"I was blown away," Jerry continued. "He invited a tramp in off the street. I must have stunk. I hadn't had a bath in months. But he invited me into his office. Made me a cup of tea and gave me some biscuits." Jerry laughed. "I wasn't gonna turn it down. Thought the bloke must have been nuts or something. But then . . ." Jerry laughed again. "I still can't believe it! He asked me if I was Jerry Ambrose. Apparently I had fought one of his fighters seven or eight years earlier. And he had reckoned I was a star for the future. But then

I disappeared for years until he read about the Jimmy Boy Levine thing and the eye injury. And then . . ." Jerry's voice suddenly broke, and tears welled up in his eyes. He continued in a whisper. "He told me he had been praying for me ever since."

Sam looked up at Jerry, who shrugged and quickly wiped his eyes.

"Who was he?"

Jerry smiled. "Gloria's old man."

Sam turned thoughtfully back toward the doors ahead. The jeers were growing louder as the fight fans became impatient at the delay.

Suddenly Sam spun around to face Jerry. "You've been praying for me since the beginning, haven't you? You and Gloria."

Jerry nodded. "Yeah. When I've had my head together. Gloria's prayed for you every day."

"You prayed for my mum, too. She told me." It was a statement rather than a question. Jerry didn't answer, wondering where this was going.

But before anything more could be said, there was another loud retort over the speaker system. A cheer went up as the announcer's voice boomed out. The double doors opened, and a huge wall of noise hit them.

"Ladies and gentlemen. The third-from-last fight of the evening is about to commence."

Another loud cheer went up, and Jerry pressed his thumbs into Sam's shoulders.

"This is a bout of ten three-minute rounds for the British

middleweight championship. The challenger, fighting out of Ilford, Essex, with a professional record of thirteen wins from thirteen fights, all by knockout. Weighing in at 156 and a half pounds. Please welcome . . . Saaamm Pennniiinngtonnn!"

There was a chorus of cheers as a steward waved Sam forward. For a heart-stopping moment Jerry thought Sam wasn't going to move. But then, slowly and deliberately, the fighter marched forward. The noise was overwhelming as the "Eye of the Tiger" theme tune crashed out over the cheering crowds. As they pushed through the throng toward the ring, Jerry dared to believe things might just have returned to plan. His plan.

/ / /

Sam climbed up to the ring and momentarily looked across the sea of faces. For the first time in his boxing career, he was scared. He didn't want to be here. Didn't want to confront his demons again. He had stepped across the threshold. He didn't want to go back.

/ / /

"And the champion, with a professional record of forty-nine fights—forty-four wins, four defeats, and one draw. Weighing in at 160 pounds. Fighting out of Bristol, England. The West Country Warrior, Daaarrennn Spennnccccer!"

A loud rock song blared out as all eyes turned toward the double doors. All except Sam's. Instead the boy looked at Jerry. "So what happened?"

Jerry looked down at Sam, bemused by the boxer's

fixation on hearing his story at such a critical time. But he was beyond frustration now.

"He fixed me up with somewhere to live and then the next weekend took me home for Sunday lunch. Took me into his house with his young family. Even though I was a tramp!"

Jerry looked out into the crowd and chuckled. His late father-in-law's faith and kindness still impressed him all these years later.

"That's when you met Gloria?"

"Yeah. I fancied her straightaway. Asked her out that evening," Jerry said, grinning.

"And she said yes?"

"No!" Jerry shook his head. "She said no. Wouldn't date a nonbeliever."

"A what?"

"I didn't believe in God."

"Oh. So what did you do?"

"I went with her to church!" Jerry said, becoming serious again. "Her church blew me away. Nothing like I'd ever experienced before. All sorts of people there. Praising God. They were so free. I immediately knew they had something I didn't. Then a preacher explained the gospel in a very simple way. And I gave my life to God that night. The rest is history."

Darren Spencer finally made it to the ring. Jerry put his arms on Sam's shoulders. "So that's it. I'm done. You've heard everything. Now let's concentrate on winning this fight, shall we?"

"What is the gospel, Jerry? Tell me about it."

Jerry swore loudly, rolling his eyes in frustration.

"Tell me!" Sam shouted urgently. "Tell me about Jesus. My mum tried to the night before she died. But I didn't understand."

Jerry shut his eyes. A tragic picture of Janet trying to talk about God in between vomiting blood flashed across his mind. It almost broke Jerry's resistance, but the referee rescued him.

"Mr. Pennington. Please come to the middle for instructions."

Sam scowled in frustration but dutifully followed the referee.

Jerry turned and reached out, gripping the top rope with two hands as his head spun. *What is going on?* He looked down at the commentators and photographers below him, trying to gather his thoughts.

Suddenly his heart froze as his eyes landed on the front row of seats. Bert! Next to Ron Donovan!

"No, God!" Jerry shouted like a madman, startling Mario and Robbie, who were standing beside him. "It was *just a dream!*"

"Jerry!" Mario shouted, shaking the trainer back to reality. The cut man pressed a mouth guard into Jerry's hand. "Get a grip."

Sam walked to the corner, looking up at Jerry with mournful eyes. Jerry automatically lifted the mouth guard and pressed it into Sam's mouth. The two watched one another, saying nothing.

The bell rang. The fight had begun.

51

Gloria walked down the stairs. It wasn't unusual for her younger daughter to wake. She was just at that age, and it had only taken Gloria a few minutes to settle her back down to sleep. As she reached the bottom step, she looked at her watch: 9:30 p.m., the time of Sam's fight.

Gloria walked back into the sitting room and sank to her knees once again. She shut her eyes and tried to bring a picture of Sam to mind. But she couldn't. Every time she tried, an image of her husband flashed through her mind instead. After a few seconds she stopped battling it as a thought occurred to her. "Is that what you're saying, God? That it's all about Jerry tonight? That he's the key to Sam?"

There was no audible answer. She didn't expect one. But a feeling deep inside encouraged Gloria she was on the right path. She focused on Jerry's face and prayed for her husband.

/ / /

The bell rang again, and the two boxers broke from one another. It had been a cagey opening round with both fighters hanging back, reluctant to trade blows. The crowd wasn't impressed. But Jerry was relieved. He had thought at times in the last hour that Sam wasn't even going to fight. At least his form and defense were there, even if he wasn't engaging properly.

"Good," Jerry said as Sam sat down on the stool Robbie shoved underneath him. "Good, Sam. That was fine. No hurry. Size him up. Pick him off. That was excellent. He hasn't dropped his right yet, but he will. When he's tired. Keep the tempo up. Go for those body shots. . . ." Jerry kept talking, determined to focus Sam's mind now that the fight had started.

Robbie fussed around Sam, toweling him down, while Mario examined his face for any sign of damage.

The break was nearly over. Jerry stopped talking and finished with a quick "Okay?"

Sam spoke through his gum shield, and all three men around him froze. Jerry pretended he hadn't understood and prayed for the bell. But Sam wasn't going to be ignored. He forced his tongue underneath the mouth shield and spat it angrily to the ground.

"You heard what I said. Tell me about Jesus."

"No! Not now!" Jerry shouted as he fumbled about on the canvas. The bell rang as he picked up the guard and tried to force it back into Sam's mouth. But the boxer turned his face away.

"Okay!" Jerry shouted. "Next round! I'll tell you whatever you want to know."

Sam looked skeptical and refused to open his mouth.

"I promise!" Jerry shouted. "Now open up!"

"Time!" the referee yelled as Sam finally opened his mouth. "That's a warning," the official added, pointing down at Jerry as he climbed out of the ring. The referee turned and, with a wave of his arms, ushered the boxers together again.

Jerry rubbed his scalp as he watched the two boxers circling above him, throwing halfhearted punches. It was all wrong. Sam wasn't even attempting to get inside, contenting himself with harmless jabs. Spencer had obviously been watching videos of Sam's last couple of fights, because he wasn't coming forward at all.

The bell rang for the end of the second round. A chorus of whistles and boos sounded out. Sam walked back to the corner, fixing Jerry with his eyes. The trainer could tell he was going to be held to his promise. "So what do you wanna know?" he said, reaching up to remove Sam's mouth guard as the boy sat down on the stool.

"I know about his birth from Christmas. But I don't understand why Jesus was killed."

Jerry took a deep breath. "Okay. He really upset the religious leaders of the time. They were all high on themselves and thought they were holy because they followed all the rules and separated themselves from normal people. But Jesus didn't. He mixed with everyone. And when the religious leaders challenged him about this, he said some pretty harsh things. They might have been outwardly living for God. But he said their hearts were full of evil."

Bang. Jerry's own words convicted him. He reeled from the realization. *That's me. A respected leader—in my community, at least. But what's my heart full of?*

The bell sounded out again.

/ / /

Over the next fifteen minutes the pattern of the fight remained the same. Lackluster rounds between breaks filled with animated conversations about Jesus. Darren Spencer was getting emboldened and throwing more punches, yet thankfully he remained wary. Sam's punch rate, on the other hand, had dropped to almost zero.

As the seventh round neared its conclusion, Mario leaned close to Jerry. "He's losing these rounds, Jerry. He's got to pick it up quick or knock him out."

Jerry nodded. He was trying to stay calm. His story of Jesus' life was almost finished. He was being obedient to God, wasn't he? Surely God would reward him with a victory in the end?

He quickly glanced sideways to where Bert and Ron Donovan sat. They both looked agitated, but Jerry breathed a sigh of relief.

"No cigars," Jerry said under his breath. "No red dress."

The bell rang again, and he jumped up into the ring.

"So the Roman soldiers whipped him," Jerry continued as Mario crowded in and began work on a small graze that had formed just above Sam's eyebrow. "And then they made him carry a big wooden cross through the town up to a hill outside Jerusalem. They fixed him to the cross with nails through his wrists. And his ankles. They shoved a crown of thorns on his head. And then they hung him up to die."

"How long did it take?"

"Hours."

"Did he say anything?"

"Yeah," Jerry said quietly. "Among other things, he said, 'My God, my God, why have you forsaken me?'"

"Why did he say that?"

"Because he hung there on the cross for us. Took on our sin. For the first time in eternity he suffered separation from God. So that we don't have to."

"I don't understand."

Jerry shook his head as he tried to explain. "At the moment he died, the curtain in the Temple was ripped in two. The curtain was what separated ordinary people from God. Only priests could go past it into God's presence. When Jesus died on the cross, it meant that we could all have a relationship with God. Not in a temple or a church." Jerry lifted his fist to his chest and beat it twice. "In here."

There was silence between them until the bell rang out once more. Jerry gave Sam one last glance, trying to read the boy's mind but failing. He climbed down as Sam stood slowly and advanced on heavy legs.

The eighth round was a disaster. Sam didn't throw a punch. Darren Spencer picked up the tempo and started clubbing his opponent from all directions. The crowd began to cheer, delighted that one of the boxers was finally doing something. Jerry watched fearfully as Sam covered up and tried to protect his head. The trainer winced as savage blows began raining down on Sam. The referee hovered, keeping a nervous eye on the battle.

"Thank God for that," Jerry said as the bell finally rang after three of the longest minutes of his life.

The referee came over and spoke sternly. "If he doesn't start throwing punches soon, I'm going to stop it."

"Okay, ref. He will," Jerry replied, nodding vigorously until the referee walked away. He watched him go and then looked down at Mario, who was working on the boy's face while Robbie toweled spilled blood from his torso.

"Talk to me, Mario," Jerry shouted to the Italian over the rowdy noise of the crowd as Mario pushed an ice bag onto Sam's face.

Mario shook his head. "Bust nose. Puffy eyebrow. But he's okay. Physically, at least." The last phrase was said with exaggerated expression. It wasn't lost on Jerry.

The trainer crashed to his knees in front of Sam and roughly pushed the ice bag away.

"*Right.* That's it," Jerry shouted in Sam's face. "I've played your game. I've told you about my life. I've told you about Jesus' life. Now. This is about *your* life. You've lost all the rounds so far and fought like an idiot. You've got two rounds left. Two rounds to redeem this thing. You've got to get out there. And you've got to smash him."

Sam spat his mouth guard out again. "Why?" he yelled at

Jerry. "What do you want from me? Why do you want this so badly?"

Jerry screwed up his face and fought the urge to hit the tormentor in front of him. Instead he jabbed Sam in the chest with his forefinger and shouted again. "Because you're too young to know what you want. You've got a chance *I never had.*"

Sam reacted angrily to his trainer's accusations and jabbing finger. "You want me to smash him?" he yelled at Jerry, their faces only inches apart.

"Yes!" Jerry shouted back, encouraged at last to see the fire returning.

"You want me to smash his head in?"

"Yes!" Jerry shouted again.

Sam pushed himself to his feet and shoved Jerry out of the way. The boy glared to the side of the ring where the officials sat. *"Ring the bell. Now!"* Sam screamed.

The crowd close enough to hear roared their approval.

His opponent sitting opposite turned pale.

52

Sam lunged forward at his opponent. Right away Jerry could tell Spencer knew he was facing a completely different proposition. He retreated into total defense. Sam abandoned all guard and began throwing enormous overhand punches at his opponent.

The crowd came alive, screaming and cheering at the savage assault. Several clubbing punches reached their mark, and Spencer staggered backward.

"*Yes!*" Jerry shouted from ringside. "Hit him. Hit him. Hit him."

But Spencer was an experienced fighter. Realizing he couldn't fend off the attack with his fists, he lunged forward and grabbed Sam, deliberately tangling their arms together. Spencer grimly held on for as long as he could until the referee forced his way between them. Finally separated, Sam launched another savage attack. Spencer dived in again and hung on to Sam like a limpet. The referee separated them again, yelling at Spencer to stop the tactic. But he continued, and eventually the referee held his finger up to the judges.

"One point to be deducted from Spencer for holding." The referee turned to Spencer and lectured him again.

Spencer nodded.

When Sam approached, the Bristol man spun out of the way and literally ran to the ring corner above where Jerry was standing. The crowd jeered, and Sam glared at his opponent with frustration and contempt. Jerry had a perfect view of Sam's face as he fixed his eyes on Spencer and slowly advanced. It was chilling.

/ / /

This time there was to be no escape. Sam anticipated the spin and swung a wide right hook just as Spencer peeled sideways. The punch nailed Spencer on the body, forcing him back into the corner. Instantly Sam was upon him, raining down blows. Punch after punch landed on his opponent's head and body. In desperation, Spencer lunged forward again, grabbing hold of Sam.

Jerry screamed in protest as the referee stepped in.

"That's your final warning. Once more and I'm stopping it."

Spencer nodded and wiped blood away from his eye.

The referee waved the fighters back together. Spencer bravely threw out a couple of jabs, but his guard had slipped and his hands were lowering as Jerry had predicted they would. Jerry looked up at Sam, hoping he had seen it.

Sam stood off for a moment, and Spencer threw another jab. Sam didn't hesitate. He launched a straight right with the strength and speed of a piston. His gloved fist caught Spencer clean on the nose. The champion's head recoiled violently, and he rocked backward into the corner. As Sam shaped to unleash, Jerry knew. This was it. He'd done it!

But Sam paused. Anguish overtook his face as he stood rooted to the spot. Everything seemed to stand still. The shrill ring of the bell sounded out.

"Aagh!" Jerry screamed as he climbed into the ring. "What was that?" he shouted as he knelt in front of his young fighter. "You had him. Why did you stop?"

Sam spat out his mouth guard and took a swig of water from the bottle Robbie squeezed into his mouth. When he looked up at Jerry, the trainer's hope drained away. The rage was gone from Sam's eyes.

"I couldn't do it," Sam said.

"Why not?" Jerry shouted.

Sam sat in silence and shook his head, refusing to speak.

"Why not?" Jerry demanded again, even louder.

Sam shook his head more vigorously and still refused to say anything. Jerry slammed his hand down on the canvas and turned away while Mario went to work on the cut above Sam's eye.

Thirty seconds passed. Mario stood back so Jerry and Sam could see each other again.

"Just one more punch. It needs just one more punch," Jerry said.

"I can't!"

"Why not?" Jerry repeated, his anger rising.

"I could see Jesus in his face. I could see the crown of thorns on his head."

Jerry was silenced for a moment before he suddenly erupted with a curse. "Sam!" he shouted, grabbing the boy's head and pointing his face across the ring at their opponent. "That . . . is not . . . Jesus of Nazareth." His angry voice carried high above the noise of the crowd. "That is Darren flippin' Spencer. From Bristol! *Now go knock him out!*"

The bell rang, and Jerry climbed wearily down from the ring. As he did so, he glanced at Bert.

He froze. Bert was bent down with his face near Donovan's cupped hands. He slowly leaned backward from his neighbor's lighter and straightened up. The promoter sucked hard on a cigar and exhaled a satisfied cloud of smoke. Jerry watched as the smoke rose above Bert's head.

Suddenly a flash of color broke through the haze. It was her.

She walked down the aisle between the rows of seats as a chorus of wolf whistles rang out. Almost six feet tall in her heels and swaying her hips in response to the stir she was creating, the beautiful woman approached Ron Donovan.

Jerry watched openmouthed as she leaned forward to kiss Donovan and then eased her red dress into the blue plastic seat beside him.

Jerry felt his legs turn to jelly. He turned back to the ring and flung his hands out to steady himself. His right hand landed on the towel where Robbie had laid it a moment earlier. Jerry's fingers instinctively gripped the material, and he lifted the towel before him.

Everything seemed to slow down as he looked at the boxers in the ring. It was exactly as his dream had been. Except for one detail.

His fighter wasn't the losing fighter, as Jerry had always assumed. His was the winning one! Spencer was finished. It would only take one more good punch.

But Jerry could see Sam was not throwing it. He had his gloves up to his face and was weaving from side to side as if looking for an angle, while his opponent stood open, waiting for his end to come. From where he was standing Jerry could see between Sam's gloves. His eyes were filled with tears.

Jerry stood, gripping the towel. It had all come to this. For the first time he understood the recurring dream; his whole life was about this moment. Glory or God. As he took one last deep breath, he heard a voice—a quiet, beautiful voice—speaking directly in his ear.

"Stop, my son. Stop."

/ / /

Immediately Jerry was carried back into a vivid memory from his childhood. He was sitting in his old single bed in the corner, with a blanket pulled up around him. Across the room sat Jerry's mother, sobbing and holding her bruised temple as blood dripped from her split lip onto the threadbare carpet. On the other side of the room his father sat, still at last. The enormous man was slumped on a chair with his elbows on his knees and his face in his hands, sobbing.

It wasn't an unfamiliar memory. It was a real image of a real incident almost thirty years earlier. But for the first time ever Jerry let himself stay within the scene. Jerry's attention turned from his father back to his mother, and he suddenly realized there was now a fourth person in the room. A man had bent down over his mother with his arm around her shoulders and tenderly held a soft white handkerchief to her cut lip. He hugged her for a long time as he whispered in her ear.

Then, ever so gently, the man let go of Jerry's mother and walked to where Jerry's father still sat, his great shoulders shaking as sobs vibrated through his body. The man squatted next to him and put a hand on his shoulder.

Jerry's father lowered his hands from his face and looked into the man's eyes. They spoke quietly for several minutes as the man gently patted Jerry's father's shoulder. Eventually his father stood and walked back across the room toward his wife. She looked at him nervously but didn't move away.

He knelt next to her and started to speak words Jerry couldn't hear. After a few minutes he stopped and lowered his face to the ground. Moments later Jerry saw his mother slowly reach out a hand and gently begin stroking her husband's head.

Jerry's eyes left his parents to see that the fourth person in the room had silently knelt beside his own bed. The little boy turned and looked deep into the man's eyes. After a moment Jerry lifted his hands, and Jesus took him into his arms and held him. Jerry shut his eyes, and all tension and fear flowed out of his body as he rested in the soft embrace.

/ / /

Jerry was back in the arena. Frustrated jeers were ringing out in response to the action in the ring, stumbling to a halt once more. Jerry looked up at Sam and could see the tears now running down his face. It was time.

He took one last look at the towel in his hand and felt complete peace about what he was going to do. Smiling gently, he nodded his head and spoke a prayer.

"Thank you, Lord. Thank you."

/ / /

The towel fluttered over the top rope and landed in the middle of the ring. Everyone stopped and turned to look at Jerry, who had climbed up to the ring's edge. The arena fell eerily quiet.

"What are you doing?" the ref demanded.

Jerry and Sam stared at one another, searching each other's eyes. "I'm conceding the fight," Jerry said.

The people at ringside erupted into a frenzy of incredulity and debate. Bert's agitated voice sounded loudest as he ran to the edge of the ring. "Rubbish! He's not conceding the fight."

The referee turned to Sam, who hadn't taken his eyes from Jerry's face. "Are you conceding the fight?" the referee said directly to the fighter.

Sam continued to look at his trainer.

"I'm sorry," Jerry said to Sam. "I've got everything so wrong. This—" he waved his hands at the arena—"this isn't important." Jerry thumped his fist against his chest twice and then lifted it up and rapped the side of his head too. "It's who's in here that's important."

Sam nodded and smiled slowly. He spat his gum shield to the canvas in front of him and kicked it over the edge of the ring.

"I submit," Sam said to the referee without taking his eyes off Jerry. The fighter walked forward and buried himself in his trainer's arms.

/ / /

The arena went wild.

"No way!" Bert shouted repeatedly as he tried to climb up into the ring. The referee bent down to talk to the judges while Darren Spencer's entourage sprang into the ring and hoisted their exhausted boxer onto their shoulders.

"You all right?" Sam said into Jerry's ear.

"Better than ever," Jerry replied. "Let's get out of here."

Jerry held the ropes apart for his fighter to climb through, and the two dropped to the floor of the arena. They put their arms around each other's shoulders and pushed their way down the aisle toward the exit. Spit and beer rained down on them as disgruntled fans and gamblers jostled around them. But they didn't notice.

"You know," Jerry shouted above the roar, "that wasn't the end of the story."

"What wasn't?"

"Dying on the cross."

Jerry ducked below an empty plastic beer cup that flew at his head, and they stumbled on toward the exit.

"Three days later they went down to the tomb where his body was laid." He squeezed Sam's shoulder. "And he was gone."

53

Gloria finally opened her eyes. She had been praying for two hours solid, and she was exhausted.

Enough.

She looked down at the TV remote on the table, knowing they would show the headline fight. Gloria hadn't had any desire to watch it, but now she felt a sudden compulsion to switch it on.

Jim Robertson, the ITV sports presenter, was in a studio speaking to an ex-boxer. The image zoomed in on the presenter as the discussion clearly ended, and he turned toward the camera. Gloria turned up the volume to hear him speak.

"So we've had a great evening already here at Wembley Stadium, with some tremendous fights entertaining the capacity crowd. Let's speak to our ringside reporter,

Dominic Thomson, and find out what's been happening. Dominic, what's going on down there? It sounds like a tasty atmosphere."

The picture switched to a commentator at ringside, who pressed his earpiece to his ear as a loud chorus of boos and jeering rang out around him.

"Well, you could say that, Jim. We've just had the most bizarre finish to a fight I've ever seen."

Gloria's heart thumped in her chest as she recognized the unmistakable figure of Robbie, standing forlornly in the ring behind the commentator and staring out into the crowd. He looked like a little lost boy, and Gloria wondered with trepidation at what might have happened.

The commentator continued. "The fight was for the British middleweight title between the holder, Darren Spencer, and his challenger, Samuel Pennington. In the tenth round Pennington had the champion in desperate trouble but just didn't seem to want to finish it. And then, when it seemed the ref might stop it in Pennington's favor, his trainer threw in the towel! Even though Pennington seemed just about to win! They conceded the fight."

"How extraordinary!" Jim Robertson's voice interjected from the studio. "What was going on?"

"I just don't know, Jim. Maybe there was something we weren't aware of. A hidden injury or something that prevented Pennington from carrying on. But whatever it was, it didn't seem to be impeding him, although he did seem hesitant and reluctant at times. I've never seen anything like it."

"Was it mental frailty perhaps, Dominic? Or stage fright?"

"I've no idea, Jim. All I know is that Spencer's still the champion, and Pennington just left the ring with his trainer to a lot of booing. You can still hear what the audience thinks of it!" The commentator held his microphone up to the air, and the noise of disgruntled and drunken boxing fans sounded through the television's speaker.

"Extraordinary," Jim Robertson said again as a stunned Gloria sat glued to the television. "Perhaps we'll hear more about that at some point. Now, what are your thoughts on this next fight?"

Gloria pushed the off button on the remote control. She cupped her hand over her mouth as her heart thudded and her mind tried to imagine what had happened. She instinctively mouthed a prayer.

Instantly Gloria felt a most wonderful peace come over her. Her heart stopped racing, and a warm rush of joy washed through her mind and body. She smiled. She had no idea what had just occurred. But she just knew, deep in her soul, that God had done it. Everything was going to be fine. She hugged herself and longed for her husband to get home and take her in his arms.

/ / /

Robbie stood next to Mario in the ring. Over the heads of the crowd, they finally saw Sam and Jerry reach the safety of the changing rooms. Robbie breathed a sigh of relief and looked down at the crowd below the ring, where Bert was pacing and muttering to himself.

"What just happened, Mario?" Robbie asked.

Mario grimaced. "I think the boy found God. And Jerry found him again too."

"Mmhh," Robbie replied absentmindedly. He examined his feelings and was surprised. It was fight nights like this at Wembley Stadium that he had dreamed about since he was a kid. But as he turned slowly, seeing Spencer and his entourage celebrating and Ron Donovan patting his boxer on the back, Robbie didn't feel sad. Even during the fight his mind hadn't been fully here. And his heart certainly hadn't been. No, Robbie realized as he watched a scantily clad model walk around the ring with a sign above her head. There was a longing deep in his stomach. But not for the girl in the bikini.

He had no real idea about what had just happened with Sam and Jerry. But with them choosing for whatever reason to throw in the towel, Robbie's main motive for being in this country had disappeared. Nothing stood in his way anymore.

Robbie turned to the cut man standing next to him, a huge grin spreading across his face. "Mario, I'm off."

"Off where?" Mario replied, looking up at the young man curiously.

Robbie smiled and hugged the Italian before standing back and lifting his fingers to his temple in a salute halfway between a Cub Scout's and an army private's. "Australia, mate!"

Robbie let out a whoop of joy. In one easy movement he vaulted the top rope, almost landing on a commentator talking into a TV camera three feet below. A producer standing nearby growled at him and moved to shove him aside. But Robbie was gone, sprinting for the exit.

ABOUT THE AUTHOR

By all standard conventions, Luke Wordley has no right to be an author. A terrible student at school, he still has to think hard to identify an adjective from an adverb. Yet his head is full of stories—inspired, no doubt, by a childhood inventing excuses to get out of trouble.

Luke came to faith in his early twenties, out of a strongly antireligious viewpoint. Inspired by Jesus' use of parables and storytelling in his ministry, and frustrated by the lack of spiritual fiction for young men in particular, he has finally found the time and motivation to put pen to paper. *The Fight* is his first novel.

He is passionate about writing honest and exciting stories that challenge readers to think beyond the normal confines of their everyday lives. He also partners with various organizations to get life-changing books into the hands of marginalized groups, including youth and those in prisons.

As well as a writer, Luke has been a farmer, a retail entrepreneur, the CEO of an international health charity, and the development director at one of the most prestigious private schools in England. Luke also suffered, and came through, a stress-induced breakdown in his early thirties, an experience which inspired elements of *The Fight*.

Luke is married and lives with his young family in the south of England.

For more information about Luke, his latest writing projects, and the story behind *The Fight*, please visit www.lukewordley.com.

DISCUSSION QUESTIONS

1. Sam's behavior in much of *The Fight* is violent and antisocial. Yet most readers find themselves empathizing with him and rooting for him. Would you feel supportive of him if you only saw his behavior and didn't know his background? There may be people around you whose behavior is similar to Sam's, yet you know little about them. Do you think your lack of knowledge influences how you feel about them? What steps can you take to avoid judging people before you get to know them?

2. What kind of a role model is Jerry? Do you believe his personal struggles or his crisis of faith should disqualify him from his mentoring role? Why or why not?

3. In your opinion, are boxing, martial arts, or other combat pursuits appropriate activities in which to encourage children—or Christians in general—to participate? Discuss your reasoning.

4. What lies at the heart of Jerry's ambition? If you were in his position, would you make similar decisions? Does

personal ambition always bring us into conflict with
God's plans for our lives and with those around us? Are
there areas of your own life where your ambition may
be getting in the way of God's plans for you—and if so,
how should you respond?

5. Do you think Jerry and Gloria enjoy a strong marriage?
What do you admire in them individually? And together?

6. The ending of the book—and, in particular, the
climactic last fight—have sparked considerable debate.
Do you think the author chose the right ending for
the book, or do you wish the book (and the final fight)
would have ended differently?

7. In between writing the first and second half of *The Fight*,
Luke Wordley suffered stress-related depression and a
crisis of faith (see his testimony at www.lukewordley
.com). Since recovering, Luke believes God has helped
him use this difficult time in his life to write about Jerry's
journey with greater authenticity, in turn helping others
who may be going through similar experiences. Has
anything like this ever happened in your own life? Are
there difficult experiences in your past that God may be
able to use to bless others?

8. Though the story is fictional, *The Fight* contains
characters with realistic struggles in hard situations.
While reading this book, were there any characters or
situations with which you could identify on a personal
level? If so, explain.